SHE LIES HERE

BLAKE LARSEN
BOOK 2

JACK SLATER

1

"Rise and shine, sweetie."

The dumb bitch's ordinarily pampered, perfect blond locks were now limp and matted. Once they had been her pride and joy. But no longer. Above her left temple, a clump of hair and blood had clotted into a dense tangle. She was wearing an orange jumpsuit, like a prisoner. He knew there was nothing underneath.

He knew because he was the one who had dressed her.

Nothing happened. She didn't move. She didn't groan. Not even her breathing changed. In fact, she made no sign to indicate she was even aware he existed at all.

They never did.

"Wake up!" he yelled, slamming his open palm against the side of the shipping container. A dull metallic thud rattled from the impact. She still didn't move. Was she really unconscious? Or was she just playing with him? Making him distrust the evidence of his own senses, his own superior mind?

A surge of pure, violent hatred rose from deep inside him. He leapt several feet across the narrow space until he was standing right over her, close enough to thrust his fingers through her filthy, oily hair.

Finally, she reacted. Just a squeak, a whimper of pain. Enough to confirm that she'd been faking after all.

"Don't make me wait again," he hissed, making a fist with his hand and pulling her hair roots away from her tender scalp. She made a low, guttural groan, her eyes flickering underneath their lids.

"What—?" she whimpered, her voice raw from her long rest. "Where am I?"

Her eyes opened slowly, still heavy from the effects of the drug he'd dosed her with. He loved this part. There would be several seconds during which she still thought she was dreaming. Where she thought she was under the influence of some horrible nightmare.

That she might wake.

"That's the wrong question," he said proudly, an evil smile turning up the corners of his lips but not meeting his eyes. "You should be asking *why* you're here."

Her breath became heavy, uneven, ragged. Her eyelids flickered shut, but he felt her entire body tense underneath him. That was the fear working. Right now, her body was dumping adrenaline into her system.

Three.

Two...

Right on schedule, the woman's back arched, and she pushed away from the ground violently with her arms and legs as she attempted to propel herself upright. She only made it halfway before the manacles around her wrists and ankles bit deeply into her flesh, the chains they were attached to rattling against the metal eyelet on the floor.

"There's no escape," he said in a conversational tone, his fist still clenched in her hair. He squeezed tighter to remind her who was in charge and was rewarded a heartbeat later with a stifled gasp of pain.

It sent a thrill through his body, starting at his loins and radiating outward. He couldn't resist doing it again, squeezing hard enough to tear the scab on her scalp and to tease free a fresh trickle of blood. It glistened on her pale, porcelain skin.

"Please," she moaned, squeezing her eyes shut. "Tell me what happ—"

He reacted instantly, slamming her head against the wall of the container. As with his palm earlier, a sound reverberated through the cramped space, this time heavy and final. She didn't make a sound. Her entire body went limp. For a moment, he worried that he'd gone too far. That he'd killed her.

But not for long.

Leaning forward, he turned his right ear to her lips and listened for the sound of breath. It was there—faint but there. She was still alive.

For now.

"It's difficult for you to understand, but now you see: There are consequences. There have to be *consequences* for your actions," he said, carefully enunciating every word so that she understood. "When I speak, you listen. That is the way of the world. Do you understand?"

She was still dazed, he saw. Her eyes were glassy, empty of life. He waited. After all, he wasn't a monster. He was a... teacher.

No, that didn't sound right.

A leader.

The roles bore certain similarities, he reasoned, which must have been why the word came to his mind. But there was also a distinct difference. A leader was a teacher, yes. His job was partly to ensure that his flock was prepared to confront all of life's many dangers. But it was also so much more. Sometimes that required more than a calm word.

Sometimes it merely required control.

When his captive's breathing steadied, he bent his lips to her ear. He knew she was paying attention. She was too taut, too tense, too terrified to be doing anything else.

"I told you once before," he whispered. "When I talk, you listen. I don't like to repeat myself. Do you understand?"

She nodded, the movements of her neck weak and jerky.

"Speak!" he snapped, furious at her wanton show of disrespect.

She knows exactly what she's doing!

Blood rushed in his ears, making it difficult for him to hear.

"Yes," she croaked. "I understand. I'm sorry."

Rage still contorted his features. He felt it gripping his chest, squeezing his heart. He wanted nothing more than to slam her head against the crate again and again and again to make her understand.

But slowly, methodically, he pulled himself back from the brink. She had a role to play. She didn't know it yet, but the whole world would soon. He couldn't kill her.

Not yet.

"Ask me," he said coldly, lifting her chin up so that she saw his face for the first time. Even in her groggy, semi-drugged state, her eyes widened with recognition and horror.

"Why?" she whispered half to herself. "Ask—ask you what?"

"Why I'm doing this."

"Tell me..."

"Don't you know?" he responded with an evil glare, twisting the knife as she visibly struggled to formulate an answer that might avoid provoking his rage. They were always the same. So predictable. They thought they could manipulate him. They all did.

But he saw through the practiced disguise they showed the rest of the world. He saw the real them.

"I swear. I won't tell anyone. Just let me go."

Disgust filled him. He physically recoiled at the sight of her, relinquishing his grip on her hair as though he'd touched a hot stove. Did she think he was that stupid? As if he could free her.

"You've had it easy your entire life," he spat, the explanation flowing out of him like water from a broken dam. She stared at him with wide, horrified blue eyes that he knew must have tricked so many men. But not him.

"I bet you screwed your college professors to get the grades you wanted. You pick and choose men like they're your playthings. How do you think your kids will feel knowing their mother was a whore?"

"What?" she gasped. "It's not—"

"Did you tell your husband where you were going tonight? *Who* you were going to see?"

"Yes!" she said, leaping onto the idea like a lifeline. "He knows where I went. He'll figure the rest out. You know he will. But if you just let me go, I swear I'll never tell. Please..."

He drew his hand back and slapped her across the cheek with enough force to make her head jerk back and bounce off the wall. A fresh streak of blood glistened where it made impact, glossy where others, so many others, were dull.

"Enough lies," he hissed. "You had your chance. You all did. And now it's too late."

2

Blake sidled into a seat at the very back of the Douglass Community Center. She was lucky to get it. The large events hall was almost overflowing. It seemed as though the entire community of Northern Pines had turned out for the special session of the Town Council.

She glanced around the room, recognizing a few faces. Shirley from Big Mike's Diner. Big Mike himself, wearing a gray T-shirt stained with cooking grease. A few others. Not many. This had always been Caleb's town. She just came to visit.

After the resolution of the events two months earlier, when Blake had helped uncover a criminal gang that had been importing illegal narcotics using military transport planes—and using the proceeds to finance a vast conspiracy that included sex trafficking, murder, and kidnapping—she'd considered never returning. The leader of the gang, Darryl Hansen, had ordered the murder of her own brother. Now that he was gone, there wasn't much left for her here. Only bad memories.

Maybe after tonight, she would wash her hands of Northern Pines for good.

An image of Ryan Walker crossed her mind's eye. She hadn't seen the one-legged ex-Green Beret in almost a month. She'd spent the last couple of weeks commuting to the North Carolina Justice Academy's Salemburg campus, getting certified as a law officer now that she was no longer a Special Agent in the US Army's Criminal Investigation Division. He'd gone out of state to get a new prosthetic foot fitted. They had just missed each other, like ships in the night.

She wondered whether she would ever see him again.

Stop kidding yourself.

Blake gritted her teeth, wishing her own interior monologue would just sometimes play for the same team. The truth was, no matter how much she tried to deny it, there was a reason she was back in town, and it wasn't just for closure.

With more than a decade of federal law enforcement experience under her belt, Blake knew that she had the qualifications to get hired to the position of her choice damn near anywhere in the United States.

And yet she'd spent the last month jumping through hoops to pass a test she could have aced in her sleep. All so she could work somewhere near a town she claimed she had no connection to.

"Yeah, I get it," she muttered underneath her breath, scowling at herself. She exhaled sharply and tried to clear her mind. She was here for a reason, not to self-litigate her love life—or lack thereof. She focused her attention on the front of the room.

It was perfect timing. The mayor, an imposing Black man with a gleaming bald head, reached for his gavel. The crowd hushed before he even had a chance to use it. Blake guessed that both its size and composition were out of the ordinary. Small-town governance meetings usually attracted only a handful of nosy gossips and those with little else to fill their time.

Then again, nothing about tonight's session was ordinary.

The mayor was seated at the center of the long table. On either side of him sat the four town councilors: two men, two women. Blake didn't recognize any of them.

Thankfully, the mayor finally dipped his head to the microphone. He looked a little strained, but Blake guessed that anyone in his shoes would be after the events of the previous two months. The town's police chief had resigned, and the officers in charge of both the Patrol and Investigation divisions had been fired in disgrace.

Half a dozen detectives and patrol officers had been arrested by the State Bureau of Investigation and were working their way through the legal system on charges of corruption and obstruction of justice. Blake suspected—and hoped—they would all go away for a very long time. The evidence found in Darryl Hansen's safe was extremely conclusive.

"Settle down, settle down," the mayor said.

About the only thing that had saved Mayor Randolph Chester was the fact that he'd only taken office a couple of months before the scandal blew up. That, and the joint investigation carried out by the Monroe County Sheriff's Department and the SBI gave him the clean slate and breathing space to decide what was to be done with what was left of the Northern Pines Police Department.

Learning the answer to that question was the reason Blake, along with everybody else, was sitting in the community center that night.

Slowly, the several hundred people packed into the hall fell completely silent. Blake peered expectantly at Mayor Chester. He cleared his throat and began to speak.

"You all know why we are gathered here tonight," he said. A muscle pulsated on his jaw. "I won't sugarcoat things. Northern Pines is a city I love. Like many of you, I was born here. I met my wife in Mrs. Kowalski's math class when I was just thirteen years old. My kids go to the same high school as many of yours. When I stood for election, I promised to make this the best place to live in the entire state. But right now, we're a long way from that. My father told me that all a man has in this life is his reputation. Well, that goes for a city also."

He stopped and took a sip from a glass of water just in front of him. He pursed his lips. Blake sensed that the hammer was about to fall.

"But right this minute, if I'd just heard of Northern Pines, I wouldn't want my kids growing up here. I wouldn't start a business here. I wouldn't want to grow old here. All a city has is its reputation. And ours is in the mud."

A whisper ran around the seated audience, which stirred as husbands and wives shifted toward their partners to murmur into their ears. Blake wondered whether the hubbub signaled dismay or agreement.

The mayor spoke over the noise his pronouncement had generated.

"The good news, ladies and gentlemen, is that you can fix a reputation." He grinned. "My boy would be the first person to tell you that, after what he got up to in college."

A quiet laugh rang out around the room. Blake sensed that some of the tension had dissipated. Nobody liked to hear negative things about the place they lived. Even if it was all true.

"But to fix what people think when they hear of Northern Pines will be a difficult—and expensive—task. I told you I wouldn't sugar-coat things, and I won't. So let me explain the proposal I am putting in front of your town councilors tonight."

He picked up an electronic switch and squeezed it. A projector on the ceiling stirred into life. A moment later, a slide appeared on the wall.

"With the town's permission, I intend to disband the Northern Pines Police Department."

Blake heard a sharp intake of breath from all around her.

"It was just a few bad apples," an angry voice rang out from a few rows in front of her. "That's no reason to close the whole department down. There's already too much crime. How will this help?"

Mayor Chester seemed unbothered, as though he'd expected the question. "The phrase is 'a few bad apples spoil the whole bunch,'" he said, a slight smile appearing on his face. "And that is what I am determined to prevent."

Another voice. "How?"

"I was getting to that..." He grinned. "Following an extensive investigation by the State Bureau of Investigation and the Monroe County Sheriff's Department, I am pleased to announce that all remaining sworn and non-sworn personnel in the existing Northern Pines Police Department are free of suspicion. They played no part in the crimes committed."

"How can you be sure?" a third voice yelled out.

"Every officer who remains with the department agreed to submit themselves to an extensive battery of interviews and background checks carried out by trained SBI special agents. Believe me when I tell you they left no stone unturned. We can trust every last one of these fine men and women. They are the best of the best and want nothing more than to protect and serve their community."

"So why are you disbanding the department?" the same voice said.

"We only have one remaining trained detective," the mayor said, beginning to tick off the reasons on his left hand. "Our patrol division is down to under thirty percent strength. The entire leadership team is gone. I'm advised that the department no longer has the institutional ability to rebuild itself."

"So what's your plan?"

Blake leaned forward, equally as interested as the entitled heckler, even if she wasn't quite so loud about it.

"The Sheriff's Department has agreed to assume responsibility for policing Northern Pines. The city will pay for this service using property tax revenue. The sheriff intends to deputize all our remaining officers immediately and put them under the leadership of Captain Gina Rogers. Captain Rogers' task over the next eighteen months is to rebuild a police department we can all be proud of and trust to stand on its own two feet."

The room—finally—fell silent as the community took a beat to digest the mayor's proposal. Blake couldn't tell from the murmuring and whispering whether the response was positive or not. She thought it was a solid idea. To get good cops, you needed great leadership, and that couldn't be generated in the blink of an eye.

"Any questions?" Mayor Chester asked.

Amazingly, there were none. Perhaps his earlier blunt appraisal of the department's parlous position had hit home.

"Then I move this proposal to a vote," the mayor said, glancing to the councilors on his right and left. "All those in favor, raise your hands."

For a moment, nothing happened. Blake held her breath, wondering if the mayor was about to be thrown under the bus. In her experience, small towns sometimes resisted change. And this was one hell of a change. Nobody liked outsiders coming in and telling them what to do—even if those outsiders were from the same county. Maybe even lived just a few miles over.

It was a matter of principle.

But she didn't see any other choice. And apparently, neither did the councilors. All four members raised their arms into the air to signal their support for the mayor's proposal.

Since it was a special session, there was no further business. The crowd filed out of the community center in dribs and drabs. Several of them—she guessed regulars at these events—moved immediately to the front to harangue either the mayor or their chosen councilor. Judging by their weary body language, they'd each heard it all before.

Blake kept her seat for several minutes after the majority of the audience departed. She thought of her brother and everything he'd sacrificed to help Cora Felton, a girl he'd barely known.

You would have liked her, she thought, a familiar heaviness clutching at her throat.

Cora had decided to stay in town with Ashley, another of the gang's victims, despite all the horrors they'd seen here. They were talking about building a women's shelter. Blake thought it was a great idea. Sometimes you needed to confront the evils you'd faced in order to heal from them. She hoped that was what she herself had done.

"You're still hiding from them," she whispered to the almost empty room.

All these weeks later, she was still avoiding truly dealing with the contents of the murder book that Caleb had somehow gotten his hands on. It had taken her years to come to terms with the fact that her father had killed their mother before turning the gun on himself.

It was almost easier to just continue believing that he was guilty, to leave that memory in a box, sealed somewhere down deep where she didn't have to think about it. Investigating the case had only two possible outcomes: Either she learned that her dad was guilty after all, or she discovered he wasn't.

The first opened her up to an unknowable amount of needless pain. The second was even worse. Because if her father wasn't guilty, then someone else was.

And they'd been walking around free all this time...

Finally, she rose and made her way out of the hall. It was dark out, and the cold February night air slapped her before she had a chance to zip up her winter coat. Taillights lit up the parking lot like fireflies as the remaining cars departed. She watched as one of the town councilors glanced around, then climbed into the passenger side of a dark black Mercedes SUV. She looked for her own car and began to walk for it.

"Ms. Larsen?" a voice called out from the darkness.

3

Blake turned, her right hand instinctively drifting toward the holster at her hip, though she made no move to draw it. She was still cautious after recent events. "Hello?"

A woman strode toward her. She was tall, perhaps five foot nine, and wore dark jeans under a padded jacket. She had an air of confidence about her. She extended her hand in greeting. "I'm Gina Rogers," she said.

Frowning, Blake tried to work out where she'd heard that name before. She was sure she'd never met this woman. Then it came to her. "The Sheriff's Department captain?"

"The one and only." Gina grinned.

"Can I help you?" she asked as she shook the outstretched hand, confused by the woman's sudden appearance.

"Yes, I think so." Gina nodded. "I want you to come and work for me."

Whatever Blake had expected her to say, it wasn't *that*. She frowned as she tried to work out whether this was some kind of practical joke.

"It won't be that bad," Gina said, an air of amusement on her lips.

"Hard work, no doubt. But something about you tells me you're not afraid of that."

"You're serious?" Blake said.

"Deadly so," Gina replied. "I have eighteen months to rebuild a shattered police department and release it back into the wild. I need people I can trust to help me do it."

"You've never met me," Blake pointed out.

"Well, since you were the one who uncovered this whole mess, you get straight As in your character reference," she said. "And besides, you know what they say."

"What?"

Gina smirked. "You break it, you own it. And you, Blake Larsen, well and truly broke the Northern Pines Police Department. They say you can see it from space. *Smoking.* So I need you to come and help fix it."

"I—" Blake stammered. "I don't think I can."

"Why not?" Gina shrugged. "You're qualified. *Over*qualified, quite frankly. You're looking to buy a place in town. You're the perfect candidate."

"How do you know all this?" Blake demanded.

"I do my research."

"Wait, candidate for what, exactly?"

"To head up the brand-new Investigation Division. Although perhaps that's too grandiose a title. Presently it consists of just one detective. And you, if you take the job."

"Detective Wilson," she replied numbly, remembering how Melissa Wilson had helped her bring Darryl Hansen and his crew of criminals to justice.

Gina nodded. "See, you already have a relationship with your team. What did I say? Perfect."

Blake closed her eyes. This was all happening too fast. She'd intended to take a couple months off before looking for a job. Maybe do some traveling or use the time to get to know Ryan a little better. Basically, anything other than diving headfirst into the burned-out wasteland that was the Northern Pines PD.

Or whatever they were going to call it.

"How soon do you need an answer?" she said, mainly to fill the space as the cogs in her mind squealed and smoked.

Gina glanced at her watch. "The mayor's vote passed, correct?"

Blake nodded. She suspected the captain already knew the answer to that question.

"Then I need you to start tomorrow. Eight a.m. We'll get the paperwork sorted out after you arrive."

"You're really serious," Blake said, staring back at Gina like she was a crazy woman.

The Sheriff's Department captain stared back at her expectantly. "I already told you that. So are you in?"

"IN FOR A PENNY," Blake murmured in the stillness of her car a few moments later, her head still swirling from her unexpected meeting with Captain Rogers. Now the lot was completely empty, the only light in sight coming from the screen of her cell phone as it stared brightly up at her. The phone number was already punched in.

She'd been putting this call off for days. But it was as if the prospect of a future had unstuck her past. She needed to know what had really happened with her mom and dad. She owed Caleb that much.

Blake pushed the call button. She pressed her phone to her ear but heard only silence for a couple of seconds as the line initialized. Once it finally connected, the ringer sounded half a dozen times without success.

She sighed and dropped the phone from her ear, almost missing the faint click and "Hello?" as the person on the other end of the line answered.

"Hello?" she said hastily, her heart racing in her chest. "Is this Mr. Hobson? Skip Hobson?"

"Who's asking?" a male voice replied. He sounded like an old man, a little short with his answers, his voice slightly hoarse.

"Sir, my name is Blake Larsen. I apologize for getting in touch with you out of the blue—"

He cut her off. "Did you say Larsen?"

"Yeah, that's right," she replied.

"Is this a joke?" he said gruffly. "Are you playing a prank on me? Because if you are, I sure don't appreciate it."

Blake's forehead knitted into a frown. She had no idea what he was talking about. "Sir, are you Skip Hobson? US Army Criminal Investigation Division, retired?"

"That's correct. Now just who the hell are you?"

"Sir, I apologize if we've gotten off on the wrong foot. See, the thing is, I'm calling about a case you investigated a long time ago. I just have a few questions. I won't take up too much of your time."

"Don't you and your brother talk?"

Her stomach clenched. How the hell did this guy know about Caleb? More than that, what did he have to do with any of this?

"Sir?"

"Your brother called me what, six, maybe seven months ago. Asked to come down to Florida and pay me a visit to talk about an old case. Never did show up."

Blake's head started to spin. She'd already known that Caleb was investigating their parents' deaths before he was murdered. But something about crossing his path on her own investigation sent a chill down her spine.

She didn't say anything. She couldn't.

"Ms. Larsen. Are you still there?"

"Mr. Hobson, I'm sorry to let you know that my brother has passed away."

This time, the pause was on his end of the line.

"My condolences," he said, a little softness intruding on his tone. "When did it happen?"

"About seven months ago," Blake said, feeling the familiar tug of grief in her chest.

Another short pause followed. "Honey, I hope you got to say goodbye."

"I'm afraid not," she replied, doing her best to push her emotions aside. "Caleb was murdered."

"What?"

No longer was there any suspicion in Hobson's voice, nor even the pity that had followed her revelation about Caleb's death. Now she heard only a keen interest, doubtless honed by Hobson's many years as a criminal investigator.

"Mr. Hobson, did my brother say why he was calling you?" Blake asked, almost holding her breath at the opportunity to hear from Caleb from beyond the grave.

"You'd better call me Skip," he said instead. "No, he didn't say anything about why he was calling. Didn't even mention your parents' case."

Blake frowned, not understanding. "But if he never showed, and he never told you which case he wanted to talk about, how did you make the connection between me and him?"

Skip Hobson sighed. He spoke like a caring father. Not that Blake had much of an idea what that sounded like.

"You don't remember, do you, girl?"

"Remember what?"

"We met. A long time ago now. I interviewed both you and Caleb on the day your parents died. I'm an old man now, but I don't mind admitting it was one of the hardest things I've done in my life."

Blake's fingers went slack around the phone. It almost slipped from her grasp. For a moment, she couldn't breathe as a long-suppressed memory wriggled its way free from the deepest recesses of her mind.

"Hey, kids," a voice said. It sounded far away to Blake, whose head was still buried in Caleb's shoulder. She hadn't stopped trembling. Not since...

"You mind if I sit down?"

"Who are you?"

Caleb had asked that. His voice was guarded and suspicious. It only made Blake more resolved to hide away from the world.

"I'm Agent Hobson. You're Caleb, right? You can call me Skip."

Blake gasped, every last breath of air in her lungs draining in an instant as the full force of the memory crashed over her. Until recently, it had been the darkest day of her entire life. She'd spent two decades hiding from the emotions it pried loose. Now it seemed as though they were all hitting at once.

"You remember, don't you, Blake?" Skip asked, his tone now soft and caring, a complete one-eighty from his demeanor at the start of the call.

"You were there..." she whispered.

"I was," he confirmed. He waited a long time for her to continue, but it was as though she'd slipped into shock. She opened her mouth to reply but found herself unable to form a single thought.

"Why did you call, Blake?" he finally asked. "Why did you and your brother want to talk after all this time?"

Blake took a deep breath to steady herself.

"I was hoping you could tell me," she said eventually. "I found the murder book in my brother's things. I was hoping you could tell me why."

A note of surprise sent Hobson's voice up half an octave. "A copy?"

"No. The original."

"That's mighty strange," he replied. A scratching noise echoed down the line, as if he was stroking his facial hair.

Blake felt a well of frustration rising in her when he didn't offer anything further. She prompted him to continue.

"Skip, what do you remember about my parents' case? I just want to know why Caleb was looking into it."

Several long, deep breaths were her only answer. "Blake, I've thought about that case most every week for twenty years. There was a time when I could recite the contents of that murder book backwards."

"Why?"

"Blake—"

"Skip, don't treat me with kid gloves," she said firmly. "I did a decade in CID. I can handle it."

He sighed. "Something about that case never sat right with me. The physical evidence all pointed to your dad as the killer. But I didn't speak to a single person who knew either of your parents who saw it coming. And of course, there was the discrepancy with the murder weapon."

"What discrepancy?" she asked quickly.

"The firearm we found with your father's fingerprints on it was unregistered. The last record of sale was to a private individual in Alabama, if I recall correctly. That person sold it at a gun fair. No background checks, no records."

"What's so strange about that?"

"Your parents owned a number of weapons. They were locked in a gun safe in the basement. Why not use one of those?"

Blake felt a flicker of intrigue in her chest pushing out the last of the shock that had briefly overcome her. "Skip, do you still have your personal case notes?"

"Sure," he said. "But I would have to dig them out. My wife made me put them into storage a few years back. I guess she got sick of me going over them. When I retired, she gave me an ultimatum."

Blake knew the feeling of obsessing over a cold case as well as anybody. The only difference, in this case, was how close it hit to home.

"Would you mind doing that for me?" she asked hopefully. "I just want to do my own due diligence. If Caleb had a reason to rake up our history, I want to know why."

"Sure. But I'm heading out of town on a golf trip for a few days. You think you can wait until I get back?"

Blake exhaled. She'd waited most of her life. What was a couple more days?

4

lake guided her truck into a parking bay outside the front of the Northern Pines Police Department's headquarters. She killed the engine but didn't immediately climb out, instead taking the time to study the police station itself. She'd driven past it many times but had never felt the need to pay the place much attention.

It was a neatly manicured, modern two-story red brick building with three flagpoles out front: the Stars and Stripes standing tallest, bracketed by the banners of both North Carolina and the town of Northern Pines itself.

The parking lot at the front was mostly populated by personal vehicles, though she could see a row of cruisers and SUVs in NPPD livery pulled up against the right-hand side, stretching around to the back of the building. Between the well-maintained surroundings, the headquarters building itself, and the abundance of modern vehicles, it was immediately clear that the town had spared little in its investment in law enforcement.

"And what did that get ya?" Blake said.

She pulled down the sun visor on the roof and glanced at herself in the mirror on the rear side. Her mouth tightened. She was wearing smart dark jeans and a matching suit jacket over a light gray shirt. She was dressed for an interview.

Blake tried to remind herself that she hadn't actually given Gina a firm answer the previous night. She wasn't committed to anything.

Yet.

In truth, she wasn't exactly sure what she would be committing herself *to*. She looked around the parking lot at the liveried police cruisers. Would they all have to be repainted? Would there even be a Northern Pines Police Department in a year's time?

She didn't know. But just sitting outside the station, Blake felt a familiar tug. She'd been out of the game almost nine full months. Longer if you counted the four months of desk duty CID had put her on before her discharge went through.

It was too long. She was itching to get back into the field.

There was only one slight hesitation in Blake's mind. *Do I have to do it here?*

"Stop procrastinating," she said firmly, reaching for the door handle. She knew that it was a complete waste of time. She wouldn't have gotten out of bed at 6:30 a.m., washed her hair, dressed herself in an outfit that screamed she meant business, and then driven herself to the station if she hadn't already made her mind up.

The moment I got offered the job... she thought.

Blake climbed out of her truck and walked briskly to the station entrance. She was fifteen minutes early. There was a small reception area just on the other side of the glass doors that led into the building. The reception desk was shielded behind a thick glass barrier.

Without hesitating, she pulled the glass door open and stepped inside. An electronic chime rang out to announce her arrival. She took a deep breath in through her nostrils and was almost knocked down by the familiarity of the scent. Disinfectant, body odor, stale coffee, and an indescribable thickness to the air. It smelled like home.

She walked up to the desk, which stood alone in the reception lobby. There were spaces for three receptionists, but only one of the workstations showed any evidence of recent occupation: a dark coffee ring on the surface, half a pack of Mentos, and a few torn scraps of shiny packaging. To her left and right were doors that led into the rest of the station.

"I'm coming!" a voice called from the office behind the reception desk.

A moment later, an African American woman in her mid-fifties bustled toward Blake. She was carrying steaming coffee in a cup that bore the inscription *My other ride is a Porsche* and had shiny black hair with impressive gold highlights.

"You must be Ms. Larsen," she said, raising one eyebrow as she set her cup clumsily onto the desk, sloshing a few droplets of coffee over the rim.

"Blake." She nodded, shooting the woman a friendly smile. "I'm here to see—"

The receptionist—Sandra Bennett, Blake learned from a brass plaque in front of her—interrupted.

"Captain Rogers," she said before leaning forward and adding conspiratorially, "It'll take some time to get used to saying that. We had the same chief of police for eleven years."

"Well, you know what they say," Blake said. "A change is as good as a rest."

Sandra snorted. "That's what I told my ex-husband. Unfortunately not until after the bastard cheated on me."

Blake kept her expression free of the amusement bubbling up inside her. She didn't even know this woman, but Sandra seemed happy to spill her whole life story.

"You can call me Sandy," she said, rapping on the glass barrier that separated them. "I'd shake your hand, but..."

"No problem. Nice to meet you, Sandy," Blake said. She gestured behind her at the rows of plastic chairs against the walls. "Should I wait back there?"

"You're to go on up to the captain's office," Sandy said, reaching for a control panel in front of her. She pushed a button, and a low buzzer sounded to Blake's right as the door to the inner sanctum opened. "Go straight on past the holding cell, and you'll hit the stairwell. Walk up and you'll find the captain's suite on your left."

"Got it." Blake nodded. She flashed the receptionist a smile. "And thanks, Sandy."

She quickened her step toward the door, feeling a hit of adrenaline shock her system as it swung open. The hallway on the other side was anodyne, the floor tiles a tacky light blue linoleum that squeaked against the rubber soles of her boots as she walked. But the feeling of familiarity only grew in her breast the farther she got into the station.

Blake had spent almost her entire adult life in law enforcement. Her time in the Army had consisted of some soldiering and a lot more policework. She'd become an adult in places like this, on military bases all across America.

Northern Pines was a small town. But police stations were the same everywhere.

A sign labeled *Patrol Division* hung on thin steel link chains from the ceiling tiles at the far end of the hallway, past the holding cells. Blake could only make out a small sliver of the office space from her present vantage point, but at least half the desks she could see were empty. It was a chilling reminder of the winds of change that had swept through this department.

She hovered in place for a second, watching as a uniformed police officer with a folder under his left arm crossed the end of the hallway without glancing in her direction. She felt a brief pang of apprehension as she wondered how her fellow officers would treat her. After all, perhaps some of those who had lost their jobs—perhaps even their freedom—had been friends. Would they blame her for what had happened here?

There might even be a few bad eggs left in uniform. The SBI investigation had been thorough, but there was no guarantee that all of the corrupt officers had been caught.

"First things first," she said softly, turning away and heading up the staircase.

The second floor was quieter. The floor was carpeted, which Blake guessed meant that arrestees and suspects were rarely if ever allowed up. To her right, she saw signs for Dispatch, Communications, Records, and several other administrative functions. She heard a phone ringing in that direction, then a low murmur as a man answered.

She turned instead to her left. A few steps down the hallway, she found the entrance to the captain's suite of offices. They consisted of a small reception room complete with an empty desk for the secretary, a closed door marked as a conference room, and another which had a dark rectangle of old adhesive a little under eye level where a name plate would ordinarily have sat.

Clearly Captain Rogers barely had her feet under the table.

Blake glanced around the reception room. The captain's office was shut, so she took a seat and settled down to wait. The tapping of a keyboard was audible through the thin door. The metronomic tick of an analog clock on the wall just above her provided the only other sound. She checked her watch instead of looking up at it. She was still six minutes early.

Another woman slipped into the reception area five minutes later. She was diminutive with mousy brown hair that was in the process of going gray. She shot Blake a tired smile but did not otherwise introduce herself, instead facing down at a leather portfolio case which she laid on her lap.

At 8 a.m. precisely, the door to Captain Rogers' office swung open with a click. Gina appeared from behind it, wearing her dress uniform: white shirt, black pants, lovingly polished boots, and a badge over her right breast.

"Blake, take a seat inside," she said, gesturing behind her before turning to the other waiting woman. "And you are Mrs. Robson, I take it? Thanks for coming in on such short notice."

"I go by Betty," the small woman replied.

"You mind waiting out here just a minute longer?"

"Not at all."

Blake disguised a frown of curiosity as she turned sideways to pass by Captain Rogers. She took a seat on the other side of the desk and waited for Gina to join her. She realized she was leaning forward with anticipation and consciously forced herself to relax.

Captain Rogers sat down a moment later. A thin manila folder sat on the desk in front of her. She met Blake's gaze, but instead of launching into a prepared sales pitch, she merely raised her eyebrow and said, "So?"

Not understanding, Blake replied, "So... what?"

"Is it a yes or no?" Rogers replied with just a hint of irritation.

Note to self: Don't waste her time, Blake thought.

She opened her mouth and said, "I guess I was expecting to hear a few more details about the role. Salary, hours, precisely what is expected of me."

The captain lifted the folder over her keyboard and slid it across the desk. Blake picked it up and opened it before realizing that it was upside down. She rectified the problem, then glanced at the single sheet of headed paper inside.

Underneath the shield of the Monroe County Sheriff's Department was printed a dozen or so lines of black text. But Blake focused on just two words. As she did, her eyes nearly popped out of her skull.

"Detective Lieutenant?" she said, spluttering with surprise. "I'm not qualified to..."

"I told you I needed your help to rebuild this police department," Captain Rogers said with a dismissive flick of her fingers. "I don't need another beat cop. I need a sharp, intelligent, and most of all trustworthy lieutenant to command my detective shop. From what I understand, you fit all those boxes. So I return to my original question. Yes or no?"

"Surely there's somebody else?" Blake said, playing for time as she scanned the offer letter. The salary was more than sufficient. Generous, even. She would be based in Northern Pines, of course, though as a sworn deputy, she would technically have jurisdiction all across the county.

"If there was anyone else, they would be sitting across from me right now," the captain said tartly. "Since they are not, you can draw your own conclusion. The Monroe County Sheriff's Department is not the FBI. I am not blessed with hundreds of warm bodies to choose from."

Thanks for the vote of confidence, Blake thought, though in truth she appreciated the captain's honesty.

Yes, she was qualified. Yes, she could do the job. No, Northern Pines wasn't Chicago or New York. Despite recent evidence to the contrary, it wasn't close to being one of the most dangerous cities in America. It was the perfect opportunity for a skilled criminal investigator without years of leadership experience under her belt.

Rogers fell silent, settling back into her chair and staring sphinxlike at Blake across her desk. Apparently, her sales pitch was over, if it had ever even started. Her left eyebrow remained mildly elevated.

"Okay," Blake said, realizing her decision was made only as she heard it come out of her own mouth. "I'll take the job."

Instead of congratulating her, Captain Rogers rose from her chair and walked to her office door.

Nonplussed, Blake looked over her shoulder as the captain called out, "Mrs. Robson? Will you join us?"

After a short pause, the woman Blake had seen in the waiting area outside the captain's office stepped into the room. She moved timorously, barely making a sound as she padded toward them carrying a Bible.

"I'll skip the formalities," Rogers said. "Mrs. Robson is a notary public. She's here to make sure everything's in line, legally speaking. Ms. Larsen, if you're happy to proceed, please raise your right hand."

For a moment Blake simply gaped, her head spinning at the pace with which everything was moving. She'd expected to have some time to think things over. But then, did she need any? She needed a job. And this was as good an opportunity as she was likely to get. She raised her hand slowly.

"Repeat after me," Rogers said. "I, Blake Larsen, do solemnly swear..."

At first, Blake stumbled over the words. But quickly she picked up conviction. A day earlier, she'd thought about leaving Northern Pines for good. But she'd never been someone to back down from a challenge. As she recited the words of her oath of office, she found herself relishing the challenge. Not just of policing—but healing—a town.

"—That I will support and maintain the Constitution and laws of the United States, and the Constitution and laws of North Carolina, not inconsistent therewith, and that I will faithfully discharge the duties of my office as a deputy sheriff of Monroe County to the best of my ability, so help me God."

"Congratulations, Lieutenant Larsen, you're now officially a member of the Monroe County Sheriff's Department," Rogers said. "I won't detain you any longer. I understand you already have a case."

5

"Welcome to Criminal Investigations," Detective Melissa Wilson said with a wry smile as she gestured around the empty office space. It was made up of four parts, taking up almost a third of the floor space on the entire second story of the police station.

Blake's eyes widened as she took in her new domain. She fully appreciated for the first time how big a job she had on her hands.

"Thanks," she offered, running her fingers through her hair and smoothing a few stray strands.

The space was split into three sections: the open-plan main office, composed of eight desks arrayed in pairs along its length with a glass wall on either side. Doors were set into each of these transparent divisions. On the left-hand side—with windows facing the parking lot out front—was the lieutenant's office. It took up about a third of the length, with the rest laid out as a conference room.

The right-hand side was similar, except in place of the office was a small breakout area with a coffee machine, refrigerator, microwave, and sink, along with a few mismatched barstools and office chairs.

Blake's overriding impression, however, was one of emptiness. Only one desk in the open plan central section of the office was occupied: Detective Wilson's. Her own new office was equally bare, a steel desk, leather executive chair, and computer monitor providing the only decoration.

"It's nice to see you again, Detective," Blake said formally. She took a few more steps into the office and set her bag down on one of the empty desks. "How have you been?"

Melissa Wilson had been one of the two Northern Pines detectives assigned to investigate the shooting of a junkie outside Blake's home several months earlier. The victim had been sent to kill her.

Unlike Wilson's partner, Ruben Ortega—who was up to his neck in the department's corruption—she was a good, honest cop. Blake had trusted her to help unravel the mess that had cost her brother Caleb his life, in the process saving almost a dozen women trafficked into prostitution.

The detective glanced around the empty office. "It's been interesting," she said dryly.

"I bet. Listen—"

Wilson held up her hand. She flushed as if embarrassed by what she was about to say but continued anyway. "I just wanted to get things off on the right foot," she said. "I don't have any resentment about Captain Rogers making you lieutenant and not me. The truth is I only made detective a couple years back. I don't have the experience to run a whole department. Hell, Ortega either buried me up to my eyeballs in grunt work or had me handling property crimes every time we caught a real case. I guess it was so he could massage the final outcome. Either way, I don't have the chops. Yet."

I'm not sure I have enough experience either, Blake thought.

"Anyway," Wilson said, flushing again, "I just needed to say my piece. I'm looking forward to learning from you, Lieutenant."

"In here, I'm just Blake," she replied. "Out in the real world, you can stick to pomp and ceremony, but in here there's no need, understood? We'll solve cases together." She grinned. "And I promise I won't hog all the good ones for myself. Something tells me we'll have all the work we can handle, at least until I can hire a couple more detectives to help fill out the department."

Wilson nodded. "You can call me Melissa too," she said. "And thanks. I'm glad you're here. I've never handled a missing persons case before."

"No problem," Blake said. "What have we got?"

Melissa looked down at her desk and consulted a page of hand-written notes.

"Dispatch got a call this morning at 7:36 a.m. from a Captain Austin Crawford, US Army, reporting that his wife Nina didn't come home last night to their house by Sandhurst Park. Captain Rogers told me to wait until you arrived before heading out."

"When was she expected back?"

"Late last night. She went to see a friend but never came back."

"Has this ever happened before?"

"Um—" Melissa winced. "He didn't say. Sorry."

"Don't sweat it." Blake shrugged. "Let's go introduce ourselves."

THE CRAWFORDS LIVED on a leafy street of one-story ranch homes on the southern edge of the town limits. American flags hung from short flagpoles attached to the outside walls or from driveway fenceposts. It was a pleasant but not extravagant neighborhood.

"Nice place to raise kids," Melissa observed as she indicated into the Crawfords' driveway. A red toddler's bike shaped like a fire truck lay on its side near the front door.

"I guess," Blake replied. She looked up from the computer console attached to the unmarked cruiser's dashboard. It had taken her half the short drive over to familiarize herself with the department's IT system.

"I ran a quick criminal records check on both Austin and Nina Crawford," she said. "Nothing worth noting. He racked up a couple of speeding tickets a few years back in Wisconsin. She seems clean as a whistle."

"I checked the department's callout records before we headed over," Melissa said as she checked her side mirror, then guided the cruiser into the driveway. "We've never visited this address."

There were already two other vehicles in the driveway: a recent model year Ford F-150 and an expensive-looking Lexus sedan. Melissa killed the engine and reached for the door handle.

Blake frowned. "This is a nice house," she said. "But if they've got the money for three cars, why not trade up?"

"I only count two."

"How did Nina go out last night if she didn't drive? I guess Austin could have dropped her to her destination, but then why not pick her up?"

"Maybe she took an Uber."

"Maybe..." Blake replied thoughtfully. She opened the door and climbed out. The air was brisk but not freezing. She adjusted the firearm on her hip. The weight was familiar yet different. It had been a while since she'd carried one of these for work.

The two detectives walked up to the house's front door. The house was fronted with white-painted timbers that appeared well maintained. Through the windows to the side of the front door, Blake spied evidence of children: scattered toys and assorted chaos. She reached up and pressed the doorbell. A muffled screech rang out, like the ring of an old-fashioned telephone.

Hurried footsteps sounded from inside the house. A moment later, a figure appeared in the hallway. Blake narrowed her eyes.

That's definitely not Captain Crawford.

"Good morning," the woman said. She had white hair and an austere, patrician bearing about her. Neat diamond studs glistened on her ears.

"Mom, is that the detective?" a voice called out from inside the house, its owner harried. A child's scream rang out, and then a muffled murmur of encouragement.

"Can I see some identification?" the woman—apparently Austin Crawford's mother—said.

Melissa and Blake exchanged curious glances, then reached for and flashed their badges. She felt out of practice with the gesture and was grateful that the woman didn't inspect her temporary credentials too closely. She seemed like the type of individual who would ask to speak to Blake's manager, and she really didn't need that on day one.

"I suppose you had better come inside," she said.

"What's your name, ma'am?" Blake asked as they stepped across the threshold.

"Jeanette Crawford," she replied, her expression hardening at the sound of boots thumping against the floorboards. "Austin's mother. Please take those off."

A man came into view as the front door swung shut behind Melissa. He had a baby in his arms that looked to be about a year old. It was sucking a pacifier and had a crown of thick dirty-blond hair. The dad was a white male, as Blake had expected from a name like Austin Crawford.

"Mom, I need you to handle the kids for the morning," he said. "I have to go search for Nina."

Blake cleared her throat. She extended her hand. "Are you Captain Crawford?" she asked.

"Austin," he said, sounding exhausted. He turned away and offered the child to his mom.

"Is there somewhere we can sit?"

"Sure. Come through to the kitchen," he replied with a lethargic gesture in that direction.

Blake and Melissa followed him out of the hallway, through a cozy but well-proportioned living room to an open plan kitchen. A steel-fronted refrigerator was covered with notes, photographs, utility bills, and magnets. Blake glanced at one of the latter objects. A photograph of a happy family was pinned on top of it.

She leaned forward and peered at the image. It had been taken on a sunny day. Austin and a woman Blake presumed was Nina stood side by side, their heads tilted slightly toward each other. Each parent carried a child in their arms: Nina cradling a newborn, while Austin crossed his arms over a blond toddler pressed against his torso. They looked radiantly happy.

But Blake needed no reminders that looks could be nothing if not deceiving.

Austin sank onto a barstool. A baby's angry cry rang out from a nearby room, followed by a shushing sound.

"Mr. Crawford—" Blake began. She stood opposite him, Melissa standing on her right-hand side.

"Austin," he interrupted. "I told you, call me Austin."

"No problem. Austin, when was the last time you saw your wife?"

"I already went through all this with the other cop."

"Yes, but not with me," Blake pointed out. She reached inside her jacket pocket and pulled out a thin notepad that she'd taken from a supply closet before leaving the station, along with a pen. "The tiniest detail could be important."

"Of course," he replied, his shoulders slumping.

She studied him closely. He looked like he hadn't slept for a week. Though he appeared to be in just his early thirties, deep lines were carved into his forehead, and his eyes were ringed with dark bags. She reminded herself that his appearance meant nothing in itself. He was an Army officer with two young children. It would be more surprising if he looked well-rested.

"She left last night about 6 p.m."

"Left for where?"

"Pinehurst," he said. A shadow passed across his face, and he glanced away.

"What's in Pinehurst?" she asked, the corners of her eyes darting to her right. Melissa had seen the same thing.

"A bar, I guess." He shrugged.

Blake's eyes narrowed, though she kept her tone even. "You don't know where your wife was headed?"

"I'm not her keeper," Austin said. "We live independent lives. Always have. Trying to raise two young kids gets tiring. Sometimes you need to blow off steam."

"Is that what Nina was doing last night?" Melissa interjected. "Blowing off steam?"

"I guess," Austin said.

That's the second time he's used those words, Blake thought. *Curious.*

More screaming sounded next door. Austin gritted his teeth and pushed himself upright. "Mom," he called out, "get the kids out of here. I need to speak with the detectives. I can't think."

"Pinehurst is a twenty-minute drive," Blake said. "How did she get there?"

"Uber."

"Did you call it, or did she?" Melissa asked.

In the background, Blake heard rustling as Jeanette Crawford gathered the children's things. She popped her head into the kitchen before leaving the house.

"I'm taking my phone with me," she said.

Austin merely grunted in response.

When Melissa had first briefed her on the call to dispatch, Blake hadn't expected much. Adult men and women disappeared for a night or two more often than many thought. Sometimes, as Austin said, they just needed to blow off a little steam. But there was something in the way the husband was behaving that set off alarm bells in her mind.

He was acting like he had something to hide.

"She did," Austin said after a short pause.

"Do you have her account details?" Blake asked.

"She uses the same email address for everything. We know each other's passwords."

"We'll need that," Blake said. She gestured at Melissa to hand over a piece of paper. The detective did so, and Austin scribbled down an email address in messy, numbed handwriting.

"Who was your wife meeting last night?"

Austin looked down at the kitchen counter. "A friend."

"Do you have a name?"

He shook his head.

Blake ground her teeth together with frustration. "Mr. Crawford, you called us to tell us your wife was missing. Do you think she could be in danger?"

He shrugged. "I don't know."

"You don't know where she was going last night. You don't know who with. You don't seem to know a whole lot."

"I already told you. We live independent lives. Nina doesn't ask me where I'm going, and I do the same."

Blake scratched her temple. Austin was definitely concealing something from them. He seemed to be shrinking in on himself with every minute that passed. She opened her mouth, then closed it. Something clicked in her mind.

"Austin?" she said to attract his attention. When he looked up, she focused directly on his eyes. In her experience, people didn't like to break eye contact of this type.

"What do you mean by independent lives?"

"I—" he began before glancing in the direction of the front door. He frowned, as if making mentally sure that his mother was gone. He grimaced and spoke in a low voice despite the fact that it was only the three of them. As he spoke, some of his uneasy tension faded. Blake wondered if that was all he'd been hiding. "Look, we have an open relationship. I see people from time to time, and so does Nina. We've been doing it for years."

Not for the first time, Melissa and Blake traded surprised glances. In her experience, jealousy was a strong motive. People could convince themselves of anything. That they were happy when they were not. That they didn't mind their partner sleeping with other people.

People could convince themselves of anything, all right. But not forever.

She cleared her throat. "Do you know who your wife was seeing?"

He shook his head. "Don't ask, don't tell. It's easier like that."

Blake scribbled down that word. *Easier.*

"You never asked?" she said quizzically. "Not once?"

"We have ground rules. That's number one," Austin said, leaning forward and placing his elbows on the counter. He began to massage his temples. "Like I said, don't ask, don't tell."

"But she told you she was going to be out," Blake said.

Austin pointed at the organizer taped to the front of the fridge.

"We put it up on there."

Blake turned and stared at the calendar. As he said, the note *Nina – out* was scribbled under yesterday's date. It was still early in the month, so she saw no other entries. She used that end of her pen to lift up the previous page. In January, she noticed two similar inscriptions. Both were for Nina.

"I don't see any from you," she pointed out before snapping a quick picture.

"I've been busy at work. It's not, it's not like an organized thing. Maybe sometimes I see somebody I like. Or Nina does. So we set up a date. It's that simple. I'm not so good with the calendar anyway."

"Had she seen the guy before?" Melissa asked. "Or girl."

"Guy, I think," Austin said. "I don't know."

"We're going to need her phone number as well," Melissa said, handing her notepad over for a second time. Austin wrote it down, a blank expression on his face.

"Is there anything else you can tell us?" Blake asked. "Any favorite bars? Any friends she might have confided in?"

As Austin opened his mouth to reply, her phone vibrated in her jacket pocket. Blake reached inside and picked it up. She didn't recognize the number and was about to kill the call when something stopped her. She stepped away to answer it.

"Is this Lieutenant Blake Larsen?" a terse male voice asked.

"Speaking."

"It's Jed Dixon here from Dispatch. Sorry for calling on your personal, but... well, we just got a call about a body. I've got a unit about two minutes out. I figured you'd want to know."

Blake took several steps farther away from where Austin was sitting and lowered her voice. "Male or female?"

"Female. It's... the caller said it was real bad."

"Bad?"

"They didn't say how. They sounded shocked. Just bad."

She closed her eyes and pinched the bridge of her nose. This day had suddenly gotten a lot more interesting. "Send me the address. I'm on my way."

6

"What?" Melissa exclaimed after Blake was done filling her in on what little she knew. "A body?"

"Yep," Blake said grimly. She reached for the radio on the car's dashboard. "This is Lieutenant Blake Larsen," she said. "I need a patrol car to sit on the following address. 518 Elk Drive. Let me know the second the owner tries to leave. Follow him if you have to."

"You think Austin did it?" Melissa asked as she spun the car around and accelerated out of the Crawfords' driveway.

"We don't know if the body is Nina yet," Blake cautioned. Even as she said them, the words sounded ludicrous to her. The coincidence was too impossible to buy.

The drive to the crime scene was a short one, barely ten minutes. The body had been found on a horse ranch just off Youngs Road, barely a mile from Fort Bragg.

The two detectives sat in silence the rest of the way, lost in their own thoughts. Blake's head was spinning. She'd expected her caseload to be relatively mild given the relatively peaceful and affluent area that made up Northern Pines. She certainly didn't anticipate handling a missing persons case and a body on her very first morning.

A patrol car was parked at the turning, blue lights flashing silently. A single officer stood beside it to direct rubberneckers. Melissa pulled up alongside him and rolled down her window.

"What are we looking at?" she asked.

"Beats me." He shrugged. "A body. Female. I hear it's nasty."

Melissa nodded and drove on. "What do you guess he means by that?"

Blake shook her head. "I don't know. But everybody keeps saying it."

Another patrol car sat about fifty yards farther down the road, which was sandwiched between two vast enclosed fields and led toward a horse-riding center. Various bits of jumping equipment lay scattered on the grass. In the distance, Blake could make out a number of figures in riding gear milling around a building.

Behind her, she heard the scream of several more sirens as new units flooded to the area. A potential murder scene was a whole lot more exciting than writing parking tickets, even for a department as undermanned as Northern Pines.

A uniformed officer nodded in recognition as Melissa pulled up near a line of blue police tape. The two detectives stepped out of the vehicle.

"This is the new lieutenant," Melissa explained as Blake gave her name for the crime scene access log. "What are we looking at?" she asked.

"Female in her late twenties or early thirties. White. Blond hair."

"Could it be an accident?" Blake asked, even as she clocked the hair color. Nina was blond, too. Experience had taught her to value the input of responding officers. Sometimes they noticed details that were gone by the time investigators arrived.

"No, ma'am," the officer replied. A muscle on his jawline tightened. "You'll see why. The crime scene team is en route. So is the medical examiner."

"Thank you," Blake replied. They returned to the car to equip themselves with blue plastic booties and latex gloves before turning in the direction he indicated.

They had to hop the fence to their left to get into the field. A second line of police tape was set up on the opposite end, cordoning off a large space about twenty yards by twenty. At the very center was a dark smudge on the ground that could only be one thing.

Blake's stomach tightened. No matter how many times she saw one, a dead body always had the same impact on her, a fact which probably had something to do with her relationship to the first two she'd ever seen.

Still, she reasoned, it would be worse not to feel anything around them. She'd seen many law enforcement personnel build armor around themselves to protect their minds from the horrors of the job. Sometimes they built those walls so thick and high they couldn't let others in—or tear them down, even when they tried.

The surface of the field was soft underfoot, but without any rain in the last week, it wasn't soggy enough to be muddy. Older indentations of horseshoes lay everywhere. It took Blake and Melissa a couple of minutes to walk to the second line of police tape.

"Detectives." A waiting officer nodded. He was facing away from the body, his hands crossed over his belt. His expression was pale.

"Hey, Frank," Melissa said.

"You get the bastard who did this, okay?"

Blake said nothing. She didn't like to promise outcomes she wasn't certain she could deliver. She lifted up the tape and ducked underneath.

"Careful where you walk," she murmured to Melissa once they were out of earshot. She didn't want to come off as patronizing.

Melissa nodded. Her posture was taut, shoulders pulled back, and her jaw set tight. Blake could tell she was consciously controlling her breathing. Perhaps she didn't trust her voice.

Blake carefully studied the turf in front of her, following her own advice instead of allowing herself to be distracted by the shape of the body up ahead. As far as she could tell, there were no footprints on the ground. It was too dry. She glanced up a couple of times, noting something strange about the way the woman's head was angled, but didn't allow it to distract her.

As they crossed the final ten yards to the body, Blake slowed even further, sweeping her gaze left and right across the grass. She couldn't see anything. No shell casings, no scraps of cloth, no murder weapon. Just a prone, unnaturally still figure lying on the grass.

"Oh my God," Melissa said as they stopped behind it. She clapped her hands across her mouth.

Blake controlled her reaction better. But she felt the same way. The woman's head had been hacked clean off, her body laid out flat on the ground like it would be in a coffin. The decapitated skull had then been placed with the neck flush to the soil, eyes facing toward the corpse's toes.

She was naked.

They stood that way for several long moments, taking in the entire situation. Blake noted that there was almost no blood: something that would be impossible if the woman had been killed here. The body also looked like it had been wiped clean, which didn't bode well for their chances of discovering forensic evidence.

But the weirdest detail was that the woman's blond hair had been spread out in a halo around her head. There was no way it had fallen that way naturally.

"Whoever did this staged the scene," Blake finally observed. "They took their time."

She glanced over her shoulder as another vehicle rumbled down the road toward the riding center. It was a white van with black lettering on the side that she couldn't read at this distance. She guessed it belonged to either the crime scene team or the medical examiner.

Blake reached into her pocket and pulled out her phone. She opened the camera app and snapped several pictures from different angles.

"Okay, let's get closer," she said.

They walked cautiously toward the body and stopped at its side. For the first time, they were able to see the woman's face. Her eyelids were open, and she was staring blankly in front of her. Blake had somehow expected her to look either terrified or angry, but the truth was that she was devoid of emotion.

"That's not Nina Crawford," Melissa said, sounding stunned.

"No it is not," Blake replied. She sank slowly to her haunches and took a close-up photo of the victim's face, as shocked by this discovery as Melissa sounded.

So who the hell are you?

The crime scene team arrived a couple of minutes later, carrying several heavy black duffel bags full of equipment which they placed on a tarpaulin sheet just on the edge of the police tape line.

The photographer, a man who looked to be in his late thirties with curly salt-and-pepper hair, introduced himself to Blake as Elijah Cummings. Melissa already knew him. The team, Blake learned, was part of the Criminal Investigations Division at Northern Pines, which meant they were technically under her command.

Elijah, along with a taciturn and diminutive woman with blue hair, climbed into white plastic forensics suits and donned similar blue booties to the ones Melissa and Blake were wearing.

"That's Robyn," Melissa explained as the blue-haired woman ushered them away from the body. She lowered her voice before continuing. "She's the department's crime scene investigator. She handles all the forensic work. She doesn't speak much, but she's extremely thorough."

The two stood back and watched as the crime scene team got to work. Elijah first walked with his back to the line of tape, snapping images that covered the crime scene from every angle before spiraling closer and closer to the body. Blake was impressed by what she saw. There wasn't a single square inch of the crime scene that wouldn't be recorded by his photographs. Robyn appeared equally thorough.

"I'll go ask some questions," Melissa said, gesturing at a small crowd gathered around the fence line nearest to the riding center. She looked a little green. "Maybe someone saw something."

"Good idea," Blake said quietly.

Her head was full of questions about what on earth was happening here. Who was this woman? What kind of rage could have compelled her killer to sever her head clean off? Why stage the body like this?

Most importantly: was there any connection with the disappearance of Nina Crawford? Was this a horrific premonition of another killing to come?

Blake exhaled deeply to clear her mind. Spinning wildly wouldn't get her the answers she needed. First of all, she needed to check in with Captain Rogers. She would have heard about the discovery of the body by now. The last thing Blake needed was her superior harrying her for information or thinking she was holding out on her.

She reached into her pocket. After withdrawing her phone, she paused for a moment, realizing that she didn't know the captain's phone number.

"Hell of a first day on the job," she muttered.

Instead, she returned Jed's call and asked to be put through to Rogers. After a short pause, she heard, "Hello?"

"Captain? It's Lieutenant Larsen," Blake said, her new title still feeling unfamiliar in her throat. "I wanted to check in. We don't know much yet, but the body isn't Nina Crawford's."

"You're sure?" Rogers replied, sounding surprised.

"Seems that way," Blake agreed. "The medical examiner just got here. I'm waiting on a preliminary time of death. We won't know much else until the autopsy comes through. But..."

"What is it?"

Blake sighed. "The vic was decapitated. The scene looks staged. I don't want to get ahead of myself, but this doesn't look like a crime of passion. And with another missing woman..."

"What can I do?" Rogers asked proactively.

"I'll forward Nina Crawford's cell number and rideshare details. We need to put a rush request in to her cell provider and Uber to find out exactly where she went last night. Right now, we're stumbling around in the dark."

"Understood," Rogers said, her tone clipped. "Send it to me, and keep me updated."

With that, she put down the phone. The line died with a quiet click.

Instead of returning her phone to her pocket, Blake dialed a different number. Her investigation into Nina Crawford's whereabouts had taken on huge added significance. Though there was no concrete connection between this homicide and her disappearance, Blake didn't believe the two events were a coincidence. They were connected. She just didn't know how.

"Blake," a friendly voice answered. "I was going to call. You still owe me that beer."

She relaxed a little at Nathan Cooper's familiar tones. He was a special agent in the US Army's Criminal Investigation Division—both Blake's own former employer and former job. He had been instrumental several months earlier in bringing to justice her brother's killers, along with those corrupt law enforcement personnel who had allowed gang crime to flourish in their jurisdictions, just so long as they got paid. He would be a friend for life, though sometimes she wondered if he was looking for something more than that.

"What beer?"

"It was worth a shot," he laughed. "How are you, anyway? And how's Ryan?"

"I'm good. So's Ryan, I think. He should be back in town with his new foot any day now. I'm working again, actually. That's why I called."

"Lucky man," Nathan replied, though it wasn't clear whether he was referring to himself or Ryan. "Sounds intriguing. Which agency?"

Blake frowned. She actually wasn't certain. "The Sheriff's Department," she said. "Or Northern Pines PD. It's kind of up in the air at the moment."

"Congratulations. So how can I help?"

She filled him in on Nina Crawford's disappearance and the body she'd just stumbled across. As she spoke, she heard fingers clacking against a keyboard in the background, along with a sharp intake of breath as she described how the victim's corpse had been arranged.

"Anything you can tell me about this Captain Crawford guy would be useful. Because right now, I've got nothing," she finished.

"O-kay," Nathan said, stretching out the syllables as he processed the information in front of him. "Captain Austin Crawford. Commands Charlie Company, 3rd Brigade Combat Team, 82nd Airborne. Born 25 February 1995. Makes him, what, 28 years old. Married four years, listed as having two kids. Both young."

"Yeah, I saw them," Blake agreed.

"I don't see anything unusual in his personnel jacket. No history of domestic violence, no red flags, nothing. Served a couple of tours in Afghanistan and saw combat both times. Purple heart. Glowing writeups from his superiors. From what I can see, he's clean as a whistle."

"Shit," she replied.

"Doesn't mean he's not involved," Nathan pointed out.

"No. But it would have given me a jumping-off point."

"That it would. I'll keep digging and send over what I can find."

"Thanks, Nathan."

"Anytime."

As she slipped her cell phone back into her pocket, the ME stood up and caught her eye. She walked over to him.

"Got anything for me, Doc?" she asked.

"Scott's just fine. I'm ready to load the body up," he said. "But I've got a time of death for you. It's preliminary, of course. I won't be able to stake my reputation on it until I get her back to the lab and run a few calculations. It was cool last night. Throws the internal temperature loss out."

Blake raised her eyebrow. Medical examiners were always the same. "Best guess?"

"The poor girl was killed between eight and fourteen hours ago," he said, pursing his lips. "Like I said, I should be able to narrow that window down for you."

"Thanks Doc—I mean, Scott," Blake said. "Anything else jump out at you?"

He hesitated, eyes narrowing slightly, then said, "This was premeditated. The initial incision was made with a sharp blade—the wound edges are visibly clean and defined—but the cuts through the cervical vertebrae are different. There's evidence of both bone particles and tissue fragments around the disrupted vertebrae that indicate both a high degree of energy transfer and an implement that is inconsistent with the original blade."

"Any guesses what could have done it?"

"I have some ideas. I'll let you know once I've made a more detailed examination," he said.

"I appreciate it. What about the autopsy?"

Scott glanced at his watch. "Most likely tomorrow morning. I'll see if I can hurry that timeline up for you. The quicker I get her into my van, the quicker you'll know."

7

"One of the stable hands found the body a little after 9 a.m.," Melissa said as she backed up the car and spun it in the opposite direction, away from the riding center. "He let the horses into the field and noticed they were acting strangely. He said he didn't go near the body. First thing he did was call 911."

"The medical examiner put the time of death at between eight and fourteen hours ago," Blake said, quickly doing the math in her head.

It was now almost 11 a.m. That meant the victim had been killed sometime between nine the previous night and three that morning. She relayed that fact to Melissa, who poked her tongue out of the left-hand corner of her mouth in concentration as she indicated back onto the road to town.

"But she wasn't killed where her body was dumped," Melissa mused. "And staging it that neatly would have taken time. Not to mention cleaning the body and practically draining it of blood. There's no way she was killed and then driven straight to that field."

Blake nodded. She'd concluded the same. "Did any of the staff say what time the center opens?"

"The owner lives here, in a house out back. She usually walks the grounds from 7 a.m. Other members of staff arrive between 7:30 and 8 each morning."

"But not today?"

"She's laid up in bed with the flu. I poked my head around the door. She looks like hell. So nobody noticed until the horses went out a little later than usual."

"But it's unlikely the killer would have known that," Blake said. The car rumbled as one of the front wheels hit a pothole. "If he staged the body that neatly, I'm guessing he staked his drop zone out ahead of time. It seems unlikely he would have left the body within a couple of hours of the ordinary start of the day. Too risky."

"It doesn't really help us, though." Melissa sighed in frustration. "Let's say he dumped the body before 5 a.m. Then he had between two and eight hours to kill the victim, prepare her body, and drive to the field where he left her. Theoretically, that could leave the site of the murder itself anywhere between Wellington and Jacksonville."

Blake grimaced. Melissa was right, though she doubted the killer would have taken so great a risk. Driving a long distance with a dead body in the back of your vehicle risked being stopped by the highway patrol. It was far more likely the homicide had occurred closer to home.

"I'm expecting a full workup on Captain Crawford by the time we get back to the station," she said. "I need you to look into Nina's background. The captain is running down her whereabouts last night. I want to know everything there is to know about her. Any online social media profiles. Dating apps. Anything you can think of that will help us get a better picture of her life."

Melissa nodded in agreement. "I'm on it."

They arrived back at the station fifteen minutes later. Blake walked in a daze toward the front entrance, her brain power focused primarily on the case at hand.

As they reached the halfway point, someone called out, "Lieutenant Larsen?"

The unfamiliar voice caused her to look up. Melissa stopped at the same time and cast the speaker a guarded glance. He was a young man, perhaps in his late twenties, and wore a dark navy blazer, tan slacks, and a red and blue checked shirt.

"He's a reporter with the *Pinecone*, the local paper," Melissa said out of the side of her mouth. "Aaron Weller. He's good. It's a cliché, but he's like a dog with a bone."

"I'll catch up with you," Blake said, quickly refocusing and putting her game face on.

The last thing she needed right now was press attention on this case. A missing military wife who had an open relationship with her war hero husband, combined with a murder as gruesome as the one they'd just left the scene of would be like catnip for the press. She couldn't imagine the moniker they would devise for the killer, but she had no doubt they would come up with something as catchy as it was demeaning to the victims and their grieving families.

"Mr. Weller," she said as she came to a stop in front of the journalist. "How can I help you?"

Never give anything away. Neither confirm nor deny. Don't say anything until you know what the other party has.

A long-forgotten piece of media training bubbled up from somewhere deep inside her. For many years, that part of her professional development had seemed pointless. Her superiors in the Army had handled all media requests. Now she was left hurriedly scrambling to remember the finer points of media sessions she'd long since dismissed as pointless.

"Ms. Larsen, the question is, how can I help *you*?" he said. "And you can call me Aaron. Mr. Weller was my father. And I never liked him."

He grinned, but Blake didn't return the favor. She wondered why he hadn't led with a question about the homicide victim.

"I'm not looking for any help, Mr. Weller," she said, the response coming across a little more icily than she'd intended.

"I want to do a profile on you," he said to her great surprise. He spread his hands wide. "Introduce you to our readers."

"On me?" Blake said, frowning. She was baffled. "Why?"

"Ms. Larsen, you might not know it, but you have a hell of a personal narrative. Most people who experience a childhood trauma as tragic as yours are unable to put it behind them long enough to just get by, let alone prosper. Believe me, I know. And then to lose your brother to a criminal gang here in Northern Pines..."

He paused to shake his head with exaggerated solemnity.

"A gang that you did more than anyone to bring to justice. Well, that all would be enough to break most people. But here you are. So imagine my surprise when I learned this morning that you're the new commander of the Investigation Division here in town. That, Lieutenant, is a story for the ages. And I want to tell it."

Blake's mouth tightened. She didn't need this today. Or any day, really, but especially not today. She stared back at Aaron Weller's expectant expression. He looked like he thought this was a no-brainer. Maybe for somebody else, it would have been. But not for her.

Most days, the pain of being the last surviving member of her family was no more prominent than a muscle ache—always there in the background but rarely debilitating. Sometimes, like right now, it was a raw, open wound.

"Mr. Weller, my life is not a story. If you'll excuse me, I have"—she paused before saying *work to do*, quickly rephrasing to something less interesting—"my onboarding to finish."

"That's where you're wrong," Weller said as she stepped past him. "Your life is a story. And you should be the one to tell it."

He reached into his jacket and pulled out a business card. He thrust it into her hands and backpedaled before she had a chance to refuse it.

"Call me when you change your mind."

The reporter walked quickly to his car without turning back. Blake ground her teeth together, tension building in her jaw.

"Asshole," she muttered under her breath.

Melissa was waiting for her inside. She had a curious expression on her face. "What did he want? Did he pick up on the case already?"

Blake shook her head. "Nothing good." She changed the subject. "What's the ETA on the vic's prints?"

"They should be back in three hours," Melissa replied. "I'll let you know the second they come in."

"Thanks."

As they walked past the lobby desk, a voice called out, "Lieutenant Larsen?"

"What's up, Sandy?" she asked, seeing the receptionist standing up behind the glass partition. Blake made a conscious effort to modulate her voice so that she didn't fire the woman a broadside of inner frustration after the conversation with Aaron Weller.

"Captain Rogers is looking for you," Sandy said. "She asked me to point you to her office as soon as you got in."

"I'll be right up."

She walked with Melissa upstairs and parted company outside the captain's office. Her partner went straight to her desk to begin the workup on Nina Crawford.

Blake walked through the empty waiting room and knocked twice on Rogers' office door.

"Enter," a curt voice sounded a moment later. She pulled the door open and stepped inside.

"You wanted to see me, Captain?"

"Your request for information came back about ten minutes ago," Rogers said. She pushed a printout across the desk in front of her.

"That was quick," Blake said, crossing quickly over and snatching up the proffered document.

Nina Crawford had called the Uber to her home at 6:21 p.m. the previous evening. She'd been dropped off outside an establishment called The Coal Yard in Pinehurst 23 minutes later. The driver's contact details were printed at the bottom of the document, along with a note indicating he'd worked over a dozen more rides that night before finishing his shift just after three a.m.

Blake bit her lip. That probably indicated the driver could be ruled out as a suspect, though she'd need to follow up with him to be sure.

"Companies tend to move quickly when you tell them a life is on the line," Rogers replied. "Guess it's a liability thing. Her cell provider is still working on pulling their records. I'll email them to you as soon as I receive them."

"Thank you, Captain," Blake said, dipping her head. She was already backing away, eager to chase down this fresh lead. Their *only* lead. "I appreciate the help."

Rogers fixed her gaze on her. "I'm requesting support from the broader sheriff's department. We're understaffed as it is. It's still your case, but you won't be working it alone."

Blake nodded. She hadn't been expecting this, but she wasn't surprised. A missing persons case connected with a gruesome murder would tax any town's police department—let alone one as short-staffed as Northern Pines.

"We could use it," she said honestly. She waved the piece of paper and started walking to the exit.

"There's one last thing, Lieutenant."

Blake turned.

"The motor pool has set you up with a personal vehicle. Go speak to Charlie. He'll get you the keys."

"Thanks, Captain," she replied as she spun away. She stopped dead, frowned, and turned back. "Where exactly would I find the motor pool?"

Captain Rogers grinned unexpectedly, the genuine display of humor breaking through the worry lines on her forehead. Blake wondered if she looked the same way herself. If not, she guessed she would by the time this case drew to a close.

"Downstairs, through Patrol to the rear of the building. You can't miss it."

Blake followed her instructions and took the stairs down three at a time, thankful for the cardio work she'd put in over the previous few weeks. At the nadir of her spiral following Caleb's death, she had barely been able to walk down the liquor aisle without breaking a sweat.

It wasn't that bad.

She flushed at the memory. Maybe it had been.

The office space allotted to the Patrol Division was significantly larger than that for Criminal Investigations, which made sense. There was a larger conference room with a projector mounted to the ceiling, no chairs or table, and a podium in one corner of the rectangular space. Blake passed by an open doorway with a brass plaque that read *PATROL COMMANDER*. The office that lay behind was empty. So were about half the desks in the open-plan office, where patrol officers filled out their arrest records and other paperwork. The same fresh wind of change had swept through here as the second floor.

Blake felt the heat of a couple of glances in her direction on the back of her neck as she walked through. She didn't stop to introduce herself. There wasn't time. She was conscious that every second that passed without a break in the case lessened Nina Crawford's chances of survival.

She found the motor pool office in the hallway on the other side of Patrol. It was a hatch in the wall, behind which sat a uniformed officer. A couple of dozen hooks were screwed into the wall behind him.

"You Charlie?" she asked.

"You got me," the sergeant—according to his uniform—replied. "Charlie Falconer. I'm guessing you're the new lieutenant?"

"One and the same." Blake nodded. "Captain Rogers said you had a car waiting for me?"

"So I do," Charlie replied. He was an older gentleman, in his mid-sixties if she had to guess. His hair was gray and fraying, but he had a muscular build. His sleeves were rolled most of the way up his forearms, and she noticed a couple of grease stains on his skin.

He spun on his office chair in the cramped cubbyhole and reached behind him for one of the keys. Blake noticed that it hung underneath a hand-scribbled label that read *UNMARKED* in all capital letters.

"I did the work on her myself," he said proudly as he handed over the keys. "She'll run nice and smooth for you, I promise you that."

"Full tank of gas?"

"Naturally," he said in a mildly affronted tone.

"Sorry for doubting you," she said with a grin. "It's not my experience at every place I've worked."

"You can't get the people these days," he said with a shake of his head. "That's why I do most things myself. Sign out the keys, handle the maintenance."

"Benefits of a small department, I guess," Blake replied.

"So long as they don't make me retire, I'm happy," Charlie said. "And it keeps me off my bum leg."

He pushed a form across the narrow surface between them, along with a cheap ballpoint pen. "If you can just sign right there on that dotted line."

Blake did as instructed.

"You got a shotgun in the trunk. AR-15 as well. That second key on the chain unlocks the gun safe. Both weapons are loaded."

"Thank you, Sergeant."

"It's Charlie." He leaned forward and lowered his voice. "Listen, I'm behind you and the captain. Most of the guys are. And gals, no doubt. Lord knows this department has needed a clean broom sweeping through it for a long, long time. If you need anything, just ask."

8

B lake indicated left and guided her new cruiser into a parking space close to The Coal Yard bar. The drive to Pinehurst had taken only twenty minutes, most of which she'd spent thinking over Charlie's parting comment. It was good to know most of the department's remaining cops were on her side.

But it would be nicer if it was all of them.

Pinehurst was a picturesque resort village developed at the start of the twentieth century by a wealthy industrialist. She knew it well, having had dinner nearby with Ryan once before their respective calendars played interference. The buildings were mostly colonial style, painted white, and only one or two stories high.

The village was surrounded by over forty golf clubs and frequently played host to US Open tournaments, a fact that was reflected in the demographic of the pedestrians she saw walking past. They were mostly older, and many were dressed in golf gear. It wasn't a sport that Blake knew much about. She doubted she had the patience to try it.

She glanced at her watch as she killed the vehicle's engine. It was hard to believe that it was only lunchtime. Today felt as if it had already lasted several lifetimes, and it was only getting going. Peering through her car's windshield, she noticed a man in blue jeans and a white T-shirt climbing up the ladder that was leaning against the exterior of The Coal Yard.

"Somebody's home," she muttered.

She climbed out of the car and locked it behind her. The door to the bar was propped ajar, but the establishment clearly wasn't open for business. Harsh electric light blared from the other side of the windows, which was quite at odds with the refined whiskey bar vibe she guessed it was going for.

"Can I help you?" the man on the ladder said as she approached the entrance. He had a screwdriver in his right hand and was fiddling with something she couldn't make out from this angle. Despite the cool winter weather, he had sweat patches underneath his armpits.

Blake pulled her jacket back to flash her badge. "Detective Lieutenant Larsen with Monroe County Sheriff's Department," she said. "I'm working a missing persons case. The woman in question was dropped off at this location last night. You the manager?"

The man looked down sharply. He pocketed the screwdriver. "Owner. Mark Lovington. I run a few bars in the area."

"You mind stepping down for a moment?"

"No problem."

She waited until he joined her on the sidewalk. Once his hands were off the ladder's rungs, he reached up and pulled a long metal screw from between his lips, which he deposited in a pocket.

"Were you working last night?" she asked.

"Every night." Mark nodded. "This place is my pride and joy. Can't seem to trust others to handle the job."

Blake knew that feeling. She nodded in appreciation. "You've done well. It looks beautiful."

"Thank you."

She reached into her jacket pocket and retrieved her phone. She pulled up a photograph of Nina Crawford. "Have you seen this woman before? She arrived before 7 p.m."

He frowned and peered at the image. "Can't say I have. But I would've been in the back doing a stock take at that time. Janie was behind the bar. That's who you should ask."

"Is she in?"

He shook his head. "She has classes during the day. Works three nights a week. I can give you her cell number."

"Yes please," Blake said, hiding her frustration. She peered through the windows. "What about CCTV footage?"

Mark's expression changed instantly. He ground his teeth together and gave a tight negative jerk of the head. "Some asshole shot them out a couple nights back. All down the street."

Blake's eyes widened instantly. "What?"

He nodded, the implications of his statement only then seeming to become clear. "Wait, you think this is connected with your missing woman?"

"You said shot out?"

Mark nodded again. He climbed quickly back up the ladder, then down, jumping the last few rungs and landing heavily on the sidewalk. He handed her a security camera housing.

"Paintball," he said. "We figured it was preparation for someone jacking our storerooms. I had my cousin's boy sleep in the bar last night, just in case. But nothing went down."

"What about cameras inside?"

"Yeah, we got a few. One in the storeroom, a couple scattered through the rest of the bar. Problem is it's dark at night. Not always easy to make out too many details in the footage. I've been meaning to upgrade them, but it's not much of a priority. Pinehurst's a safe neighborhood. We don't see much trouble."

Until now, Blake thought.

"Can you show me?"

He gestured for her to follow him inside and led her behind the bar and past the rows of whiskey bottles on backlit shelves that faced the room. A door opened onto a small office area and then to the storeroom. Mark ushered her into the office.

He sat down at a neatly ordered desk and logged onto a computer. After a few moments, he turned the monitor toward her. A quadrant of security camera feeds were shown on screen, under a label marked *INTERIOR*. "What time did you say she arrived?"

"Six-forty p.m. Can you fast-forward it from then?"

He grunted his acknowledgment and scrubbed along the time marker, stopping at 6:40:32. He pressed play, then set the feeds to fast-forward at 8x. The numbers on a digital clock at the bottom right of the screen ticked up at pace.

The storeroom camera at the bottom of the quadrant didn't change, but Blake watched as a woman—she guessed Janie—walked left and right serving drinks on the feed focused on the bar itself. The other two cameras at the top of the screen were focused on different seating areas.

They were mounted high, on the ceiling or at the very top of the wall, judging by the camera angle. Her heart sank as she realized that Mark was right. You could see what people were wearing, the tops of their heads, occasionally a blurry flash of their face, but little else.

Still, Blake leaned forward as a flash of blond hair appeared on the top right camera feed. "Wait! Pause it there."

Mark tapped the spacebar, and all four feeds froze. Blake peered at the screen. "Play it in real time," she said.

He did so. Blake watched, holding her breath, as a woman wearing a dark, tight-fitting dress walked into shot. Judging by the way she was standing, she was dressed in heels.

It could be her.

She watched as the blonde walked to a pair of armchairs in the very center of the shot and turned as if to sit down. Then a man wearing a tan jacket and a baseball cap followed her into the image and tugged her gently by her left elbow, pulling her to a more secluded spot at the very corner of the video feed. It was right by the walls and almost out of sight.

He sat down facing away from the camera. The woman joined him. Her face was lost in shadow. Blake glanced to her left and checked the other video feed, but it was pointed in completely the wrong direction. She grimaced with frustration.

"Did he know where the camera was pointed?" she said out loud.

"Could be," Mark replied, not recognizing that her question was rhetorical. "Want me to put it on fast-forward?"

She nodded, and he tapped the keyboard once more. They watched as the woman behind the bar walked up to take the drinks order, disappeared, then returned holding a silver tray with two cocktail glasses on it. She set them on the table and returned to the bar. The couple drank slowly.

"I'm guessing you wash all your glassware each night?" Blake ventured, hoping they might be able to retrieve a fingerprint.

Mark nodded. "I run a tight ship."

"I guessed you might," she sighed.

She continued studying the video. About all she could make out was that the man was tall and broad-shouldered. He was wearing a tan jacket. Perhaps a Carhart worker jacket or similar.

After half an hour, the couple stood. Blake watched as the man walked to the bar to pay the bill, then as they walked outside. She grimaced as she saw he paid cash. Neither face became visible on camera the entire time. Acid singed the back of her throat as her indigestion kicked into high gear after she watched Janie thoroughly wipe down both the seats and the bar after they left—basically anywhere that could have retained a fingerprint.

"The new normal." Mark shrugged apologetically when he saw her face.

"It doesn't matter. I guess this place gets busy at night?"

"Yeah."

"I doubt the fingerprint would have stuck around anyway. This is a high-traffic environment."

"Want me to email you the footage?"

Blake nodded, then realized she was still holding the broken security camera. "I need to take this."

Mark shrugged. "No problem. Damn lens cracked on impact anyway. I'm going to have to replace it. Here, let me get you Janie's phone number too. Maybe she can shed some light on this."

The footage was uploaded directly to an online system, which meant all Mark needed to do was send her a link to allow access. He added Janie's number into the same email. Blake gave her thanks and left her phone number in case either of them remembered any further details.

After leaving, she walked to her cruiser and pulled out a thin plastic evidence bag from the well-stocked trunk. There was no chance the suspect had handled the security camera, so she didn't worry about leaving prints. She closed the trunk after she was done, then forwarded the camera footage to Melissa so that a fresh set of eyes could comb over it.

Blake walked the street for the next 45 minutes, speaking to every business owner and pedestrian she came across. By the end, she was no more informed than she had been at the start. Nobody had seen anything. There was no reason why anyone should remember passing by a single couple, after all. Neither was there any camera footage. Their suspect had been meticulous, somehow identifying every single CCTV camera on the entire street and disabling all of them in the middle of the night without being seen.

"With a paintball gun," Blake said out loud.

Whoever had done it was a hell of a shot. Most of the cameras had been taken out with just one or two paintballs. She wondered whether the culprit had a military background. Possibly. Perhaps it tilted the scales toward Austin as her suspect—if the homicide case was even connected to her missing person. But she wasn't sure how much crossover there was with paintball accuracy and real-life marksmanship.

And besides, even if the suspect was current or former military, that didn't narrow the pool of potential suspects down much. Half the population this close to Fort Bragg fit that category.

Her phone buzzed in her pocket as she returned to her car. She ignored it for a moment as frustration built inside her. This case wasn't opening up. All they had was a few minutes of grainy video footage of the tall, muscular man who might or might not be their suspect. It was always possible that Nina had been taken after her date.

But not likely.

She brought her phone to her ear and answered, "Larsen."

"It's Melissa. You need to get back here."

"What's up?"

"I'm not exactly sure," Melissa replied. "But I just got a strange call from Austin Crawford. He sounds real shaken up. He said something about a video, but he was blubbering down the phone."

Blake's blood turned ice cold. "Have you seen it?"

"No."

"Okay, I'm on my way over. I'll be fifteen minutes."

"I'll meet you there."

9

With anxiety vibrating through her body, Blake flicked on her siren and lights and drove to the Crawford home in record time. She arrived only a few seconds after Melissa and parked just behind the other detective's car as she was climbing out.

"Any news?"

Melissa shook her head. Her ponytail danced left and right behind her. "Nothing."

Blake walked briskly up to the front steps. She raised her hand to knock on the door, but it swung open just before she brought her knuckles down.

Austin Crawford appeared on the other side. His eyes were red-rimmed with tears. He looked in shock, face devoid of color. He was holding a cell phone. The screen was on, but Blake couldn't make out what was on it.

"Mr. Crawford?" she said, peering behind him, her hand automatically going to the side her holster was on. "Is everything okay?"

His head jerked left and right. "They have her," he said, his voice thick. "My God, they've taken Nina."

"Who has?" Blake said, suddenly alert. "Have you received a kidnap demand?"

Kidnap for ransom was very rare in the modern age. The FBI was *extremely* good at hunting down kidnappers, and decades ago, the practice had largely fallen out of use. The risk/reward ratio was simply too high. But that didn't mean it never happened. If there was one thing Blake had learned over the years, it was never to overestimate the intelligence of the average criminal.

Tears streaked down Austin's cheeks. His mouth bobbed open and closed a couple times before he could bring himself to speak. "Terrorists."

Blake and Melissa traded stunned glances. At first, Blake wondered whether she'd heard the man right. What he was saying simply didn't make sense.

He lifted up his arm and showed the two detectives the screen of his cell phone. "They sent me this video," he said.

Blake snatched the phone from his fingers. At first, all she could see was a flash of orange on a white background. She scrubbed the video all the way back to the beginning and pressed play. Melissa inched closer to her side so that she could see.

"Austin..." stammered a woman Blake recognized from the photos on the Crawfords' fridge. "I'm going to die. I'm sorry. Please take care of—"

An audible crack rang out. Blake watched in horror as an arm clad all in black snapped across the screen. Nina's head jerked backward as she was hit with a powerful open-hand slap. In front of her, Austin flinched at the sound. She wondered how many times he'd replayed this video. That crack would have been drilled into his skull over and over again.

She jerked her attention back to the video. Nina was dressed in an orange jumpsuit, like she was a prisoner. Her blond hair cascaded around her face. As she looked back toward the camera, a trickle of blood flowed from her left nostril. She looked dazed.

"God..." Melissa whispered.

Nina glanced off-screen, her eyelids flickering as though she was receiving instructions. When she returned her attention to the camera, she swapped between staring at the lens and somewhere down, off screen. Blake noticed a flash of white at the bottom of the shot. Perhaps a piece of paper.

"I am a prisoner of the Islamic State," Nina said—read—in a quavering voice. "I am accused of supporting the Great Satan and its soldiers. I will be tried for my crimes. If merciful—" She broke off and looked away from the camera. Her face drained of life. Blake guessed she was staring at her captor.

A click echoed through the phone's speaker. A metallic click. Blake would know that sound anywhere. It was the noise made when a round was chambered. She imagined the man on the other side of the camera raising his arm and aiming the weapon at Nina. Imagined the paralyzing fear that must have seized her.

Nina continued, her voice strangled in her throat.

"—if merciful Allah finds me innocent, I will be set free. If he does not, then I will be executed." Nina looked dead into the camera. Her eyes were glassy with tears. "I'm not the first, and I will not be the last. America has spilled much blood. Now that debt will be repaid."

The video file ended after 27 seconds. The screen went black.

Blake blinked slowly, stunned by what she had just seen. She'd already played out dozens of possible scenarios for this case in her head. But she'd never come close to predicting this. She let out a slow, shaky breath. She knew instantly that everything was about to change. A circus of three-letter agencies would descend on Northern Pines. So too would the media. Before long, this would be the leading news story on every station in America.

Finally, she looked up. Austin Crawford was still standing in front of her. He was trembling violently. He looked as though he might be sick.

"Mr. Crawford," she said gently. "Why don't you sit down?"

When he didn't respond, she and Melissa led him to the nearest chair and pushed him into it. He stared blankly into space.

Blake pulled Melissa aside. "Go to the kitchen," she whispered.

"Make him a coffee. Black. Lots of sugar. And as strong as you can, okay?"

Melissa nodded and hurried to the kitchen. Blake returned to Austin. She knew she should call this in, inform Captain Rogers so that she could bring in the FBI, Homeland Security, the State Bureau of Investigation, and who knew who else. But she hesitated. The moment she made that call, the case was no longer hers alone to work. Things would get complicated, fast.

"Mr. Crawford?" she said.

No response.

She tried again, reaching out and squeezing the officer's shoulder. She spoke in an authoritative tone she knew would get his attention. "Captain? I need you to listen to me."

Training kicked in, and he looked up. His eyes were still empty.

Better.

Softening her tone, she said, "Austin, I need to know who sent you this. How did you receive this video?"

"Email," he whispered.

Melissa returned a moment later. She was carrying a steaming cup of instant coffee. She handed it to Blake, who dropped to her haunches and offered it to Austin. He closed his palms around the cup and didn't seem to notice the stinging heat.

"Drink some," Blake urged.

He lifted the cup automatically to his lips and drank. He flinched as the hot liquid coursed down his throat. The pain seemed to shock some life back into him as Blake had hoped. The sugar would help ease his shock, too.

"From who?"

Austin shook his head. "I don't know. The email address is just a jumble of characters. I don't recognize it. When I tried to reply, my email bounced back."

"What else did the message say?"

"Nothing. Just that I should watch the video. I could see Nina's face in the still. Of course I was going to watch it!"

He crumpled forward, and half of the cup of coffee spilled onto the floor. He started to sob and rocked back and forth. "I can't believe it. They're going to kill her."

Blake indicated to Melissa to console him. She returned her attention to the phone screen, which still displayed the paused video. She exited it and returned to the email inbox. The address was exactly as Austin had described: a meaningless string of letters and numbers. Underneath the initial email was a bounce back confirming the second half of his story.

The timestamp on the email also fit with when Melissa had called her less than twenty minutes ago. As far as Blake could make out, Austin was telling the truth.

Austin fell silent. Melissa winced with guilt but stood up and rejoined Blake. They stepped a few feet away where they could speak in private. "What do we do?"

Blake shook her head, still staring at the phone in disbelief. "We don't have a choice. The department's held together with string and sticky tape, and the town has barely recovered from Hansen's crimes. It's time to call in the cavalry."

10

B lake entered the basketball court at the Hercules Fitness Center on the grounds of Fort Bragg and found that it was already abuzz with activity. The smell, stale sweat cured with disinfectant, yanked her back in time. She'd spent years in rooms just like this, sprinting up and down to the sound of a discordant, totalitarian electronic beep. She shook off the feeling. Now was no time for reminiscing.

There were dozens of command centers and other office buildings within the sprawling military base, but apparently, this was the space that could be made available for a multi-agency task force most quickly.

And right now, speed mattered.

Only three hours had passed since Austin Crawford had received the kidnap message from his wife. In that time, the FBI's Joint Terrorism Task Force, based out of its Charlotte Field Office, had spun up a quick reaction unit. The first units were just starting to arrive—mostly law enforcement personnel from local police and sheriff departments, CID special agents, a handful of DHS and ATF personnel, and a large number of military police and other soldiers.

The latter were mostly engaged in setting up workstations,

running electrical line, carrying in desks, and setting up Internet routers.

Charlotte was a two-and-a-half-hour drive from Bragg, so only a few FBI agents had so far arrived. A minivan containing four of them in tan slacks and navy blue yellow-stenciled polo shirts had pulled up just as Blake walked inside.

She found CID Special Agent Nathan Cooper directing traffic. Blake was pleased to see him. There were very few people in the world whom she trusted implicitly. Nathan was now one of them. Not just because he'd been instrumental in bringing justice to her brother's killers, but because he was a good man.

"Any news?" he asked as she joined him.

Nina Crawford was an Army wife. She knew that for Nathan, that made this one personal. Partners, male and female alike, were an intrinsic part of the fabric in communities like these. Their other halves knew the hazards of serving their country. But the threat wasn't supposed to reach into their own homes. It was as though a Rubicon had been crossed.

Blake shook her head. "I'm waiting on the victim's fingerprints. I've got images of her face for you to pass around. Maybe your guys can turn something up. Right now, she's a Jane Doe."

"Shit," Nathan muttered. He put his arms on his hips and surveyed the room. "What a mess."

Since Blake could still see discarded sweat towels by one of the walls, left by a PT group that must have been cleared out at a second's notice, she wasn't so disappointed. The burgeoning command center was coming along quickly. Rows of desks were already in place. The electrical wiring was being taped down. In no time, the budding operation's nerve center would be up and running.

But she knew Nathan wasn't referring to the building project in front of them.

"We'll find her," she said with more confidence than she felt. She bit her lip, an image of the murder victim's face floating across her vision as she did so. She said it again, this time for her own benefit. With meaning.

"We'll find her."

"You're right," Nathan sighed.

"Who's taking the lead on this one?" Blake asked. "CID?"

Nathan snorted, genuine amusement on his face. "Who do you think?"

FBI, then, Blake thought.

Maybe that wasn't such a bad thing. There was a Joint Terrorism Task Force in every FBI field office across the country. The units were designed as nerve cells, bringing in the DOJ along with local, state, and other federal law enforcement agencies under one roof to share information and coordinate operations.

And the fact of the matter was, Blake knew, this case would require resources that were far greater than those either the Northern Pines Police Department or even the Sheriff's Department could offer. Still, the cop in her rankled at the thought of having her own case taken from her.

Which is exactly what's going to happen.

Both of them turned to the doors at the front of the room as a commotion sounded. A tall, broad-shouldered man in suit pants, a white shirt with rolled-up sleeves, and a red tie strode into the makeshift command center. He was trailed by a dozen other individuals, a roughly even mix of men and women in their late twenties and up. Most were dressed in dark suits that screamed FBI just as loudly as the stenciled windbreakers the remainder wore.

"I guess the cavalry just arrived," Blake muttered.

The leader of the pack stopped. Blake studied his face but didn't recognize him. That was no real surprise. He was in his late forties or early fifties, if she had to guess. Dark hair turning white at the temples. Handsome, but with a shine in his eyes that marked him out as a real hard-charger.

"That's ASAC Carl Granger," Nathan explained. "He heads up counterterrorism in the Charlotte office."

Blake had guessed as much. The ASAC—or assistant-special-agent-in-charge, to give him his full title—was one of the deputies to a field office's SAC. He, in this case, would be a senior and experienced leader given wide latitude to get things done.

And usually, they knew it.

Granger didn't waste any time. As his minions came to a halt behind him, he cupped his hands around his mouth and bellowed, "Ladies and gentlemen, your attention please."

All activity in the bustling basketball court came to a stop. Nathan and Blake traded glances but turned their attention to the front. Granger waited until you could hear a feather drop before continuing.

"Excellent. My name is Carl Granger. Many of you know who I am. For those who don't, nice to meet you. I lead the JTTF in Charlotte. And until we bring Nina Crawford back home alive and well, I'm going to be working, eating, and not getting a whole lot of sleep right by your side. So if you want to see the back of me, do the work. Go beyond. Be the person who sees what no one else does. Now let's bring this woman home."

He paused and turned to an aide, who whispered something to him. After nodding his understanding, he said, "I'm looking for a Detective Blake Larsen. Is he out there?"

Blake caught Nathan flashing her a raised eyebrow. She hid her reaction, instead stepping forward and clearing her throat.

"I'm Lieutenant Larsen," she said with just the right amount of emphasis on both words.

Without a hint of embarrassment, Granger said, "I want you to bring us up to speed on everything you know."

Blake nodded. At first, she assumed he wanted a private briefing. After feeling the heat of his expectant gaze on her cheeks for several long seconds, she hurriedly added, "Now?"

"If you'd be so kind."

She cleared her throat to buy a second to think. Public speaking wasn't a huge fear of hers, but she preferred to be given a heads-up ahead of time. But cases this size didn't care what you preferred. You either rolled with them or they rolled right on over you.

"Northern Pines dispatch received a call first thing this morning from a Capt. Austin Crawford," she said, recounting the plain facts. "He reported that his wife failed to return home last night from a social engagement."

"Why did he wait until this morning?" an FBI agent called out.

Keeping her expression flat, Blake said, "According to the husband, the Crawfords are engaged in an open relationship. Capt. Crawford did not consider it unusual when Nina didn't return home before he fell asleep. He only raised the alarm when she wasn't back in time for breakfast."

A shocked murmur echoed around the room. Nathan glanced at her, surprise written on his face. She shot him an apologetic look. There hadn't been time to bring him up to speed.

"You're sure of that?" the same agent asked.

Blake raised an eyebrow. "Do you have any particular reason to doubt me?"

He said nothing in response.

She continued, "I interviewed Capt. Crawford this morning with my partner. While I was interviewing him, I received a call that alerted me to the fact that a body had been found in a field south of town. The victim remains unidentified—but is not Nina Crawford."

Another murmur ran around the edges of the room. ASAC Granger's face remained inscrutable. A number of more junior agents behind him were scribbling notes.

Blake waited for questions, then cleared her throat to silence the room.

"The body was found naked with a severed head. The crime scene was staged neatly. It's my initial assessment that the victim was not killed at the scene but was instead transported from elsewhere."

She glanced at her watch. "Time of death is estimated at between 11 and 17 hours ago. My team is working on a fingerprint search as we speak. I'm expecting results any moment now."

"Have you made any progress in tracing Nina Crawford's movements?" Granger asked.

Blake nodded. "She was last seen in a bar called The Coal Yard in Pinehurst, about a twenty-minute drive from her home. I have low-quality video footage placing her with an unidentified and likely unidentifiable male inside the bar. All cameras on the street outside were vandalized within the last couple of days."

"Do you have anything else?" Granger said brusquely.

Blake shook her head. "Not at present."

"Okay. One of my team will help you transfer your case files over to the JTTF database." He turned away from her, returning his attention to the rest of the crowd. "That's all for now. We'll have a full briefing at 4:30 p.m."

"No problem," Blake muttered. She wasn't surprised by the FBI man's cavalier attitude to local law enforcement, but it still put her nose out of joint.

"He takes some getting used to," Nathan observed.

She pulled out her phone and selected several images of the victim. She added them to an email and clicked send.

"I just fired over those pictures of the victim," she said. "You mind passing them around? Maybe we'll get lucky."

"I'm on it," Nathan said. He pulled out his own phone and spent a few moments forwarding the message on, his tongue poking out of the corner of his mouth in concentration as he did so.

Blake's phone beeped to signal she had an incoming message.

"That was Melissa, my partner," she said after she read it. Lowering her voice, she continued, "The medical examiner is ready to carry out the autopsy. Want to tag along?"

From the flash of excitement on Nathan's face, Blake had her answer before he opened his mouth. He glanced over at Granger, who was in a huddle, surrounded by his FBI clique and half a dozen other mostly men in DHS and ATF windbreakers.

Seems the feds like to stick together, she thought. *Well, two can play at that game.*

"Shouldn't we let the ASAC know about the autopsy?"

She grinned. "I won't tell if you don't."

11

Blake crossed the parking lot with a sense of foreboding in the pit of her stomach. She could already taste the disinfectant, the copper tang of blood, and the general aroma of human decay on the back of her tongue.

She took her time opening the large glass door that led inside and used it to take a final, deep breath of fresh, clean air. It would be her last for some time, and she wanted to make it count.

As prepared as she was likely to get, Blake stepped inside. The eyes of a young man behind the reception desk widened as she presented her badge. She guessed that either he was new at the job or had learned about the gruesome state in which the body was found.

She inclined her head in thanks and followed his instructions to Dr. Meyer's lab, where she found the medical examiner and his assistant already dressed in scrubs. The assistant was a young woman with startling pink hair and heavy eye makeup. She wore matching pink scrubs, in contrast to the more ordinary medical green favored by her boss. She was holding a metal clipboard in her hands and filling out some paperwork.

"Thank you for moving this up, Dr.—I mean, Scott," Blake said as she entered. "I really appreciate it."

"No problem," Scott replied. "I understand there have been some unpleasant developments on the case."

Blake wondered how he had heard that. She guessed he was probably plugged in to the various local police departments—and the sheriff's department, for that matter—much better than she was. Detectives tended to owe medical examiners favors. Either that or he was fishing for information.

"Unfortunately," she agreed, making a face but not adding any more detail.

"Then we had better get started." He shrugged.

He rolled up his sleeves and walked to a large sink on the side of the room, thoroughly scrubbing his hands with antibacterial solution before drying them and donning surgical gloves. The assistant followed suit, then both added a thick rubber apron to their ensemble.

Nathan joined a few moments later, apologetically mouthing, *Traffic.*

The assistant, who had an access badge on a floral lanyard around her neck, handed each of them a surgical mask and hairnet. She opened a drawer and pulled out a box of blue plastic nose plugs, which Blake refused. It was stupid, but she felt a point of pride about being able to handle watching autopsies without shielding herself from the horror.

Or perhaps not pride, exactly, but respect for the victim. She felt as though it was somehow wrong to try and hide away from what had happened to the men, women, and children whose last, most vulnerable moments fate had allowed her to observe.

"Good to see you again, Special Agent Cooper," Dr. Meyer said. Blake remembered that Nathan had watched Kyle Thompson's autopsy several months ago in the previous case they'd worked together.

"Likewise." Nathan nodded.

Scott bowed his head as he pulled a green paper sheet off the body on the autopsy table.

"Okay, young lady," he murmured softly, "let us uncover what was done to you."

Blake pursed her lips as she saw the victim's face staring up at the ceiling. The severed head had been steadied with blocks on either side, leaving only an inch or so of gap between the two ends of cut flesh. A passing glance might leave the impression that she was still whole. With her body cleaned and prepared for the autopsy and no visible signs of blood, she could almost be asleep.

Who are you?

Melissa had searched state, local, and federal databases of missing persons that morning but had yet to turn up a trace of the young lady lying in front of her. Perhaps it was too early for her to have been reported. Or perhaps no one cared enough to notice she was gone.

But Blake didn't think so. The body in front of her was young and healthy. Watching the care and respect Scott paid the victim, she shivered. This was someone's daughter. Maybe someone's sister. She had been loved. Now she was gone.

She watched as the medical examiner carefully examined the woman's body from head to toe. He took his time, not narrating his thoughts, perhaps spending five or ten minutes on his task of simply familiarizing himself with the body. Only then did he speak.

"Charlotte, we've got bruising on the left wrist," he said.

Charlotte made a notation on her clipboard, then approached with a digital camera and took several shots. "Same on the right," Scott intoned as his assistant circled the autopsy table.

After examining similar injuries on the victim's ankles, Scott said, "This woman was bound before she was killed. Perhaps using thin canvas straps or plastic cuffs, though it's difficult to be certain."

"How long for?" Blake asked.

"I can't say," he replied. "The marks are faint but definitely there."

She grimaced but fell silent. She'd hoped he might be able to shed some light on how long this woman had been held captive. Anything might prove useful in determining her identity—or whether she was connected to Nina Crawford's disappearance. It was difficult to guess how the two horrific cases could be unrelated, but they had to be sure.

"I also have hypodermic entry wounds," Scott said without looking up from his examination. "Three of them, no, four. The last one was successful."

"Are they recent?" Nathan asked.

"Indeed. I suspect they were administered shortly before this young lady's untimely death."

The medical examiner gently ran his gloved fingers down the victim's skin, searching her wrists, the crooks of her elbows, and other major veins for evidence of further injection sites but reported none. Neither was there evidence of prolonged or historical needle usage—no scar tissue or evidence of use of dirty needles. As far as he could reasonably be sure, the woman wasn't a drug user.

Blake watched at Nathan's side as Scott directed Charlotte to take a variety of samples, including blood and scrapings from underneath the victim's nails.

"No evidence of defensive wounds," he said after carefully studying her fingers and nails. He pulled a bright overhead light and magnification glass down and studied the steel tray of nail scrapings. "Nothing of interest here, either."

Next, Scott turned his attention to the victim's severed head. He pulled the overhead light across and lowered it close to the woman's closed eyelids. He gently pushed them open, holding the left one back as far as possible as he intently studied the eyeball underneath.

Blake caught a glimpse of it through the magnification glass and forced herself to look away. She only barely restrained a shudder. There was no life in the woman's gaze. Just cold emptiness.

"Interesting," Scott murmured.

Blake opened her mouth to ask what, then forced it shut. She saw Nathan doing the same thing beside her. Her heart rate picked up in anticipation of what the medical examiner had discovered.

"Charlotte," Scott said, looking up at his assistant instead. "Is the camera ready?"

She said nothing but instantly appeared at his side holding a high-resolution digital camera.

He murmured, "Petechiae. Do you see?"

Charlotte nodded and bent down. She snapped several photos from different angles of each eyeball as Scott retracted the eyelids. Then she returned to a work surface on the opposite wall to where Nathan and Blake were standing. She scribbled notes onto a diagram of the human face.

Still Blake and Nathan kept silent. They watched intently as Scott studied the victim's face through his magnifying glass, paying close attention to her nose and mouth. Then he opened the mouth and peeled back her lips. He called Charlotte over a second time, and she snapped multiple images of the interior of the victim's mouth.

Finally, Scott looked up. He rolled his shoulders and beckoned them over.

"I believe I have a preliminary cause of death for you, Detectives," he said.

Nathan wasn't technically a detective, but he didn't correct the medical examiner. Blake guessed that, like her, he was too interested in his discovery.

Even so, his face knitted over. "This might be a stupid question, Doc, but isn't the cause of death pretty obvious?"

"How so?" Scott asked curiously.

Nathan glanced at Blake, then back at the medical examiner. "Someone cut her head off."

"Yes, but before she was killed or after?"

Blake watched as the CID special agent's mouth opened wide, then shut just as quickly. He closed his eyes and swallowed reflexively. She guessed he was imagining what had happened to the poor victim.

"Shit," he muttered.

"Come take a look," Scott said, pushing the magnifying glass a couple inches upward so that it once again focused on the victim's eyes. "She has conjunctival petechiae in both eyes. In layspeak, they are bloodshot. There was damage to the capillaries caused by high pressure in the blood vessels."

He pushed the magnifying glass down. "Do you see these marks around her nose and mouth?"

Blake squinted. Slight reddish-brown marks were only just visible even with the addition of the high-power light and magnification. "I see them."

Next, leaving her still none the wiser, Scott shone the light inside the victim's mouth, where dark red and purple discoloration on her gums and underneath her lips was much more obvious.

"This unfortunate lady has subcutaneous contusions around her mouth and nose here," he said, pointing at the exterior of her face, then dragging his finger down and placing it between her lips. "Here you see abrasions on the inner aspect of the lips and contusions on the gums."

"What does it mean?" Blake asked.

"I believe your victim was killed as a result of mechanical asphyxiation of the mouth and nose. She was smothered. There are no lacerations, so perhaps it was done with a soft item: a pillow or a cushion."

Blake closed her eyes and tried to work out how all this stacked together. The victim had been tied down, likely drugged or sedated, then smothered to death. "You said her head was severed postmortem?"

"From a cursory examination, I believe so," Scott agreed. "There's little evidence of bleeding, which indicates the cuts were made after death. It's possible that she was smothered into unconsciousness and then killed in some other way, but I believe that scenario is unlikely."

"Can you tell how it was—severed?" Nathan said haltingly.

"Likely a saw, given the amount and disposition of bone particles within the wound surface. I will include that information in my preliminary report. I'll have to confirm my hypothesis with a microscopic investigation before I can say for sure."

Nathan nodded his thanks, but Blake noticed an expression of disappointment on his face. Details like that could prove vital to breaking open an investigation. But there was no hurrying science. It was better to get a result right rather than fast.

Scott completed his examination of the woman's head. Blake watched with trepidation as Charlotte fetched the bone saw. She knew what was going to happen next: the medical examiner was going to open up the victim's chest cavity. The smell would be... unpleasant. Though she had a strong stomach, even it had its limits —and they were about to bump up against them.

She reached into her pocket and pulled out a scrap of paper and a pen, then scribbled down her phone number and personal email address. She really needed to get business cards. And find out how to access her official email.

"Would you call if your investigation throws up any additional information?" she asked. "Or if you change your mind on the cause of death?"

"Of course, Detective."

"Thank you." She smiled. She walked around the autopsy table and left the scrap of paper near Charlotte's notes. She deliberately kept her pace slow and measured, though she was desperate to breathe fresh air once again.

"I think we've got enough to work with. We'll leave you to it."

The two investigators stayed silent until they were outside. Blake noted that Nathan matched her increased pace stride for stride. She pulled up and sucked fresh oxygen into her lungs, not stopping until she felt completely flushed through. She turned to face Nathan, who looked as green as she felt. There was something unsettling about this case that went way beyond a garden variety murder.

Blake shook her head. "Something's off about this, right?"

Perhaps sensing she needed to work things through out loud, he replied, "Go on..."

"Okay. Our victim was sedated, bound, asphyxiated—and only then was her head removed. Does that feel like a revenge killing to you? I'm not so sure. It feels too cold. Too...meticulous."

"What are you saying?"

"When ISIS was taking over in Syria and Iraq, they lopped off plenty of people's heads. But they did it while they were still alive, with chainsaws and axes. I saw some of those videos back in my Army days. There was real anger. *Rage.* This is different."

Nathan chewed his lip. "You're right. But if this isn't a terrorist attack, what is it?"

12

B lake waved her hand as Nathan's SUV pulled out of the parking lot outside the medical examiner's office. He was headed back to the task force headquarters at Bragg to update the rest of the team on the preliminary findings. She sat in the front seat of her car for a few moments instead, head spinning from what they'd just learned.

The murder victim's body had the key hallmark of an ISIS publicity killing—a severed head—but without the propaganda video that had accompanied Nina's kidnapping. Why? And for that matter, why wasn't she killed execution-style? ISIS wasn't usually queasy about inflicting violence to serve their own ends. Why go to the lengths of drugging, asphyxiating, and only then severing the head?

Maybe our suspect is a lone wolf.

She glanced up, her eyes flickering as she considered the thought in greater detail. The Islamic State the world knew, the one that had swept across Syria and Iraq leaving mayhem and devastation in their wake in the middle of the previous decade, was only barely clinging on in mountainous pockets of Syria and in a variety of war-torn African countries.

While there had been a number of ISIS-claimed attacks in the United States and Europe since the so-called Caliphate was beaten back, they were mostly "lone wolf" attacks. The perpetrator, usually male and radicalized online, went to a public space with a gun, knife, even a car with the intention of killing as many people as he could before being taken down.

The key feature of these attacks, however, was that the perpetrators received no training. They chose their own targets and used whatever weapons they had to hand.

Perhaps Nina Crawford's kidnapper—and the murderer of her Jane Doe, if they were indeed one and the same—was such a lone wolf. The profile was of an isolated young male, typically with psychiatric instability. Was it possible that such a killer could adopt his own unique style, much like a serial killer?

She jerked back to life as she heard her cell phone's ringtone. She glanced at the screen and saw Melissa's number flash up.

I need to add her to contacts, she thought as she answered the call.

"Lieutenant?" Melissa asked. She sounded breathless with excitement. "Are you driving?"

"Not yet. Why?"

"Good. I didn't want you to crash. The victim's fingerprints just came back."

Blake guessed instantly that the victim's identity had to be important. "Who is she?"

"Private First Class Piper Hicks, US Army. She's in the 82nd Airborne. And get this: Guess who her commanding officer is?"

Groaning, Blake said, "You're kidding me. Austin Crawford?"

"The one and only," Melissa said. "The husband in our kidnap case has a direct connection to our murder victim. That could just be a coincidence, but…"

"Yeah, right," Blake snorted. "Okay, where does she live?"

"Base housing. Should I get a warrant prepared to search her accommodation?"

Blake thought for a second, then said, "Don't bother. We only need permission from someone in her chain of command. Special

Agent Cooper can arrange that for us. Have you sent this information to the task force?"

"Not yet. It only just came in."

"Okay. Give me a twenty-minute head start, then send it over in an email marked urgent."

"Will do. I'm trying to track down Piper's movements."

"Thanks, Melissa."

Blake killed the call and immediately searched for Nathan's contact in her phone. He answered after two rings, a roar in the background like waves crashing on a beach indicating that he was using hands-free.

"What is it?" he asked. "Did the ME figure something else out?"

"Not yet. But I have a lead."

AN EVIDENCE TEAM from CID was already waiting outside Piper Hicks' barracks as Blake pulled up. It was a five-story building with dark window frames. The first floor was built of red brick, and those above had a smooth tan finish.

Nathan was already parked outside. As Blake climbed out of her department-issued vehicle, she saw that he was concentrating on the screen of his cell phone. As she watched, he pumped his fist with satisfaction, then popped the door.

"Battalion commander just emailed over permission to conduct the search."

"That was quick," Blake remarked. Years of experience over Army bureaucracy had left her expecting a long wait.

He shook his head ruefully. "Once the Lieutenant Colonel heard the letters FBI, he seemed to decide holding things up was well above his pay grade. Wish I had the same juice."

Nathan gestured at the waiting evidence team and pointed toward the barracks entrance. They seemed to recognize him.

"We're going to get an earful after this," he commented as they approached the entrance door.

Blake raised an eyebrow. "Want to call it in, let the Bureau take the lead?"

"Hell no." Nathan grinned. "Just wanted to make sure we are both on the same page."

"They'll bitch and moan." Blake shrugged. "But until somebody tells me different, it's still our case."

"We didn't exactly give the ASAC an opportunity to alter the running order..." he commented.

"That sounds like a him problem."

Piper's room was on the second floor. A soldier with chevrons on his biceps was waiting with a set of keys. Blake held back as Nathan flashed his identification badge and let the sergeant read the battalion commander's email. After a short wait, the man unlocked the door and allowed them inside.

As much as she itched to be the first one inside, Blake knew better. She formed her hands into fists and dug her nails into the flesh of her palms as she waited for the evidence team to don gloves, forensics suits, and blue plastic booties. The sergeant watched with curiosity in his eyes but said nothing.

Finally, they were ready. The two-man team entered with cameras poised. Blake peered past them as they entered. The room was small and resembled a college dormitory. A single bed was pushed against the wall on the left-hand side. To the right was a desk, a single chair covered in blue fabric, a small TV, and a wall-mounted corkboard covered in pinned-up photographs, letters, and other paraphernalia.

The room was neatly arranged, despite—or perhaps because of—the fact there was only enough floor space to lay down a yoga mat. Blake shivered at the sight.

"Takes you back, huh?" Nathan said in a low voice.

"I guess it wasn't so bad at the time," she replied, watching as the two crime scene techs circled the small space, documenting every square inch of it with rapidfire clicks from their digital cameras.

"But you wouldn't actually go back?" he said. "I don't blame you."

It took the techs about twenty minutes to photograph the room and take fingerprint and DNA samples. There was no obvious sign of forced entry or any kind of disturbance to attract further attention. Piper Hicks had been a neat woman. Her single bed was made with hospital corners. Blake still made hers the same way. The habits instilled in you in basic training took a long time to fade. In her case, she wasn't sure they ever would.

"Room's all yours," one of the two technicians said as they exited. He pulled off his gloves. "We'll get those fingerprints scanned in today. We didn't find any computers, tablets, or phones."

"Call me the moment you have results," Nathan said after giving his thanks. Then he turned back to Blake. "Let's take a look."

They each took half of the room. Blake naturally gravitated to her left, to the desk and clothing storage. She drew open the desk drawers at first, one by one. The topmost contained half a dozen tightly rolled charging cables for various electronic devices.

There was also a thin red notebook, about fifty pages thick. Blake picked it up and flicked through it. Though she was initially hopeful that she'd found the dead woman's journal, it was little more than a to-do list.

Buy running shoes, Blake read in neat cursive.

Other notations referenced different types of makeup and various toiletries, a note to buy *new underwear* underlined twice, and reminders to perform basic tasks.

Call mom, and *wash clothes.*

Blake grimaced as a stab of guilt jolted through her. They needed to inform Piper's next of kin of her death. It looked like the woman had at least one living parent. She didn't see any references to her dad, but the to-do list was only half a dozen pages full. It looked relatively new. She set it on the otherwise bare surface of the desk so that she would remember to bag it up as evidence before leaving.

"Come take a look at this," Nathan said.

She turned around to see he was crouching by the head of Piper's bed. A wastepaper basket sat between the bed and a small bedside table containing a couple of drawers. The bottommost was ajar, which Blake guessed meant Nathan had already searched through it and found nothing.

"What?"

"Look in the trashcan," he said.

Blake peered over. "Shit," she said.

"My thoughts exactly."

Blake reached into her pocket and drew out her cell phone. She snapped several photographs of the contents of the trash just in case the crime scene techs had somehow failed to do so. She doubted it. They were thorough.

Finally, she reached inside and pulled out a pink and blue rectangular cardboard box about the length of the toothbrush, and not much wider.

"Was she pregnant?" Nathan asked, staring at the pregnancy test kit in Blake's hand. He went to the door, where the crime scene team had left a container of evidence bags, and retrieved one. He returned and held it open for Blake to drop the box inside.

"Early, maybe." Blake shrugged. "I'll ask Dr. Meyer. He should know once he finishes his examination."

"So she was sexually active," Nathan mused. He set the sealed evidence bag down on the desk beside the red notepad and returned to the bedside. He continued as he pulled back the covers and searched them thoroughly. "Who with?"

Blake returned to the desk. She opened the remaining drawers but found little of interest. Just paperwork, a couple of Army manuals, and a popular thriller novel with a blue and yellow cover that she had recently read herself. The same was true of her wardrobe. It contained neatly folded utility uniforms, a couple of hanging dresses, and a dress uniform, along with her civilian clothing. She checked every pocket, but nothing fell out.

"Where's her cell phone?" she sighed, frustrated. "We have to find out where she went before she died. Maybe that will help narrow down who she was with."

Finding nothing else on his side of the room, Nathan turned and eyed Blake. "We need to speak to her CO. Which brings us right back to Capt. Crawford."

13

"Private Hicks owns a dark blue 2012 Toyota Highlander," Nathan announced after climbing out of his car. He was still holding his cell phone, having apparently just ended a call.

Both he and Blake had parked a little way up the road outside the Crawford home as the driveway was now occupied by a large black SUV along with the vehicles she had seen on her previous visit.

"Location?" Blake asked as she fell in alongside him.

He shook his head. "Unknown. I've put a BOLO out. Bragg installed automatic license plate recognition at all the gateposts several years back, so I know the vehicle drove off base late Friday afternoon. That's it."

"Do you have footage? Maybe she didn't leave alone."

"Working on it."

They stopped in tandem as they spotted a black SUV reversing out of the Crawford driveway, now just twenty yards up ahead.

"Bureau," Nathan muttered.

"Looks that way," Blake agreed. The SUV reversed around the corner toward them, but just before the driver spun the wheel, she caught a glimpse of a man in a dark suit occupying the driver's seat and a flash of light hair in the passenger's.

"Trust but verify," he said with a raised eyebrow.

Blake didn't reply. If the FBI wanted to check her homework, that was fine with her. She was confident in her abilities. Just so long as they shared anything they found.

As they reached the front door, it swung open fast. Austin Crawford was standing on the other side. He wore light jeans and a thin insulated jacket. His car keys were clutched in his right palm.

"Going somewhere, Captain?" Blake asked pleasantly.

He stopped dead, eyes widening as he processed the unexpected appearance on his doorstep. "What are you doing here?" he said.

"Is this a bad time?" Nathan asked. Blake saw her fellow law enforcement agent's eyes flickering from side to side, scanning Austin's face and the scene behind him for anything of interest.

"No." He shook his head vehemently before seeming to force himself to relax. "It's nothing like that. It's just the other cops only just left. I got worried something had happened. Can't you guys work together?"

"The FBI?"

"Yeah."

"Don't worry," Blake assured him while matching his gaze and holding it. "They're the very best. If anyone can track down your wife, they can. We're here following up on a different lead."

She studied him carefully after she finished speaking. A muscle pulsated on his temple. He seemed nervous. Or maybe just anxious. Maybe she was reading too deeply into the connection between Piper Hicks and her CO. Maybe he was exactly what he seemed to be: a consenting adult who just happened to engage in an open relationship with another consenting adult.

Yeah, right.

He took a half step back and straightened his shoulders. "Well?"

Blake frowned. "I'm sorry?"

"You said you were here to follow up a lead. What is it? Have you found my wife?"

"Captain," Nathan interjected. "Is there somewhere we can sit?"

"We sat last time," Austin snapped. "Here is just fine."

Blake nodded imperceptibly at Nathan. She sensed Austin would respond better to a female touch.

She softened her posture and said, "Of course. I need to prepare you, Austin, but we found a body. It's not your wife," she added hurriedly. "But we have reason to believe you knew the victim."

A succession of emotions flashed across his face, mostly too quickly to read. "What? Who?"

"Do you know a woman called Piper Hicks?"

Austin's eyes went wide. He reached out and held the door frame for support. His mouth opened, then bobbed shut again. He seemed stunned, lost for words.

Blake watched intently as he visibly pulled himself together. He swallowed, then seemed to notice he was still holding the door frame and pulled his hand away as though dropping a hot pan. It seemed an intense emotional reaction to the death of one of his soldiers. She wondered how long she had been under his command.

"Piper's dead?" he said, his voice a half octave higher than usual. "How?"

Blake made a mental note that he'd used her first name. "Capt. Crawford, when was the last time you saw Private Hicks?"

"I don't know. A few days ago."

"Do you know if she had plans this weekend?"

A flicker in Austin's eyes gave Blake the impression he was holding back. "I'm not sure. Family, maybe."

"Do you know where? Her vehicle is missing."

"I don't know. I command a lot of soldiers."

"Of course," Blake said soothingly. "Anything you can remember could help us find her killer."

"Oh God, Nina," Austin said belatedly. He turned away, then sank to his haunches, clutching his face. His voice muffled he said, "You think this is related, don't you?"

"We're considering the possibility," Blake said.

"They're going to kill her," Austin said. He started to tremble. His voice came out in an anguished moan.

"We don't know that for sure, Austin," Blake said. "But you need to tell us anything you know. Was Piper Hicks dating anyone?"

Austin said nothing for a few seconds. Finally, he said, "I wouldn't know. You should ask her platoon leader. He would have a better idea than me."

"She never mentioned it to you?"

"I'm her commanding officer," Austin said. "She doesn't come to me to gossip. I can't believe she's dead."

He stood up. His face was ashen. He didn't make eye contact. "Have you told her mom?"

Blake shook her head, slightly surprised by the sincerity of the question. "The family hasn't been contacted yet. The Army is putting together a notification team."

Austin finally met Blake's gaze. "How did she die?"

"Mr. Crawford—"

"Just tell me, dammit. My—wife is missing. Piper's death can't be a coincidence. I deserve to know what I need to prepare myself for."

Blake spared the gruesome details. "She was asphyxiated. We believe she was sedated when she was killed. It's likely she didn't feel anything."

At least not while she died, she didn't say. There would have been a whole lot more terror before that.

Austin's face grew black. Blake noticed he was clenching his fists. "You need to find the bastards who did this."

"We will. And we're doing everything possible to find your wife."

"Is that it?" he said, gesturing toward his car. "I have to go get my kids."

Blake nodded. Just before she turned away, a thought occurred to her.

"Oh, can I get a cellphone number?" she said. "Just in case I need to follow up with anything you told us. Time's of the essence, and it could save us a trip."

"Of course," Austin said. His eyes were slightly glazed over. He seemed to be in shock. "I'll go get it."

"We have a number on file," Nathan interjected.

Austin shook his head. "I lost my phone earlier this week. My mom went out and bought me a replacement just this morning. It's probably in the house. I've looked everywhere. But maybe I'm not in the right state of mind to find it."

He disappeared back into the house and returned a few moments later with a scrap of paper with a phone number scribbled on it. He handed it to Blake, then closed the door behind him.

Nathan and Blake said their farewells and walked out of the driveway. As they did so, a white work truck with a logo on the side that said Hartmann Construction entered the driveway. The driver was about Josh's height, though perhaps a fraction shorter. Blake didn't get a great look but saw a hairline that was just starting to recede, and the type of puffy yet low body fat-percentage face that indicated a heavy reliance on steroids.

Less than a minute later, the same truck screamed out and sped down the road—definitely above the speed limit, and now with two faces behind the windshield.

"That was weird," Blake said, stopping to watch the car disappear behind the pines that rose up on either verge, giving many of the towns in the area their name.

"Uh-huh."

"Do you have Piper's personnel jacket?"

Nathan nodded. He reached for his phone and started flipping through emails. "What do you want to know?"

"How long was she in Crawford's unit?"

"Looks like..." he murmured. "Since last March. About a year."

"Hell of an emotional reaction to the death of a woman he probably encounters once a week at best. He has what, 100, maybe 150 soldiers under his command?"

"Something like that."

"Used her first name, too. And there was something else he said," Blake muttered, her eyes narrowing as she replayed it in her mind.

"He referred to her mom. Not her parents. That's kind of specific, don't you think?"

Nathan scrolled on his phone. He was silent for a few moments, then said, "Her father is listed as deceased."

"I think Austin knew that," Blake said, meeting Nathan's gaze as he looked up from his phone. "The question is, why was he pretending he didn't?"

14

Blake's phone rang just as she finished the short drive from Piper's barracks to the task force command center at Hercules Fitness Center. She swung the car into the closest parking bay and picked up her phone while the engine was still running. Her forehead kinked slightly. She didn't recognize the number.

She answered the call anyway. It was difficult to break the habits of the past eight months, and she brought it up to her ear half expecting to hear the mechanical tones of a spam autodialer.

Which accident was I in today?

"Lieutenant?" a voice said instead.

It took Blake a second to place the voice. "Captain?"

"Gina," she said, continuing without any small talk. "I just got off the phone with Assistant Special Agent in Charge Carl Granger."

"Yes, ma'am," Blake said noncommittally.

"He's spitting feathers about you attending Piper Hicks' autopsy without informing the task force ahead of time. Not to mention the fact that you subsequently searched her quarters without an FBI team present."

Blake cleared her throat. She couldn't get a read on her superior's emotional state. The older woman kept herself within tight bounds. That wasn't unusual for a high-ranking female police officer. Despite all efforts to the contrary, law enforcement could still be a boy's club.

She decided to play it cool. "Yes, ma'am. I'm investigating my homicide case. I was following up a lead as fast as I could. Would ASAC Granger prefer me to sit on my hands instead?"

There was a short pause. Then, with dry humor that rustled down the phone, Gina said, "You took the words out of my mouth."

Blake relaxed against her seat. "Thank you, ma'am."

"I made it quite clear to our friends from the Bureau that Piper Hicks' homicide is a Monroe County Sheriff's Department case, and that while we gratefully appreciate their assistance, we do not intend to restrict the activities of our investigators. But Blake—try and play nice."

"Yes, ma'am. I will."

Gina ended the call. Blake sat in her car for a moment, just thinking. It was good to know that the department had her back, and that the captain would go to bat for her if needed.

She also knew that the captain was right. It would be easier to work with the FBI rather than against them. The sheriff's department might be taking the lead on Piper's homicide, but Nina Crawford's kidnapping was squarely in the Bureau's jurisdiction. ASAC Granger could make things more difficult for her than they needed to be.

Blake climbed out of the car and quickly walked inside. In the few hours since she had last been in the command center, it had materialized into something much more coherent. Rows of desks filled the entire room, each with laptop computers, desktop workstations, and freestanding monitors on top. Bundles of wires criss-crossed the floor. Some were marked with yellow and black danger tape; most were not.

Melissa was waiting for her inside. She shot Blake a warning glance and subtly nudged her head in the direction of the quickly-approaching—and furious-looking—Carl Granger. Blake reminded herself of the captain's parting words.

Play nice.

"Sir," she said pleasantly, inclining her head as he came to a stop in front of her.

"Lieutenant," he replied through pursed lips.

Blake decided to get a word in first. "Sir, I think we need to interview everyone in Piper Hicks' unit. We believe that she might have been sexually active. Finding out who with could be our best lead."

Granger blinked several times in quick succession. A flicker of irritation ran across his face. "Special Agent Cooper is already putting the arrangements in place."

"Excellent," Blake said with a wide smile. "How soon can we get started?"

He ignored her. "Lieutenant, from now on, you are to coordinate your activities with my agents. It's important that we don't tread on each other's toes. This is a fast-moving investigation. Your captain agrees."

Strictly speaking, that wasn't exactly what Gina Rogers had said. But Blake thought better of arguing.

"Of course, sir."

Granger turned slightly to his right and beckoned a man and a woman over. Blake narrowed her eyes. She recognized them as the two she'd seen departing Austin Crawford's home.

"Quinn, Madden, you can take it from here," Granger said curtly. He turned away and was immediately accosted by half a dozen different agents requesting his input or signature on different matters.

The man offered his hand and a friendly smile. "Special Agent Victor Quinn."

"Detective Lieutenant Blake Larsen," she said in response, wincing at the firmness of his handshake.

"Emily Madden," the female agent said as Melissa introduced herself to the woman's partner. She had a faintly apologetic look on her face. Blake couldn't work out whether that was for her boss or for the punishing strength of her partner's handshake. "Call me Emily."

"Nice to meet you," Blake replied. "And yeah, I'm just Blake."

Emily handed over a business card with her details on it. Blake grimaced in response. She shrugged and said, "I'm working on it..."

The agent flashed her a curious glance but said nothing. "What's your email address?" she said instead. "CID has drawn up a rota for Piper's unit's interviews. There are 137 names on it, so we need to spread them around."

"Great," Blake groaned, seeing a similar expression of mild hopelessness on Emily's face. She sensed that they were about to dive into a very deep haystack without even knowing whether there was a needle to be found.

Half an hour later, Blake, Melissa, their new friends from the Bureau, and over two dozen other agents from various federal law enforcement agencies filed over to a nearby meeting center which had been cleared for their purposes.

She had to admit, the FBI's pull could be kind of helpful.

Just a couple of moments before, Blake's phone had buzzed at the same time as Melissa's. They'd checked the email to discover they had been assigned eight names. Six men, two women. Their names and ranks were listed on the left-hand side of the paper. On the right was their availability status and contact information.

Only the final entry, a Private First Class Diana Stetson, was listed as unavailable. To the right of her name was typed: WHEREABOUTS UNKNOWN.

A flicker of concern ran through Blake at the sight. Was it possible that another woman with connections to the 82nd Airborne was missing, and somehow nobody had noticed?

She relayed her concerns to Melissa as they entered the meeting room they had been assigned. Three soldiers were already waiting in a line outside. All men. They'd stiffened as the two detectives approached.

Melissa set a Dictaphone onto the table and flicked a switch. A red light glowed on the side to indicate that it was recording. Blake pulled a small notepad from a pocket along with a pen and set it in front of her.

"Okay, let's get the first one in," Blake said, glancing at the document in front of her. "Corporal Michael Litman."

"At ease, soldier." Blake smiled to put him at ease as the man stepped inside and came to a halt in front of the meeting table, his posture rigid and eyes facing dead ahead. "We're not officers. This shouldn't take long. We just have a few questions. Take a seat."

"Yes, ma'am," he replied. If he relaxed, it was only fractionally as he pulled a chair back and sat across from her.

"Call me Blake," she said. It was always better to use a person's preferred first name. Titles and formality were barriers, the enemy of any good detective's work. This was especially the case in a place like the military with its rigid and hierarchical command structure. "Do you prefer Michael?"

"Mike," he said.

"Okay, Mike. Like I said, this won't take long. And you're in no trouble."

Mike's eyes quickly flickered between Melissa and Blake. He seemed nervous but not unreasonably so.

Blake continued. "Do you know why you're here?"

Mike shook his head.

"Do you know a woman called Piper Hicks?"

He shrugged. "She's in 1st Platoon, right?"

Blake nodded.

"Yeah, I've seen her around. Don't think we've ever talked one on one. I'm 3rd Platoon."

"When was the last time you saw Piper?"

He made a face, and his eyes flicked toward the ceiling as he thought. "Not sure. Could be a week, maybe two. Maybe I seen her around, but not so that I'd remember. It's a busy place."

"It is," she agreed. "Do you know any of her friends? Who she hangs around with?"

He shook his head. "If I were you, I'd ask Sgt. Wiley. He would know better than me."

"We will," Blake replied, making a note of the name. It didn't appear on the manifest she'd been assigned. But Mike didn't need to know that.

"Why you asking?" he said, leaning forward with interest.

Blake paused for a second and studied the soldier's face. She sensed only genuine curiosity on it, not any deeper malice. She exhaled slightly. "I'm sorry to report that Piper was found dead this morning."

He blinked. It looked like it took a few seconds for him to process the news.

Definitely not guilty, Blake thought.

"Damn," he breathed. "How?"

"That's what we are attempting to determine," Blake said. "I just have one last question before I let you go."

"Shoot."

"Do you know a soldier called Diana Stetson?"

This time, she saw a flash of recognition on Mike's face. He nodded vigorously.

"Hell yeah," he said before visibly pulling back. He brought his hand to his mouth and coughed.

Blake raised an eyebrow. "Hell yeah?"

"Dammit," he muttered. He ran his fingers nervously through his short cut hair. "I just meant. Well, it's that she's kinda fine. Least, she was."

Melissa and Blake swapped glances.

"Was?" Melissa pressed.

"Shit, she got hit with a golf cart a couple days back. She's in Womack. Heard she hit her head pretty bad. Concussion or something."

Melissa's face screwed up. "A golf cart?"

"Yeah, they're always driving around here. Stetson's a road cyclist. Pretty hard-core. I heard she was going to go pro before she signed up for the Big Green Machine. Cart clipped her back wheel as she was cycling around the course. Tore her up real good."

"So this was on-base?" Blake said. She wrote the words *Womack*

Medical Center and underlined them three times in her notepad. It was the base military hospital.

"Sure." Mike nodded. "We have two golf courses. I see near misses all the time. Bad luck if you're on a bicycle, though. I guess she would've been going real fast."

"Does Diana know Piper?"

Mike cocked his head to one side. "Now you mention it, I guess I seen them together from time to time. They are in the same platoon. Shit, were. Man, that's crazy."

"So they were friends?" Blake pressed.

"I think so." Mike shrugged. "Like I said, ask Sergeant Wiley. He would know better than me."

"Thanks for your time, Mike," Blake finished. She leaned back against her chair, knowing she wouldn't get anything more from him. "Head out left when you leave. Please send the next guy in. Don't say anything else to him. Just direct him in."

Mike stood. "Yes, ma'am."

As he left, Blake tapped out a quick note to Nathan outlining what she'd just learned and asking him to fast-track an interview with the famous Sergeant Wiley.

"Coincidence?" Melissa murmured as the door whooshed closed behind the first interviewee.

"I'm not sure," Blake said slowly as she tapped send. "As far as we know, Piper left the base of her own accord, and Nina was never on it. But that doesn't rule out a suspect who lives or works on-base. Perhaps Private Stetson knows something. Maybe that's why she's currently in the hospital."

"Or maybe it was just an accident," Melissa said with a tired sigh.

The following interviews told a similar story. Piper Hicks and Diana Stetson were indeed friends. Close friends, according to at least two of the soldiers. One of them, from the same platoon, said they'd taken a vacation together to Puerto Vallarta in Mexico earlier that year.

But a golf cart crash didn't fit the profile, such as it was. It stood to reason that Piper had been taken before she was killed. Nina had certainly been kidnapped, although either she wasn't dead, or the body was yet to be located. Diana's accident shared little in common with either incident.

As the final soldier departed the meeting room, Blake ground her molars together with frustration. "We need to speak to Diana," she said.

Blake's phone buzzed on the meeting table in front of her. She reached urgently for it and flipped it over. It was a text from Nathan. Her stomach sank as she read the message.

Bad news.

15

It was late evening by the time Blake and Melissa returned to the task force command center. Exhaustion tugged at Blake's bones. This day seemed to have lasted forever. The atmosphere inside was quiet. It was only about a third full.

Melissa found a desk to type up her notes of the interviews and upload them to the shared database. Blake made a beeline directly for Nathan, whose cryptic text message had piqued her curiosity. He was hunched over his laptop, elbows hemmed close into his sides, stabbing furiously at the keyboard.

"You shouldn't do that," she observed as she leaned against the desk to his side. "You'll give yourself carpal tunnel."

He didn't look up. "Already did."

"You keep going like that, they'll have to amputate."

"Maybe they'll give me a fancy prosthetic like Ryan's." He grinned, finally pushing the laptop away and closing the lid theatrically. "I'm done."

"So what's the problem?"

"I spoke to Diana Stetson's doctors. She's currently sedated. She developed some kind of swelling on the brain after her crash. It's subsiding, but they want to keep her under for at least another 24 hours, just to be sure."

"What's your read?"

"I looked into it. MPs filed a full report, and I spoke to the responding officers. She was hit by a cart on the Ryder course the day before yesterday around 6:30 p.m. The MPs took one driver and a single passenger into custody. Blood-alcohol tests put them well above the limit. They were drinking out of a hip flask, and half a dozen crushed cans of Bud Light were found in their golf bags."

"Careless assholes," Blake muttered.

It was another stick with which to beat golf. Blake added it to the fact she couldn't keep her elbow straight, or whatever the damn coach kept bleating at her. The last and only time she'd picked up a driver, she'd ended up hurling it straight down the range and storming off in a huff.

"You can say that again," Nathan agreed, his face black. "They could have killed her. It's not even clear if she'll escape lasting damage. Won't be until she wakes up."

"Tell me you're charging them."

"Oh, you better believe it. Unfortunately for the investigation, I think we need to chalk this one up to coincidence."

The command center was slowly filling up around them. Agents returned in dribs and drabs to type up their notes just like Melissa. Judging by the glum expressions on most of their faces, nobody had had a major breakthrough.

"Any luck on finding Piper's vehicle?" Blake asked, searching around for a lead.

The metronomic tick of a second hand of a large clock above one of the basketball nets at the far end of the hall beat down on her eardrums like a hammer. Every passing second reminded her that Nina's life could be draining away.

"Nope," Nathan replied, his expression looking even more glum than it had before.

She saw that he was under the exact same strain as she was. Perhaps more. She had no doubt that the Army's top brass would be

paying close attention to this one, and as the senior special agent in
Bragg's CID detachment, he would be under the microscope.

"We'll find her, Nathan," Blake said softly.

Mostly she was trying to convince herself.

An agent stood up at the far end of the room. His startled rendition of the word "Shit!" echoed around the cavernous basketball hall.

Blake and Nathan traded worried looks. Whatever this fresh hell was, it didn't sound good.

Along with most of the other law enforcement personnel in the command center, they clustered around the agent's desk. He had a widescreen monitor propped up on top of a cardboard filing box.

"You all gotta see this," he muttered several times as he brought up a webpage. He shook his head and mumbled darkly to himself as he did so.

Melissa sidled in beside Blake. "Do you know what this is about?" she whispered.

Blake shook her head. "No idea."

It soon became clear. Blake vaguely recognized the homepage of the *Pinecone*, the local newspaper. She realized with a jolt that the story was written by Aaron Weller—the reporter who had introduced himself to her earlier that very same day.

The headline was stark: *LOCAL RESIDENT TAKEN HOSTAGE.*

Underneath was written: *TERRORIST MOTIVE SUSPECTED.*

"The wires are already picking this up," the agent who had first discovered the story stated glumly. "It'll be on every major network in a matter of minutes. This is going to screw everything up."

"Play the video," ASAC Granger growled. Blake hadn't noticed he was even in the room.

The agent quickly put a halt to his editorializing and clicked the play button on a video that sat just underneath the headline. The format was very similar to the demand video sent to Austin Crawford.

"My name is Nina Crawford," she sobbed. Like before, she appeared to be reading from a script somewhere off-screen.

"My husband is Captain Austin Crawford. He was deployed to

Afghanistan three times. He should not have gone there. Afghanistan is a Muslim land. Now I will pay for his crimes."

"Somebody send this to the computer forensics lab, dammit," Granger muttered as Nina closed her eyes for a moment and took a steadying breath.

"A woman is already dead. The man who—"

She stopped and once again looked off-screen, a flicker of fear in her eyes. When she looked back at the camera, her tone was flat. "My captors have already killed a woman. The police know this. They are hiding the truth from you. Many more will die unless the following demands are met."

The agent at the desk grabbed a yellow legal pad and a pen. He held it expectantly above the paper.

Nina sniffed and looked away from the camera once again. Blake studied her face closely. She looked confused, as if she didn't understand what she was reading. Her face drained of blood, and she began to tremble. When she next looked at the camera lens, her pupils were dilated, like she was going into shock.

"I don't want to die," she whimpered, starting to rock back and forth on her chair. "Please, just let me go. You don't have to—"

The screen went black for several seconds as the camera feed died. When it resumed, Nina was once again staring at the camera. Her eyes were red-rimmed and bloodshot from crying.

Blake wondered how long the gap between the two segments of video was. What had her captor done to her in the interim?

Nina resumed, her voice hoarse and crackling. "Mr. President, at this moment, there are thousands of American troops in the Middle East. Every one of them is an abomination. Every inch of Muslim land they tread on is an insult to millions of devout believers. Every day they are there compounds the offense. It should not be tolerated. It *will not* be tolerated."

She swallowed. Her voice grew weaker and more hesitant.

"But Islam is a merciful religion. My captors are not unreasonable men. Mr. President, they will grant you 48 hours to begin removing all American troops from the Middle East. If you do not appear on television before that time to announce this is happening…"

Nina began rocking forward and back once again. "Then another woman will die."

The feed went black for a second time. For a moment, nobody in the command center even breathed. The only sound was the scratching of the FBI agent's pen on the yellow legal pad in front of him.

Then all hell broke loose. Agents and deputies split in every direction, either bringing cell phones to their ears or else beginning to talk among themselves in excited tones.

"Qui-et!" Granger yelled in a booming baritone, elongating the middle vowels until the entire command center fell silent around him. When he was certain that he had the entire room's attention, he beckoned them closer. His expression was stern. Resolute. Blake couldn't help but be impressed by the authority he exuded.

"Everyone put their phones away, right now," he instructed. He waited several moments until his command was followed, making eye contact with almost every person present in the process.

"Okay. I'll keep this short and sweet because we have work to do. Most of you have never worked a case of this magnitude. The attention of the entire country is about to focus directly on the people in this very room."

He said the last three words slowly, emphasizing them as he stabbed his index finger into his left palm.

"It will be like the eye of fucking Sauron hovering overhead. Our actions will make front pages across the nation. Careers will be made and broken by the decisions we make and the leads that we miss. We need to bat a thousand. Better than that. We make one mistake, and Nina Crawford is the one who will suffer. So first things first: Until Comms is up and running, all media requests go through me. Is that understood?"

He rotated in a full circle, once again making eye contact with everyone. Blake felt a chill run down her spine when it was her turn to face him.

"This task force needs to be leakproof. Be careful with every word that you say. You shouldn't have time to be out in bars. If someone asks you questions while you're standing in line at Starbucks, just ignore them. Better yet, report them. This job is going to be hard enough as it is. Don't make it any harder for the rest of us."

A general murmur of assent ran around the room. Blake spied looks of determination on almost every face—along with a not inconsiderable level of concern. She guessed that it was hitting home with them, as it was with her, that this was likely to be the most high-profile case most would ever work on.

"Our first task is to control the narrative. I want a press conference set up by 7 p.m. I will need representatives from Homeland, Monroe County, and CID standing behind me. The country needs to know that we have our best working on this.

"Finally, sometime in the next few minutes, all of you need to call home. Tell whoever's waiting for you there that they won't see you for a while. It's nothing personal. A woman's life is on the line."

He clapped his hands together to signal that his impromptu speech was over. Everybody stood stock still for a moment to process his words. And then the bustle resumed.

Blake exchanged a look with Melissa. "Holy shit," she muttered.

Melissa just nodded. She looked shellshocked. Blake didn't blame her. Neither of them had expected to be working a national-level terrorism case when they woke up that morning.

The next couple of hours felt almost like a dream. The atmosphere inside the task force center was one of renewed determination. Agents and other law enforcement personnel rushed in every direction or else tapped furiously at their keyboards.

But it was all busywork. They had few leads. Nothing concrete. It all felt hopeless.

Blake stood behind ASAC Granger as he addressed the media on the grounds of Fort Bragg. Just before they stepped in front of the cameras, an FBI communications expert had handed her a navy-blue windbreaker with *POLICE* stenciled over her chest and advised her to make sure her badge was prominently displayed.

Despite the short notice given, almost 20 journalists and reporters had fired a barrage of questions at Granger for almost a quarter hour. For Blake, it was a crash course in dealing with the press—not a skill she'd acquired in her decade plus in the Army. Granger handled them masterfully, giving her an appreciation for his talents that she hadn't previously had.

After working until 9 p.m., she called it a night. She was bone tired, and until certain people got back to her, she had no leads to follow up.

Her car's radio started automatically as she fired up the engine. The familiar tones of a local radio news presenter filled her ears.

"—Crawford is still missing after a bombshell FBI press conference just a couple hours ago. There is still no word from the White House about the terrorists' demands, but—"

Blake reached forward and stabbed the power button. The last thing she needed was to be reminded about the case. She closed her eyes for a second and drew in a deep, cleansing breath, slowly exhaling before she put her hands on the wheel and began to back out of her parking space.

But there was no escaping the whirlwind. As she guided her car through the gate post on the edge of Bragg, she was confronted by a sea of flickering lights.

Candles.

She blinked dumbly several times, bringing her vehicle to an almost complete stop as her exhausted brain attempted to process what it was seeing.

"What the hell?"

As she lifted her foot off the brake, the shimmering pinpricks of light slowly came into focus. About fifty men, women, and children were standing dead still a few yards in front of the security post.

Blake reached for the window control. As the sheet of glass disappeared to her side, she expected to be greeted by a murmur of conversation. Instead, she was met by an eerie and total silence. Even the whoosh of passing cars was somehow muted, as if they were slowing with respect.

The hairs rose on the back of Blake's neck. She felt individual goosebumps prickle on her skin as she drank in the scene. Even the children were quiet, cupping candles to their chests and occasionally looking up at their parents as they aped their posture. Their tiny figures were like shadows in the dark.

"Please," she whispered to herself in the darkness, "just let me find her."

She left the last part of her prayer unsaid.

Alive.

16

Blake's phone buzzed twice on the dashboard as she drove home. She was so dog tired she didn't even glance at the screen as she climbed out of her car and walked inside. She held it loosely in her left hand as she pulled open the fridge. An empty wasteland stared back at her, a vast expanse of white plastic and no food.

She grabbed a bottle of beer instead. At least that was one thing that wasn't in short supply. The fridge door rattled as she swung it closed with disgust.

A couple of message notifications vied for her attention as she unlocked the phone. Instead of checking them, she dialed a local pizza joint and ordered a medium pepperoni pizza. She threw her head back and took a large swig of beer as the employee tapped her details into the system.

On second thoughts...

"No, make that a large."

Since it wouldn't arrive for half an hour, she grabbed her laptop and sought out the couch. Finally, she turned her attention to the notifications. One was from a number she didn't recognize. The other she remembered belonged to the medical examiner.

After taking another swig of beer to steady her nerves, she returned the call. He answered after one ring.

"Scott, it's Blake Larsen."

"Thanks for getting back to me so quickly," he said. "I have some additional information that might help your investigation."

"Shoot."

"First of all, Piper Hicks was not pregnant. I found no evidence of a fetus in my examinations, nor any of the physical changes or blood markers that you would expect to find in the early stages of a pregnancy."

Blake's head slumped forward. She let her eyes fall shut. Another theory had bitten the dust. Perhaps Piper wasn't sexually active after all. Perhaps there was no man in her life.

Then why buy a test?

Either it was a false alarm, or the test had been taken by somebody else. Until Diana Stetson woke up, there was no telling which. Maybe not even then. After all, there was no guarantee that her friend knew those details.

"Lieutenant Larsen, you still there?"

Blake nodded, then slowly mumbled her assent.

Scott continued, "I confirmed my initial suspicion else after you left. I believe that Ms. Hicks' head was indeed severed with a saw, rather than an edged blade."

"How can you tell?"

"The initial cuts are consistent with a large, edged blade rather than a surgical scalpel or similar weapon. However, the marks on her vertebrae are different. Using a microscope, I detected fine striations in the bone which I believe were generated with the push stroke, as well as deep furrows as the saw was retracted," he said.

His tone was studied and unemotional. But Blake also detected a complex mix of pity and sorrow lurking beneath the surface. Scott Meyer truly cared for his patients, even if he only saw them after they were already deceased.

"What kind of saw are we talking about? Are you able to tell?"

"With great difficulty," Scott admitted. "There's no national or international database for this kind of wound. At this juncture, all I can tell you with absolute certainty is that the marks were left by a hand tool, rather than a powered construction saw."

"Because you can see the, what did you call them, furrows?" Blake said, wrinkling her forehead.

"Exactly. A powered implement would have left far neater cuts in its wake."

"What a psychopath," Blake murmured.

"I have no argument with that characterization," he replied. "As I was saying, there's no database of this type of cut. I am currently cross-referencing journal articles to try and narrow down the exact implement used on this poor woman. There's no guarantee I will have any success."

"Thanks, Doc," Blake said softly. "I appreciate it."

"Any time. And Lieutenant?"

"Yeah?"

"Make sure you get some rest. That's my professional opinion. You'll have better luck finding out what happened to your victim if you can think straight."

Blake laughed and ended the call. A quick glance at the digital clock on her phone's home screen told her that the pizza was at least twenty minutes out. Despite the growing desire inside her to simply fall asleep on the sofa, she tapped the other number that had attempted to call her. A male voice answered.

"Aaron Weller."

Instantly, she sharpened her focus. ASAC Granger's instructions about how to handle the media still reverberated in her mind.

"How did you get my number?" she said curtly.

"Lieutenant Larsen," Weller said smoothly. "Thank you for returning my call so quickly."

"I asked you a question," she said.

"I have my sources," he replied.

"I already told you I'm not interested in assisting with your profile," Blake said. Her stomach growled with hunger. It felt like it was eating her from the inside. "Now if you don't mind, I'm going to hang up. It's been a real long day."

"This isn't about the profile," Weller said quickly. "Well, not only, anyway."

"What are you talking about?"

Weller spoke hurriedly, as though he was worried she would follow through with her threat to kill the call. "I saw you on television earlier. Standing behind the assistant special-agent-in-charge. I figured you must be working on the task force."

"No comment. If that's all—"

"It's not," he cut in. "I remember the time at the bottom of the screen when the press conference started. It was 5:53 p.m."

"So?"

"I received the email from the terrorists almost five hours earlier. At 1 p.m."

Blake blinked stupidly. She was too tired to process the meaning of this with her usual alacrity. "Wait, what did you say?"

"The terrorists emailed me a copy of that video, the one with Nina Crawford. And a short message that I haven't seen anywhere else."

"What was it?" Blake said urgently. "And why didn't you call the police?"

"I'm speaking to you right now," Weller said defensively. Blake thought she detected another emotion in his voice as well.

He's embarrassed.

"The message, Aaron," she snapped.

"It said, um..." She heard tapping on a keyboard. "*This is our town now. We're not finished.* Just that, all in capitals. *This is our town now. We're not finished.*"

All sensations of tiredness slipped away from Blake's mind as she processed what he'd said. Fresh adrenaline slipped into her bloodstream.

She frowned. "What time did you say you received the email?"

He cleared his throat. Again, she sensed embarrassment.

"At 1:01 p.m.," he said simply.

"But you didn't publish your first story until hours later," she stated. "You were only a few minutes ahead of the major networks. We figured you just had fewer editorial hoops to jump through."

She could practically hear him flushing down the phone. He cleared his throat again.

"I was busy," he said. "You think it's every day a story like this breaks in Northern Pines? Usually I'm fending off press releases about a café opening, not missing a terrorist demand."

"What were you doing that was so important that you almost missed breaking the story of a lifetime?" she asked in disbelief. She shook her head. "In fact, I don't care. Email me everything the terrorists sent you."

"It's just one email. I tried to reply but didn't get a response."

"Just do it," Blake said. She read out her email address, grimacing as she realized Weller now had free license to contact her. Although since finding her cell number had proved little challenge, she wasn't sure it mattered.

Weller paused. She didn't hear any clicking or tapping to indicate that he was following suit.

"About that profile," he ventured.

"No," she replied firmly. "Don't you have enough to write about at the moment?"

He sighed. She heard him typing her email address. A moment later, her phone pinged to acknowledge receipt. She already wanted to end the call. She needed to get this information over to the task force immediately.

"You're a story, Lieutenant," he said. "It's not just what happened to you earlier this winter, not now that you're leading a case like this on your first day in the job. People have a right to know."

"People have a right to feel safe in their homes," Blake said. "That's my job. Thank you for your assistance, Mr. Weller. The sheriff's department appreciates your cooperation."

She ended the call. Before slumping back against the sofa, she forwarded the journalist's email to the task force using an address that could be picked up by every agent in the command center, along with a short summary of her phone call.

When she was done, Blake opened her inbox. She read the terrorists' email to Aaron Weller back once again. The 'from' field was filled out with a random sequence of letters and numbers before a Gmail.com suffix. It was clearly a throwaway email address. It was possible that the FBI's digital forensics technicians might be able to work out who had sent it, but she doubted it.

The careful staging of Piper Hicks' body indicated that the killer was a careful and meticulous individual. Lone-wolf type terrorists were often not the sharpest knives in the drawer. They knew little about fieldcraft or information security.

But she sensed that this one was different. He, she, or they would not make elementary mistakes. They would have masked their IP address with one or multiple VPNs. Probably used a burner cell phone to send the email from a busy location, too.

Her eyes were drawn to the body of the email. The words that Aaron Weller had read out over the phone caught her attention.

THIS IS OUR TOWN NOW. WE'RE NOT FINISHED.

"Our town," she whispered, reading the first part out loud.

The term reverberated in her mind. But she couldn't say why it jumped out at her. The same went for the fact that Nina Crawford's captors had reached out to Aaron Weller, a local journalist, hours before contacting major news networks.

It was significant. Both things were.

I just don't know why.

Blake gave up trying to work it out. Instead, she idly clicked on a hyperlink in the footer of Aaron's email. Though she had no intention of granting the persistent young journalist's request to assist with any feature he wrote about her, she sensed that this wouldn't be the last she heard of him. She doubted the *Pinecone* had a large newsroom, which meant that it was likely she would cross paths with Aaron frequently in the course of her new role.

The link took her to his bio on the *Pinecone*'s website.

"Aaron Weller," she murmured to the empty room. "Graduated East Carolina University's communications program in 2015, with a particular focus on journalism. Two years on the investigations desk for CNN's digital team, then a year at the *Washington Post* before returning home to take up his current role as chief reporter for the *Pinecone*. Teaches a journalism class at his alma mater."

Underneath the bio was a list of Aaron's recent stories in chronological order. The nine or ten most recent were all about the murder of Piper Hicks, the kidnapping of Nina Crawford, or the supposed terrorist threat to the residents of Northern Pines. Blake noticed that sprinkled among those were stories that appeared to focus more on Aaron himself—mostly video clips of his apparently frequent appearances on major national news networks explaining the crisis developing in his hometown.

The doorbell rang, and Blake pushed her laptop aside. She gave the delivery boy a twenty-dollar tip, then found after only a couple of slices that she was no longer hungry. She toyed with the idea of another bottle of beer as she stuffed the uneaten pizza slices into the otherwise empty fridge, but she resisted the urge. She needed a clear head the following morning.

As she drifted off to sleep a few minutes later, an image of Nina in her orange jumpsuit painted the inside of her eyelids. Nina's terrified words echoed in her exhausted mind.

"The man who—" she had said before being cut off. She'd been on the verge of revealing something her captor didn't want out in the open.

But who was she talking about?

17

B lake arrived at the Hercules Center just as Melissa was climbing out of her car. The detective waited for her to park.

"How did you sleep?" she asked as Blake approached.

"Do I look that bad?"

Melissa smiled. "I think we all do."

It was only 7 a.m., but the converted basketball court was already a riot of sound and activity. Blake caught her partner up on her suspicions about the call with Aaron Weller the previous night.

"It's weird," she agreed with a thoughtful expression on her face. "It's very... possessive. 'Our town.' Right?"

"My thoughts exactly." Blake sighed. "But I'm not sure where that gets us. And we only have thirty hours to figure it out."

They had barely walked in before Granger clapped his large, meaty hands together. A sharp echo rang off all four walls. The room instantly quieted. Like everyone else, they turned their attention to where he was standing. A projector whirred into life, plastering a large square blue light onto the wall behind him as it started up.

"Okay, let's keep this brief. Overnight, JTTF worked up a terror threat matrix ranking potential suspects in order of likelihood of involvement. The DC field office is taking the lead on combing chatter for evidence of involvement by an international terror organization.

"Our job is to investigate and clear domestic cells and individuals. In the past five years, the Charlotte JTTF has investigated two dozen persons of interest with sympathies or connections with fundamentalist Islamist terror organizations. In the last twelve hours, we have confirmed the present location of all of them. Seventeen still live within a hundred miles of Fort Bragg. Fourteen men and three women."

Blake instantly dismissed the three women in her head, if only as primary suspects. Something about the way Piper's body had been staged told her that the suspect was male. Carrying her through the field, at the very least, would have required significant strength. That didn't preclude female assistance, but she would focus her attention on the men first.

"After this meeting, Special Agent Quinn will hand out assignments. I want each of these men and women interviewed in person. Make sure their alibis stack up hour by hour for the last week. Go in pairs with backup from local police. Agent—and officer—safety is paramount. Understood?"

A moment of agreement echoed back.

Granger cleared his throat. "Excellent. That brings us to the other order of business on the agenda. The Bureau's Intelligence Branch has flagged up signs of far right and white nationalist groups intending to protest in Northern Pines over the coming days in response to these terrorist threats."

An agent cleared his throat. Granger raised an eyebrow.

"Sir, why Northern Pines, not Bragg?"

"First, our kidnap victim is a Northern Pines resident. Bluntly, she's attractive, white, and blond, everything these groups think they are trying to defend. Second, Piper Hicks was found in the town."

Granger sought out Blake's and Melissa's attention.

"We'll forward you the intelligence reports as a matter of urgency. JTTF will provide any assistance required in policing the protests.

The biggest appears to be one organized on Facebook by a local resident named Dwaine Hilton. Has he already crossed your radar?"

Blake glanced at Melissa, instantly feeling aware of her own inadequacy. She didn't know anything about her new department or the area and population that it policed.

"We know him," Melissa said. Blake felt an irrational sense of gratitude that she'd used the plural. "He's a troublemaker. Couple of arrests for assault a few years back. And his ex-wife reported him for domestic violence before retracting her claim. That was about eighteen months ago."

Blake nodded sagely at the detective's side as if she had the faintest clue what Melissa was talking about. She resolved right then and there not to be caught like that again. She would know more about Northern Pines and its citizens than anybody else. Even if she had to go through the department's crime reports month by month to do it...

"Good. His protest is scheduled for 6 p.m. this evening. About fifty RSVPs so far, but it's growing. And it looks like among them are representatives from known violent militias."

"We'll handle it," Blake confirmed.

Granger pivoted away, already turning to the next topic. Blake briefly closed her eyes.

Great.

Her job was getting more difficult by the minute, let alone the hour. She drew in a steadying breath. Granger's briefing came to a close.

Agent Quinn walked over, cradling a stack of manila folders. He lifted the one on top and handed it to Blake. "Abdul-Malik Azizi. Afghan national. Thirty-two years old. Came over with his wife and two kids following the fall of Kabul. Used to work as a translator for coalition forces. Green Berets, I think. That's how he settled here."

Blake frowned. "So he must have passed security background checks?"

"Correct. But we received an anonymous tip three months ago

that he was seen hanging around Fayetteville Regional Airport with a digital camera."

Her frown deepened. That seemed like thin evidence to mount an FBI counter-terrorism investigation. "Was he?"

"The investigating agent found no evidence to substantiate the claim. We received three similar tipoffs around the same time, all relating to refugee families. Could just be a disgruntled local resident trying to cause trouble. But we still need to check it out."

"Understood," Blake said. She tucked the folder underneath her arm. "We'll get right on it."

Quinn nodded his thanks and turned away in search of his next victims. As she and Melissa left the task force HQ to return to Northern Pines Police Department, Blake caught a glimpse of a TV that had been mounted on a stand at the edge of the room. It was playing a rolling national news channel.

An image of Nina Crawford flashed up on the screen. It was taken at what looked like a family barbecue. She was wearing casual linen shorts and a white tank top. No shoes. She looked happy.

But that wasn't what caught Blake's eye.

"Classy," Melissa muttered, apparently noticing the countdown timer at the bottom right-hand corner of the screen at the same moment.

29:46:52.

Nina Crawford had fewer than thirty hours of life remaining.

Blake ground her teeth together. "We need to move faster."

They rocketed back to Northern Pines with lights flashing. Every second counted. They went straight up to the second floor to brief Captain Rogers on the upcoming protest and the current status of their investigation into the murder of Piper Hicks.

That part didn't last long.

Just as they reached the office space set aside for the Investigation Department, Blake's phone buzzed. She sat down on one of the unused open plan desks rather than in her own office and answered the call. It was Nathan.

"Tell me you have something," she said, dragging a keyboard toward her and typing in the login details she'd been provided with.

"No guarantees, but Diana Stetson's awake."

Blake shot upright, reaching for the keys she'd tossed onto the desk a few moments before.

"Hold your horses," Nathan cautioned. "Her doctors won't give us access for a few hours. Maybe not until tomorrow morning."

"We need to speak to her, Nathan," Blake insisted.

"I know. But Nina Crawford's life isn't the only one on the line here. Private Stetson has suffered a serious traumatic brain injury. Her care needs to be handled with great caution if she wants to come out without permanent damage."

She lowered herself slowly back into her chair. A glum expression settled on her face, though she knew Nathan was right.

"You'll—"

"—Call you the moment we're allowed to interview her?" Nathan chuckled. "Of course."

Blake ended the call. Melissa sat a few desks down from her, pulling up everything they knew about Abdul-Malik Azizi. While she did, Blake chose a different avenue of investigation. She opened a familiar database: the FBI's ViCAP system, which stood for the Violent Criminal Apprehension Program.

It had been built to facilitate information sharing between the thousands of different state, local, and federal law enforcement agencies all across the United States. If a violent homicide was carried out in the tiny community of Milner, Colorado, the local sheriff's department could consult ViCAP to learn whether a killing with similar characteristics had already taken place anywhere in America.

It was a long shot, but something had bugged her ever since the discovery of Piper Hicks' body. The staging was too neat, too meticulous. It felt more like the MO of a serial killer rather than a terrorist.

She typed a series of queries into the blank search box. *Decapitation, female, naked, staged scene*, and so on.

The computer made a groaning sound, and the system hung for several seconds before a list composed of hundreds of hits populated.

Too many.

Blake narrowed the query, searching only for crimes that had happened in North Carolina and neighboring states within the past ten years. This produced a more manageable list of crimes that numbered under half a dozen. She quickly clicked through the case reports of each in turn, navigating first to the crime scene photos.

None matched.

She let out a frustrated sigh which attracted Melissa's attention and a concerned narrowing of her eyes. She gestured that she was fine and returned her attention to the keyboard. Her fingers hung over it for several seconds as she considered her next move.

"Okay," she muttered under her breath. "What if he's escalating?"

Many serial killers did just that. They started out abusing animals before moving up the food chain. Some were frozen in amber, forever doomed to attempt to relive the rush of their first kill; others meticulously and continually refined their techniques.

She removed the first keyword in her search string. A decapitation was a statement: the kind of homicide that made headlines. If their killer had previously used the same MO, she would almost certainly have heard about it. Therefore: either this was his first time, or he'd changed tactics.

Blake simply didn't buy the idea that the individual they were looking for had popped their cherry with Piper Hicks' murder. The crime scene had been too clean, too clinical, too perfect.

The computer repeated its hard-done-by bit but eventually spat out a new list. This time seven results flashed up.

Blake instantly dismissed the first three. One was an actress quite literally killed on a theater stage in Wilmington. The others just didn't feel right.

She clicked the fourth. A PDF opened, and she scrolled down to the crime scene photos. The moment she saw the first one, she sat bolt upright. A shiver ran down her spine, like someone was dragging an ice cube down the length of her body.

It's the same.

Except for the cuts to the neck, the crime scene looked almost identical to where Piper Hicks was found. A woman in her mid-20s had been stripped naked. She was lying on her back in an open field, her blond hair spread into a halo. The only difference was that the photo appeared to have been taken in summer, and the grass underneath her was pale and straw-like rather than verdant and green.

Blake inhaled sharply and urgently scrolled through the remainder of the case report. She learned that the woman's name was Hannah Sanders, a student at East Carolina University. She had been 22 when she died.

Melissa looked up. "What is it?"

Quickly scrolling through the rest of the document, Blake took a few seconds to reply. "Take a look at this."

"What am I looking at?" Melissa murmured softly from behind her. "No shit."

"Same cause of death. Asphyxiation due to smothering. She was found with traces of Rohypnol in her system, too."

"This can't be a coincidence."

Blake saved the case report to her computer, then quickly checked through the three remaining bulletins on ViCAP. The first two didn't seem connected. The third, however, was an almost carbon copy of Hannah's killing. Same cause of death—manual asphyxiation —though the toxicology screen was inconclusive.

"Mandy Yates," Melissa murmured, reading the girl's name out loud. She pointed at the screen. "Wait."

"What is it?"

"Hannah Sanders' body was discovered in a field just outside of Ayden, right?"

"Um, I think so."

"Mandy was found about twenty miles north in Bethel. The two towns are just on the edge of Greenville."

Blake opened Google and pulled up the map of the area. Melissa was right. Ayden and Bethel were sort of satellite towns to Greenville, about ten miles south and the same distance north respectively.

She leaned back in her chair, head spinning from the implications of her discovery. "Our suspect has killed before. At least twice, but maybe more. He didn't stop with Piper, and he damn sure won't with Nina. I think he's just getting going."

"What do we do with this?" Melissa asked.

Blake quickly scanned through the two case reports a second time. The murders were still unsolved. Hannah had been killed just over nine years ago and Mandy six months after that. No DNA or fingerprints were found at either crime scene. The two women had not been sexually assaulted. The chilling similarities with the murder of Piper Hicks only mounted up with every line she read.

Except for the obvious problems.

Melissa's fingers danced over her own keyboard, then fell quiet as she studied the results of her search. "I don't get it," she muttered. "There was no terrorist link with either of the Greenville killings. Nothing out of the ordinary. Except the fact that two women died."

"And why the change in MO?" Blake asked, chewing over the discrepancies herself.

"With Piper?"

"Yes. Why cut off her head?"

"Maybe it's a copycat raising the stakes. Leaving their own mark," Melissa suggested.

"Have you ever heard of these murders before?"

Melissa shook her head.

"Copycat killers feed off publicity. I wasn't here at the time of these killings. Was there any?"

"I'll look."

"Okay. And get the contact details for the detectives that worked each of these cases." Blake stood and reached for her keys. "I want to speak to them both. There's something here, that's for sure. But I'll be damned if I know what it is."

"Where are you going?"

"To interview Abdul-Malik Azizi."

"I should go with you."

Blake shook her head. "This is more important. I'll take backup with me. I won't be long."

18

Blake glanced up into her rearview mirror. The Northern Pines police cruiser trailed about twenty yards back. They were about twenty minutes west of town, heading to the home that had been fixed up for one of the several Afghan refugee families that had settled around Fort Bragg over the past eighteen months.

Mostly they were sponsored and supported by vets and currently serving soldiers from units they had worked alongside during the long war in Afghanistan. She remembered her own brother, Caleb, spending vast amounts of time during the chaotic fall of Kabul coordinating the exits of translators and other specialist personnel. These individuals, mostly men, had worked and gone into battle at the side of American soldiers day after day for years.

The radio on her dashboard crackled as a bend in the road emerged through the pine trees. Jed's now familiar voice filled the vehicle's cabin.

"All fire and rescue units respond. BREAK. Smoke reported south of Foxfire, coming from a construction site off Hoffman Road. Waiting on address. Over."

Blake ignored the broadcast. Her thoughts returned to Caleb. Her brother had seen it as his duty to repay the favor to men who had saved the lives of him and his brothers many times. Leaving them to face the consequences of torture or death at the hands of the Taliban for the crime of working with the Americans was never even an option.

She gently tapped the brakes as the turn in the road approached. As she fed the steering wheel to the right, a white truck spun around the corner heading in the opposite direction. It was traveling so fast she scarcely believed it would stay on the road. Wind buffeted her vehicle as it briefly passed her.

"What the fuck?"

Her eyes automatically jerked up to the mirror. The truck was already disappearing into the distance. Its plates were impossible to make out. She guessed it was probably a Ford F-150, possibly with writing on the side of the chassis, though she wouldn't have put money on that last detail.

"Great," she grumbled as the vehicle finally disappeared from sight. An F-150 in white was probably the most common truck type in the entire United States. It would be nearly impossible to find the offending driver.

Her radio barked, "Lieutenant, did you catch those plates?"

She reached for it as the turn finally ended and the straight road through the trees resumed. "Negative."

Blake frowned. Above the canopy of the pines on either side, she could see a trail of dark smoke stretching up into the sky. The source couldn't be far away. She remembered the earlier radio broadcast. Her eyes widened as she glanced at the satnav on the dashboard.

I'm on Hoffman Road.

"Dammit," she muttered, stepping on the gas.

She still held the radio in her left hand. "This is Larsen," she broadcast. "I see the fire. Responding."

Belatedly, the unit behind reported the same. Blake flicked her lights and sirens on. The needle on the speedometer touched a hundred miles an hour. Thankfully, the road was completely empty as it stretched out a couple of hundred yards ahead of her. She couldn't be more than a mile away from the source of the fire.

Thirty seconds later, she rocketed past a Baptist church to her left. The tree cover broke, and an empty green field of grass appeared on her left. The smoke was coming from a fenced construction site on the far side of it.

As she looked back at the satnav on her dashboard, a sinking feeling gripped Blake's stomach. It was coming from the Azizi address.

The realization redoubled her determination. The needle hit a hundred and ten miles an hour, and still she kept her foot pushed all the way down on the gas pedal. The rev counter in front of her was slowly ticking up all the way to the red zone.

Blake braked hard as the turning for Shaver Lane appeared on her left. A thick pyre of black smoke was coughing into the sky. She could smell it now, like sandpaper grating the back of her throat. She spun her wheel into the turn, immediately gassing the engine to pull the car out of a skid as it hit the apex.

She could see the fire itself now. It was bursting out of the windows of the first in a row of brand-new single-story homes built into a copse of trees about fifty yards up ahead. She stamped on the brakes to bring the car to a stop right next to a large sign that proudly announced the construction of a dozen new homes, courtesy of Hartmann Construction. The sign gave her a strange rush of recognition, though from what she couldn't say. She could barely hear the squeal of rubber on asphalt over the pounding of her own heart and the rushing of blood in her ears.

As she flung open the car door, the satnav calmly reported, "Your destination is on the left."

Horror greeted her as she sprinted for the fire. The amount of smoke pouring into the sky was almost impossible to believe. It was as though a volcano had erupted out of the green and pleasant land of North Carolina.

She passed three small children to her left. Their cries of fear were heart-rending. It took everything she had not to stop and sweep them into her arms.

As she got within thirty feet of the burning home, the heat of the flames scorched her cheeks. Flakes of ash were thrown into the sky like chunks of volcanic rock, flaring bright white before turning black and floating toward the ground.

A man staggered out of the burning house clutching a bundle of cloth to his chest. He took half a dozen unsteady, stuttering steps before collapsing to the ground. He turned his body at the last moment so that his right shoulder took the brunt of the impact.

Blake sprinted toward him. She rolled him over and realized with shock that he was carrying a baby, perhaps only a year old. It was wrapped in white cloth that was stained dark from smoke and ash.

She sank onto her knees at his side. As she reached for his face, she said loudly, "Are you okay? Is anyone else inside?"

He stared up at her, eyes bright and dark and uncomprehending. He tried to answer but only coughed, his entire body twitching violently as his brain attempted to expunge the smoke that had infiltrated his lungs. With what seemed his last reserves of energy, he pushed the baby into Blake's arms.

"Please," he finally breathed, his accented voice ragged and wheezing. "My wife..."

"She's still inside?" Blake asked sharply.

The man—who had to be Abdul-Malik—nodded. He attempted to push himself upright but evidently didn't have the strength. He collapsed back against the ground. His expression was raw and imploring. "Please!"

Blake nodded furiously, as much for her own benefit as his. A loud pop echoed from the direction of the house as something shattered inside. Fresh plumes of smoke swirled into the sky.

She clutched the child to her chest and ran a dozen yards away from the house, placing the baby down on the ground for safety. She heard boots thundering toward her—the officers from the patrol car that had followed her to the house.

"Get him away from the house!" she yelled, already turning back. "Lieutenant, what are you—?"

The rest of the man's question was lost to the adrenaline pumping through her veins as she ran back toward the flaming house. The windows glowed from the flames inside. The front door was open but only to a vast expanse of smoky blackness on the other side. Freshly painted wood blistered from the heat on either side of the frame.

Don't you dare, a voice inside her yelled.

She ignored it. Spying a tap for a garden hose attached to the wall, she flicked it on. It spluttered several times before a stream of clear water spat out. She pulled off her jacket, then her blouse, caring nothing for her modesty. All that was left underneath was a plain black bra.

She dunked both items underneath the spout of water and soaked them thoroughly. She flinched from the cold of the water as she hurriedly shrugged the jacket back on over her shoulders and buttoned it.

Behind her, she heard fire truck sirens and a desperate cry of, "Lieutenant!"

Blake ignored him. She thrust the soaked shirt over her mouth and nose, muttered a quick prayer, then ducked through the front door.

She stepped into hell. The room she entered was wreathed in smoke. There was almost no visibility. She flicked the light switch on the wall to no avail. She quickly got her bearings. She was in a combination kitchen and living room. The kitchen space was to the right, and a couple of over-stuffed leather sofas to the left surrounded a small television.

The house was one long rectangle. The bedrooms—she guessed three of them, judging by the layout—were past the living space. A hallway beckoned from the other side of the room.

Which was exactly where the flames were coming from. They glowed from the very far end of the building. Some were already beginning to punch through the external walls, which she estimated were made of nothing stronger than wood and drywall. They might only last a few seconds longer.

Smoke already filled Blake's lungs. It was everywhere, so thick she could barely see across the room. She pressed the soaked shirt more firmly against her mouth and tried to breathe through the filter it created. She resisted the violent urge to cough and dropped lower to the ground, where the smoke was marginally less thick.

She removed the cloth from her mouth for a moment and yelled, "Is anyone in here? Hello?"

After the last word died in silence, Blake's straining lungs automatically demanded a fresh breath. The instant the smoke hit her lungs, she doubled over and retched. It burned the back of her throat, and tears stung her eyes.

But she tried again. "Hello? Can anyone hear me?"

This time, a plaintive cry rang out from the bowels of the burning building. It was a woman's voice, Blake was certain of it. It descended into a burning, wracking fit of coughing. She sounded pitifully weak.

"Where are you?"

No answer.

Shit.

Blake ducked as a crack rang out somewhere above her. The force of the noise buffeted her. It felt as though she was standing inside a large marching drum as sticks beat on it from either side. Heat singed her skin from overhead. The fire must have run up the building's walls toward the roof. The whole structure might collapse at any moment.

"Then move," she muttered.

She crossed the living room as fast as she dared. Timbers and other chunks of debris had fallen from the ceiling, presenting hazards underfoot. The sofa smoked where embers had landed on it. Tiny fires were springing up in every direction she looked. Her hair smelled as though it was singeing.

Snatching the life-giving shirt away from her mouth for just a second, she yelled, "Keep low. Try and cover your mouth with something."

That was all she could manage before the heat of the burning building singed her lungs. She thrust the shirt back over her lips. It was already visibly drying, though it had been soaked through just a few seconds earlier.

Nerve endings all over Blake's skin screamed with agony. It felt as though a thousand tiny whips were raining down on every inch of her body. Finally, she made it to the hallway. She crouched there for a moment, hiding behind the wall to its side. She dared to snatch another glance down it. Her eyes sprang wide.

Nobody could pass down there. It was suicide.

Another cry rang out. The woman sounded close to death. Blake spun and rested her back against the wall. She closed her eyes. Her brain was begging her to run. Every survival instinct cried out that this was hopeless. Even if she made it through the hallway, there was no guarantee the woman would still be alive when she got there.

Enough excuses.

Blake pushed off with her right foot. She rounded the corner and stepped into the hallway. The walls and the ceiling funneled the heat from the far end toward her. It was like stepping into an oven. To her right was a single doorway about halfway down the hallway. On the left, there were two: the master bedroom and another.

"Where are you?" Blake called out.

Nothing.

She gritted her teeth, cursing with anguish before yelling, "Come on, give me something!"

The door to the master bedroom was closed. Something had fallen against it, a timber beam from overhead. It was charred and smoking with tiny flickers of flame bursting into life up and down its length.

Blake drew closer toward it. She saw that the doors to the small bedrooms were both open. If anyone was still in here, then they had to be behind the lone blocked doorway.

"Crap, crap, crap, crap," she said underneath her breath as she stopped in front of it.

She crouched down low, where both the heat and smoke were

less intense. She had to move fast. It might already be too late. The structure above her was making ominous creaking and groaning sounds, as though it was decades old rather than brand-new.

Blocking out her growing fear and desperation, Blake attempted to calmly analyze the scene in front of her. The doorframe opened outward into the hallway. That meant the fallen beam was definitely blocking it. It had to weigh a hundred pounds easy. The way it had fallen left it propped up in an A-frame against the door, rendering it impossible for anyone inside to escape.

Blake could only imagine the fear of the woman on the other side as she faced imminent death with no means of escape. But she didn't have time to contemplate it. She was in a bind of her own.

Another crack. One more beam fell from above her, toppling to the ground at the far end of the hallway. She had only seconds to act.

Inspiration came to her.

She tore the jacket off her body, whimpering slightly at the pain inflicted by heat of the flames above on her bare skin. She wrapped the wet cloth around her right hand like an oven glove and then pushed against the beam, stretching as tall as she could to maximize her leverage.

The beam rocked but otherwise stayed stubbornly in place. Blake's shoulders protested at the effort. She tried again. Same result. The third time was no luckier.

"Dammit," she cursed. She took a step back. A sudden, almost overwhelming urge to drop everything and run almost overcame her.

I can't do this with one hand, she realized.

But since her other hand still held the damp shirt over her mouth and nose, she was stuck. It was a choice between finding the strength to move the beam and losing her oxygen entirely.

She made her choice. Better to do it quickly while there was still a chance of success.

Blake filled and emptied her lungs several times in quick succession, flushing as much smoke-infused oxygen into her bloodstream as possible. She took one final, deep breath, filling her lungs as if preparing to blow up a child's birthday balloon.

And let the shirt fall to the floor.

Time slowed. Blake knew that this was the final roll of the dice. She placed her left arm against the back of her right hand so there was some protection against the smoldering beam. She resumed her earlier position, lowered herself into a half-crouch, and jumped upward, pushing all her strength into one specific spot.

Again, the beam rocked. It didn't fall, but it slid several inches to the left.

She tried again. It slid farther. She tried the door handle. It opened a few inches, but not enough to get inside—or anybody out.

One more heave.

Blake resumed her crouch. It was like some kind of strange shotput posture from the Olympics. She thrust herself upward. Finally, the beam shifted before hurtling toward the ground. She didn't wait until it hit before yanking the door open.

As it came toward her, the body of a young woman with dark hair came with it, sprawling out into the hall. She was wearing blue jeans and a thick hooded sweatshirt. She was completely unconscious. The room was filled with dense smoke. Just barely visible on the other side was the window, which was like a scene out of Dante's Inferno.

Flames licked up the side of the building, completely swallowing the view. All that Blake could see was fire. She stared it with horror for a few seconds, her face blanching as she understood why the woman had been unable to escape through the window.

No time.

Blake snatched the wet cloth from the ground. She sucked in a greedy breath, then dropped it again. She needed both hands. One breath would have to do.

She bent down and maneuvered the woman into a straight line before stretching her arms out in front of her on the ground and rolling her up onto her shoulders. She had a slight frame, but even so, it took all of Blake's strength to hoist her into a fireman's carry.

She ran for the exit, the weight easier to bear now that it was up. The cracking of timber and hissing of flame behind her gave her all the adrenaline she needed to run far faster than her body had any right to do. She weaved through the smoke and the furniture, hurtling over several fresh fires, and stumbled outside.

Her last thought before collapsing into unconsciousness was: *What the hell happened here?*

19

"Lieutenant, how you feeling?"

Blake shot him a weak smile and a thumbs-up. She didn't have the energy for much else. She clutched the oxygen mask to her face and gratefully sucked in the life-giving gas. The bed in the back of the ambulance was raised, and she slumped back against the bolster. Her chest rose and fell shakily.

The officer standing at the back end of the ambulance shook his head in disbelief. "With all due respect, ma'am, you're one crazy sonofabitch."

The world outside the ambulance's rear doors was a picture of chaos. Firefighters, police officers, and EMS technicians swarmed around the row of newly built homes, the first of which had been reduced to a smoldering shell by the intensity of the blaze.

A siren wailed in the distance, and a hissing, sputtering sound produced by water tamping down the last of the flames that had consumed the structure provided a backing track of static that hung behind everything. Two more of the houses were smoking, so presumably the fire had spread while she was unconscious. It was a miracle the fire department had responded quickly enough to prevent the entire development being destroyed.

Blake let her head fall back. She closed her eyes. She flinched as images of flame and smoke appeared in the darkness. What the hell had she been thinking? She could have been killed.

"Open your mouth," the paramedic at her side instructed. Her eyes flickered open, and she did as she was told. He shone a high-power flashlight between her teeth and manipulated her cheek and jaw with blue-gloved hands. He spent almost a minute conducting a detailed search.

"Okay, now look up," he said.

This time, he shone the flashlight up her nose, pulling her nostrils left and right to get a better look. Blake was too beat to ask him what he was doing.

"You got lucky," he finally said, clicking the flashlight off and tossing it into his bag. "No thermal damage. I don't see any signs of blistering or burns. No soot, either. Promise me one thing?"

Blake raised an eyebrow as he shot her an expectant look.

"You won't ever do that again..."

"I'll—" she began before breaking out into a fit of coughing. She took another deep breath from the oxygen mask and forced her chest to relax. "I'll think about it."

"How is she, Jack?" a man she didn't recognize bellowed as he stopped at the rear of the ambulance.

He was wearing firefighting gear, though the flame-retardant jacket was open to the chest. He looked to be in his late 50s, his hair already mostly gray, and a two-day stubble covered his chin.

"The lieutenant will live," the EMS tech said, shaking his head in disbelief. "But she needs to go to the hospital to get checked out. They spray all sorts of chemicals onto building materials these days. You don't want all that crap in your lungs."

"You're telling me," the firefighter said with a knowing chuckle. "Pete. Pete Donahue. I'm the fire chief here in town."

"Nice to meet you," Blake said as she shook his hand. Her voice was muffled, but as long as she kept the oxygen mask plastered to her face, she had the energy to speak. She shrugged. "I'd get up, but..."

"Stay where you are," Donahue boomed. "You're one brave

woman, you know that, Lieutenant? Dumb as all hell but definitely brave."

"I did what I had to," Blake said.

She winced as the paramedic pulled her sleeve back, revealing a two-inch burn on her forearm that she didn't remember receiving. He sprayed it with a cool mist that stung, causing a vein on her temple to pop out.

"You saved that woman's life. No doubt about that."

Blake coughed. "How is she?"

"On her way to RightHealth. She sucked down a lungful of smoke, but she should be okay in a couple of days."

"Her husband?"

"Still here. He's answering a few questions from my guys."

"I need to speak to him," Blake said. She tried to sit up but instantly felt woozy. She braced her palms against the stretcher and struggled to remain upright.

"Lieutenant, I need you to lie back," Jack said, letting out an irritated sigh. She felt a tug on her right arm and looked down to see he was in the process of dressing her burn.

"I need to take a statement," Blake insisted.

"One of your guys already did," Donahue said. "Listen to Jack. You'll do yourself no good overexerting yourself before your body has had a chance to clear the smoke. Trust me."

He waggled an eyebrow.

"Fine," Blake said, relenting. "Bring him to me."

Donahue kept his eyebrow raised but didn't argue the point. He stomped away, bellowing fresh instructions to his men.

While she was waiting, Blake settled back against the stretcher and closed her eyes. She didn't protest as Jack cleaned and dressed the rest of her wounds. Donahue was right. The longer she kept herself hooked up to the oxygen, the better she felt.

"Lieutenant?"

Her eyes snapped open, and she saw Melissa looking back at her.

"I came as soon as I heard," her partner said. Her face was woven with worry lines. "Are you okay? You could've been killed!"

"Coulda, shoulda, woulda," Blake replied, flicking her thumb dismissively against her forefinger. She pushed herself upright, using the stronger muscles in her thighs to lever herself up the stretcher.

Definitely feeling better.

"What happened?" Melissa asked.

Blake shrugged. The truth was, she had no idea. She blinked and remembered the white pickup truck she'd seen speeding away from the crime scene. "The truck—"

"Officer Casey put out a BOLO," Melissa said. "But without plates..."

Slumping back, Blake grimaced. "Whoever was in that truck was the arsonist," she said. "They could have killed all those kids. We need to catch them. They need to be put away."

"We will," Melissa said soothingly. "But we got lucky. All the children are okay."

"This time," she replied.

Blake hadn't dealt with many arson cases while she was with CID. But she knew that many arsonists got a powerful thrill from setting fires. In some, it could be as powerful as taking drugs. It drove them to set more and bigger blazes.

Donahue returned a moment later with Abdul-Malik Azizi in tow. The Afghan former translator looked shaken and had a shiny foil blanket wrapped around his shoulders. He was clutching something to his chest. On closer examination, Blake realized it was the baby he'd carried out of the fire.

The fire chief grunted, "He's all yours" and departed, still barking orders to his men.

Dropping the mask from her face, Blake took a couple of experimental breaths. She filled her lungs a couple of times without feeling the overwhelming urge to cough. It felt like the worst of the smoke had been cleared from her chest. She wouldn't be running marathons anytime soon, but she hadn't planned to, either.

Finally, she said, "How are you?"

"Alive, thanks be to God," Azizi said.

"My name is Blake Larsen," she said. "I'm a lieutenant in the sheriff's department. What should I call you?"

Despite the shock of the morning's events, she noticed a flicker of interest on Azizi's face. He was evidently an intelligent man. That much was clear just from his eyes.

"Abdul is fine," he said. He clenched his jaw, then unlocked it and spoke. "I want to thank you for what you did, Lieutenant. You saved my wife's life. If it wasn't for you..."

"I did the same as you," Blake said. She felt the eyes of both Jack and Melissa on her, and her skin prickled with awkwardness.

"They are my children," Abdul said. "It is my responsibility to protect my family. Not yours. So I thank you."

Blake inclined her head, then turned to Jack. "You mind giving us a moment?"

He nodded. "You're all patched up. But you really need to go to hospital to get checked out. And keep breathing through that mask!"

"Thanks, Jack," Blake said genuinely as he extricated himself from the cramped confines of the ambulance. She pressed the mask to her face and took a deep breath before continuing. Melissa took her place on a small stool to her side.

"Abdul, first of all, please accept my most sincere apologies for what happened to your family today, on behalf of both me and the whole of Monroe County." She took another deep, steadying breath, feeling a little like a fraud proclaiming that she spoke for a public she'd only just begun serving and yet feeling deeply that someone needed to say it.

"This attack goes against everything our community should be about. Please know that Detective Wilson and I, as well as the entire sheriff's department, won't rest until we catch the person responsible."

"Thank you, Lieutenant," Abdul said, the blanket on his shoulders making a crinkly sound as he gently swayed from side to side. The baby in his arms burbled a few times, then settled.

"I know that this was just some madman," he said. "I don't blame anyone in the community. America has welcomed us with open arms. Mr. Hartmann gave us this house. For free."

Blake recognized the name. She frowned, then remembered it was plastered over construction sites all across town. Hartmann was on the town council. He was also one of the wealthiest residents of Northern Pines, courtesy of the construction company that bore his name.

Abdul's shoulders slumped as the enormity of what had been taken from him crashed home. "We've only lived here for two weeks. Our house was the first to be finished. But we will survive. My family has lived through worse."

"I know you have," Blake said. "But that doesn't make what happened okay. We should have protected you."

"Lieutenant, my cousin was also a translator for your special forces. He was a proud man. A good one. I got my family out. He was unable to. Six months ago, the Taliban dragged him out of his house, strung him from a tree branch by his ankles, and used him for target practice. Nobody stopped them. Nobody helped. Today you did. You saved my wife's life. That is the difference."

Blake inclined her head. She matched his fierce gaze and didn't look away. "Tell me about what happened today," she said.

Melissa pulled out a notepad and pen and waited expectantly.

Abdul closed his eyes as if replaying the events in his mind's eye. "My wife was preparing lunch. I drive rideshare at night, when the fares are better, so I was asleep when I heard her cry out. There was already fire everywhere. All around the house."

Blake stayed silent.

His voice grew hoarse. "We got the older children out together. I told them to run far away. But Aaliyah, our newborn, was in our bedroom. My wife went back inside. She took our baby out of her cot, but before she could escape, the beam fell, and she was trapped inside. I did what I could to move it, but I had already breathed too much smoke. I didn't have the strength."

Tears formed at the corners of his eyes. Blake said softly, "Take your time."

He shook his head and carried on. "I could only pull the door open a few inches. Just enough to pass Aaliyah through. My wife begged me to take her and run. So I did. And I left my wife to die."

"You saved your baby's life," Melissa interjected firmly.

Blake waited a moment, then asked, "Did you see anything else? I know you were asleep, but what about your wife?"

"I saw who did this!" Abdul snapped.

"What?"

"When I ran out the first time, I saw a man standing in the trees near the road. He was dressed all in black and had something pulled over his face. He was staring at the house. I waved my arms and begged him to help, but he just... stood there. When I came out the second time, he was gone."

"Can you describe him?"

Abdul shook his head. "I've tried to remember but... no. He looked tall. Maybe six foot, perhaps a little less. Or more. It was hard to say. But he was wearing a baseball cap, and I couldn't see his face."

Melissa scribbled down the details. Blake fought the urge to grimace at Abdul's description. All they had so far was a description that could account for half the men in America and a sighting of a vehicle that just happened to be the most popular pickup truck in the entire country.

"Have you seen this man before?"

He shook his head, then made a face. "We received letters..."

"What kind of letters?" Melissa asked.

"Threatening ones. Telling us to go home. Five of them, maybe more." He looked indignant. "This is our home now. We cannot go back."

"Did you keep them?"

He gestured back toward the smoking house. "Only the last one. It was in the kitchen."

"When did you receive it?"

"Last week."

"Did you report this to the police?" Blake said.

Abdul shook his head. "No. Maybe I should have. I thought... I thought it was nothing compared to my cousin's troubles. I was wrong."

Blake fell silent. She couldn't think of any more questions to ask. They would need forensics to take a look at the charred remains of the house once the fire department was finished. She was almost certain that her reason for being here in the first place was a wild goose chase. She'd seen the anger on Abdul's face when he spoke of the Taliban and of what had happened to his country.

He was no terrorist. He was a victim.

"Lieutenant Larsen, can I ask you a question?"

She nodded. As she spoke, her phone buzzed in her pocket. "Of course."

"Why were you here?"

Blake winced. The last thing she wanted to do was add to his anguish right now. But she also had a job to do. "Abdul, where were you two nights ago?"

His lips tightened. "Driving. I told you, I work every night."

"Can anyone attest to that?"

"My passengers. The app records all of my journeys. You think I was responsible for that woman's disappearance?"

"I do not. But we have to follow every lead."

"I've never met her," Abdul said tightly. "I will send you my records. Now I must go be with my family."

He turned and walked quickly away. Blake's chin fell to her chest, and she let out a groan. She sucked in a breath through the oxygen mask, then said, "I feel like an asshole."

"You had to ask," Melissa replied, her expression matching the way Blake felt. "But I don't like him for it."

"Me neither. But now we've got a second major crime to solve." She grinned bleakly. "I hope you like overtime."

"Well, I was thinking about a trip to the Bahamas..." Melissa replied. "But now we've got a hate crime to add to our murder and kidnapping cases, I'm guessing I won't find the time."

"You think that's what this was?" Blake asked.

"You didn't see?"

"See what?"

Melissa gestured for her to follow. Blake walked gingerly behind her as she was led back to the large sign she'd passed at the entrance to the site. It still triggered the same strange sense of déjà vu in her. On the front, just under the words HARTMANN CONSTRUCTION, somebody had spray-painted a much less pleasant message.

"Immigrants go home," Blake muttered blackly. "Real nice."

"Tell me about it," Melissa replied.

Blake finished scanning the sign. The graffiti had been sprayed over the logos or names of over a dozen organizations and individuals, the most prominent of which was the Hartmann Foundation.

"What is this place?" she asked.

"The town came together a couple of years back after the Afghanistan withdrawal. Lot of people around here deployed over there. Gabriel Hartmann's been building homes for some of the refugees who came over."

Blake nodded, now understanding what Abdul had been referring to.

"Better hope he's good for the repairs, too," she said as she fished for her cell phone. She quickly scanned the message she'd received while talking to Abdul. It was from Nathan.

"What's up?" Melissa asked.

"It's about Diana Stetson. Her doctors have okayed an interview."

20

B lake probed her bandaged forearm, wincing as the burn lashed out with a savage blast of pain.

"You okay?" Melissa asked, glancing over the central console, apparently concerned by her sudden intake of breath.

"Fine," she said. "But it stings like a bitch."

"Make sure you take it easy," Melissa replied.

She snorted. "Lucky we're not working our fingers to the bone, right?"

Melissa flicked a switch on the dashboard to flash the grille lights, then stepped on the gas and sped past an ancient gray Mercedes. As soon as she was ahead, she turned off the lights and backed off the accelerator, though at a faster pace than before.

"Okay," Blake said, placing a hand on her chest to test her breathing. It was coming easier now and improving with every few minutes that passed. "Tell me about Dwight Hilton."

"Dwaine."

"Okay," she repeated with a wry smile. "Tell me about *Dwaine* Hilton."

"What do you want to know?"

"First off, do you think he's capable of setting fire to the Azizi place? Seems kind of coincidental; he organizes this rally, and suddenly we have a hate crime on our hands."

Melissa frowned. "I looked at his file back at the station. His first arrest record was for an attempted Ponzi scheme. He was pushing an online timeshare scam. He set the whole thing up himself. Raked in over $200,000 in deposits before it all came tumbling down. Spent three years in Lanesboro Correctional Institute."

Blake rolled her eyes. "Let me guess, he found white nationalism behind bars?"

"Something like that." Melissa nodded. "I asked around. As far as anybody knows, he wasn't outwardly racist before he went inside. By the time he came out, he had Aryan Brotherhood tattoos."

Prison could be a deeply traumatic place, Blake knew. Many inmates initially fell into prison gangs for protection, not because they truly believed in the deranged ideologies espoused by the lifers who ran them. A person could go into prison with a relatively normal outlook on life and come out completely altered.

It was one of the contradictions of the job she'd always wrestled with. She took bad people off the streets to keep the rest of the community safe. You couldn't have a dozen Dwaine Hiltons running around scamming grandmothers, after all. Many people went behind bars and came out with a resolve never to break the law again.

But not all.

Blake asked one last question as they entered the grounds of Fort Bragg. "You think he could be responsible for this?"

Melissa considered the question for a long time before responding. "I think he's smart. His timeshare scam couldn't have been pulled off by just anybody. We also know he's got priors for violence—both domestic and random. No history of arson, but maybe he just didn't get caught."

They drew up in front of Womack Army Medical Center a few moments later. Melissa parked, and both detectives stepped out. Blake was grateful to take the elevator up to the third floor. Her legs already felt heavy by the time they reached Stetson's private room.

Nathan was waiting there.

"Have you spoken to her already?" Blake asked.

He shook his head. "Her doctor told me she's fragile. Figured it could use a woman's touch."

"Okay. Does she know why we're here?"

"Just that you need to ask her a few questions."

"And she doesn't know anything about Piper?"

"She does not."

Blake briefly closed her eyes. She hated death notifications. This wasn't exactly the same as informing a wife that her husband was dead, but it burned up the same emotional fuel. "Let's get it over with."

Nathan nodded at a nurse standing behind a desk at the end of the corridor, then reached for the door handle. He twisted it, and all three of them entered.

The room had a large window and contained a single hospital bed. It stood in front of a large bank of electrical outlets and hookups for oxygen. Diana Stetson was lying in bed, her eyes closed. She was a young Black woman in her early 20s. Her head was swathed in a white bandage, and she was connected to a variety of drips and a pulse oximeter that measured her heart rate and blood oxygen levels. A quick glance at the display revealed that both were in normal bounds.

A wheeled table hung over the bed. On top of it was a small jug of water, a single plastic cup, a cell phone, and a get well soon card. The lights were turned down low, and the blind was drawn most of the way across the window.

"I'm just resting my eyes," Diana whispered. "Still hurts when I open them."

"That's just fine," Blake said softly, matching the patient's tone. "This won't take long. I know you were in an accident."

"Hit my head."

"So we heard. Diana, my name is Lieutenant Blake Larsen. I'm with the Monroe County Sheriff's Department. I just need to ask you a few questions."

Diana's voice sharpened. Her pulse shot up ten beats on the display. "Am I in trouble?"

"No, it's nothing like that," Blake said soothingly. "It's about your friend Piper."

She frowned, then winced, as if the movement pulled against her wound.

"Piper?" Diana repeated. "Is she okay?"

Blake ran her hands through her hair. She bit the bullet. No sense dragging it out. For either of them. "Diana, I'm sorry to tell you that Piper was found dead while you were unconscious. I'm trying to find out what happened to her."

Diana's heart rate spiked to over ninety beats a minute. The monitor let out a warning chime. Blake made a face, knowing that she needed to keep the woman calm—not just for the sake of her health but because her doctors would end the interview. She couldn't let that happen. Right now, they needed a lead.

Any lead.

"Take a deep breath, Diana. With me. In, one, two. Pause. Out, three, four."

They breathed slowly together for almost a minute before Blake was satisfied that she was in the right state of mind to continue.

"What—what happened?" Diana finally asked. She opened her eyes a crack, and Blake could see that they were filled with tears which clung to her lashes like morning dew on grass.

"That's what we're trying to find out," Blake said without showing her cards. "Diana, do you know anyone who would have reason to hurt Piper?"

Diana stuttered again. "You—you think she was murdered?"

"We have to rule everything out," Blake said. A white lie. "Take another deep breath, think about it."

She did as she was told. A single tear rolled down either cheek. "No. Everybody liked Piper. Why would anyone hurt her?"

Blake studied the woman's face intently. Everything about her reaction seemed genuine. "We don't know. One of the soldiers in your company said they thought she packed a suitcase. Do you know where she was going?"

Diana stiffened. Blake glanced at the display above her. Her heart rate noticeably started to climb, though not as steeply as during the initial shocks.

Interesting.

"Anything you can think of might be useful," Blake said. "Did Piper tell you about her plans?"

"She—" Diana began before her mouth ground to a halt. "Oh my God, I can't believe she's dead."

For the first time, Blake began to suspect that she was holding out on them.

"The other soldiers in your unit said that you two were tight," she said. "They said you shared everything with each other."

Diana's heart rate climbed a few more beats. She swallowed hard. Her mouth made a dry, rasping sound.

"I don't know who killed her," she said. "I promise, I don't know who might have wanted to hurt Piper. Like I told you, everybody liked her."

An image of the attractive blonde flashed into Blake's mind. It wasn't a surprise that everybody liked her. But someone hadn't.

"Diana, another woman is missing," Blake said. "She's been kidnapped. We need to find her before it's too late. Anything you can remember might help."

She started weeping. Tears coursed down her cheeks. "Who?"

Blake glanced at Nathan and Melissa, then back to the patient. "Her name is Nina Crawford."

Diana's heart rate rocketed past a hundred and twenty beats per minute. The monitor screamed a warning. She gripped the bedsheets with both hands, scrunching up the fabric. Her entire body went rigid.

Hearing commotion out in the hallway, Blake gestured at Nathan to run interference. He headed hastily for the door.

She knows something.

"You know her," Blake said firmly.

"She's Captain Crawford's wife," Diana said lamely. "I've met her a couple of times on base."

"Diana, if you know something, you have to tell us. It's important. It could save a woman's life."

Not to mention defuse the ticking time bomb that was the rally scheduled to take place in the center of Northern Pines. But she kept that part to herself.

"He's—" Diana began. "They are..."

"You can tell me," Blake said softly. Melissa edged forward a couple of feet, and Blake saw that she had her cell phone out and was recording the entire thing.

"They're sleeping together," Diana said before breaking down into a series of heaving sobs. "She told me not to tell anybody. She made me swear."

"Detective!"

Blake spun around to see a doctor storming into the hospital room. He had a sulfurous expression on his face. Nathan stood behind him with his palms up, wearing an expression that said, *I did everything I could.*

"Diana, take a deep breath," Blake said, turning back to the bed. She felt adrenaline pulsating inside her. They needed to know whatever was inside the woman's brain. This couldn't wait.

"Detective, get out of this room right now," the doctor snapped.

"Deep breaths, Diana," Blake said, her gaze fixed on the heart rate monitor. She set her own feet wide apart, almost daring the medical staff to drag her out of the room. "You're not going to be in any trouble, okay? We just need to know what Piper told you."

Slowly, Diana's heart rate dropped. It dipped below 110bpm, then 90, then 70 before plateauing just above fifty. Her tears stopped. She looked like she was in some kind of catatonic state.

"They're sleeping together," she finally whispered, her eyes screwed shut. "Piper and Captain Crawford. She told me I had to keep it a secret. He would lose his job if I told anybody."

Blake's own heart began to race at the vindication of her suspicions about Austin. She recalled the way he'd reacted when they'd first mentioned Piper to him—the sense of familiarity, rather than concern.

"They were having an affair? For how long?"

"Three, maybe four months," Diana said. "Piper said they were in love."

"Is that what she was doing this weekend? Going to see Captain Crawford?"

"Yes," she whispered, her face knotted with anguish as though she was revealing a great secret. "He had a hotel room booked. I guess it was a surprise. He texted her Friday, real last minute. Said they were going to spend the whole weekend together. She was so excited. I... I can't believe she's gone."

"Do you know which hotel?"

"The Carolina," she replied affirmatively. "I remember because it looked real fancy."

"Diana, did Piper ever mention whether the captain was violent toward her?"

She shook her head. The movement was almost imperceptible. "No. I'm sure he wasn't. Piper would have told me."

"Do you think that the captain could have hurt your friend?"

"No!" Diana exclaimed. "He isn't like that."

She ground her jaw together as if to prevent herself from saying anything else. Blake grimaced. She sensed that the woman was still hiding something. But what?

"How do you know?"

"He—" she started. "Piper, she sent me a picture. God, she promised I could never show anyone. But she said she didn't want to hide it from me. She was happy. *They* were happy."

"Can you show me?"

"I need my phone."

Blake stepped forward, picked it up, and held it up in front of Diana's face. The device unlocked.

"Go into messages," Diana said.

It only took a few seconds for Blake to locate the picture. It had been sent three weeks earlier. Piper—alive, happy, her hair all messed up—was lying in bed next to a male form that was unmistakably that of Captain Austin Crawford. It looked like it had been taken in a motel room.

Blake's breath caught in her throat. This could be the break they needed. Austin had lied about his relationship with Piper Hicks. At the very least, he'd concealed the truth. She quickly forwarded the image to her own number, then put the phone back down.

"But you knew that Captain Crawford was married, right?" she said, taking a different tack. "Piper knew, too."

Fresh tears. "They were unhappy. I guess they had an open relationship. But they were staying together for the kids."

"Piper told you that?"

"Yeah. Yeah, she did."

"Detective, I'm going to need you to cut this short," the doctor finally said, as if shaking himself out of a reverie. "My patient needs to rest."

"One last question," Blake said, holding up a finger. "Diana, we found a pregnancy test in the trash in Piper's barracks room. Did she think she was pregnant?"

Another spike in heart rate. Diana answered in a low, pained voice, as though she'd taken a blow to the stomach. "No."

"That's enough, detectives!" the doctor said harshly, starting toward them. "Get out."

Blake kept her gaze focused intently on Diana's face, shocked by the devastation she saw written on it. The penny slowly dropped.

The test wasn't for Piper. It was for her. And judging by the grief written on to her features, the tears now leaking from her eyes, the baby was gone.

Blake didn't resist as the doctor physically pushed her from the room. Though she knew she had to ask, she felt sick at having caused so much pain to a woman who was already suffering.

The three investigators stood outside Diana's hospital room in silence for several seconds after the doctor finished cursing them out in a voice designed not to carry through the door. Judging by the expressions on all their faces, Blake guessed they'd reached the same conclusion.

"We need to get Austin in for questioning," she said finally, hating the coldness of moving so quickly past such pain, yet knowing she had no other choice.

Melissa was already raising her phone to her ear, an expression of relief on her face that someone had broken the spell. "I'm on it."

Blake pushed her guilt aside and returned to the bare facts they'd just learned. Austin Crawford, husband to their kidnap victim, was also having an affair with their murder victim. Why hadn't he told them? Was he hiding the truth to protect his career?

Or does he have something darker to hide?

21

Blake jerked out of a half-sleep as her phone trilled in her pocket. She reached automatically forward, wincing as the action caused nerve endings in her burned forearm to cry out in agony. As her eyes came back into focus, she realized that they were only about a minute away from the station in Northern Pines.

"You shouldn't have let me fall asleep," she muttered to Melissa as she answered the call.

Her partner said nothing in response. But Blake could almost hear the knowing roll of the woman's eyes. She was exhausted. They both were, but Blake was also suffering from the physical aftereffects of her brush with death earlier that day.

Blake answered the call, glancing at the screen but not recognizing the number before she said tightly, "Larsen."

"Lieutenant Larsen?" a gruff male voice asked. "Lieutenant Blake Lawson with the Northern Pines Police Department?"

"The one and only. Who's calling?"

"Name's Keaton. Captain Sidney Keaton. I run the CIU down here in Pitt County."

For a moment, Blake's mind was empty. Where the hell was Pitt

County? At first, she thought it had something to do with her parents' case and former CID agent Skip Hobson.

"I understand you requested information about the murders of Mandy Yates and Hannah Sanders."

Comprehension hit her like a speeding truck. She felt her chest tighten with anticipation. "That's right. Thanks for calling, Captain."

"No problem. This have something to do with the case you're working over there? Didn't put two and two together until your partner sent over that request for information, but—what's her name? Nina something?"

"Crawford."

"That's right. Crawford. She looks just like they did. A little older, sure, but the resemblance is there."

The car rocked as Melissa spun the wheel and guided it over the sidewalk into the parking lot to the front of the station. Out of the corner of her eye, Blake saw a small press pack snapping photos and shooting B-reel footage. She recognized the face of Aaron Weller, but nobody else.

"Captain Keaton, right?"

"Call me Sid."

"Listen, Sid. You know how it is," Blake said as Melissa guided the car into a space. As her partner killed the engine, she shot her a look that said, *I'll see you inside.*

"You can't comment on an active investigation," Sid chuckled. "And sure as shit not one with the Bureau's fingerprints all over it. I'm not asking you to. Listen, if you think there's a connection between your case and my cold ones, I'll tell you whatever you want to know. Those two stuck with me."

"Tell me about them."

Melissa's door swung shut behind her, and her partner disappeared into the station. Blake looked out through the windshield and listened to Sid emit a heavy sigh.

"There's not much to tell. I'm guessing you've read the case files. I was a detective back then, still with Pitt County sheriff's office. Ayden PD called us in after they found Hannah Sanders' body, since they only had a part-time investigator who was more used to dealing with property crimes. Hannah was a student at East Carolina University. The dean put a lot of pressure on law enforcement to close the case fast. It's a big employer around here."

Sid sighed ruefully. "But we had nothing. Poor girl was drugged then smothered to death. No defensive wounds or evidence of sexual assault. Her body was bleached, and her fingernails scraped clean."

"Who was your prime suspect?"

"We didn't have one. Hannah didn't have a boyfriend. No evidence of any arguments with friends, either. But I always wondered whether she knew her killer."

"Why?"

"She went missing after class. She wasn't intoxicated. She just up and vanished. The next day, her body was found on the edge of a field outside of Ayden, twenty miles from where she was last seen. And since there was no evidence of a struggle, I always figured she climbed into a car with someone she knew. But I never found any proof to back that theory up."

"What about Mandy, um—" Blake said, struggling to recall the girl's surname.

"Yates." Sid's teeth audibly ground together, and it was a few seconds before he continued. "I failed that girl. And that was when everything went crazy."

"Crazy how?"

"One pretty blond girl dying's a tragedy," he said. "Two's a pattern. A serial killer who goes after coeds? That's catnip for the press. The student paper started calling him the Blonde Butcher. One of their writers emailed me for comment every day for a year. We had parents threatening to pull their kids out of college. Girls wouldn't walk home alone at night."

"I don't blame them," Blake said.

"Me either," Sid said firmly. "I have girls that age now myself. They were younger back then. But you can't help but worry."

"Was anything different with Mandy's case?"

"Same MO. Same lack of forensic evidence. I had no doubt that it was the same killer. We never released images of the way Hannah's body was found to the press, but Mandy's was staged the exact same way. Only difference between the two cases was that Mandy disappeared after meeting someone for a date."

"Meeting who?"

"We never found out. By all accounts, Mandy was a quiet kid. Didn't have many close friends. But her roommate said she was excited. Said she met somebody. And then she never came home."

"Any suspects?"

"None. I figured that whoever killed those girls was a student also, though," he said. "Both murders occurred during semester time, a school year apart. I spent the last eight years waiting for a third. My guess is that whoever killed them graduated, then went back home. Time to time I check ViCAP looking for similar killings."

"Can you think of anything else I should look into?"

"Yeah, the blog," Sid said.

"What blog?"

"It was called *She Lies*," he said. "Hosted on an anonymous blogging platform. We subpoenaed them, naturally, but it was hosted in some shithole. We never got anywhere with it."

Blake stayed silent, waiting for him to continue.

"It was real unhinged shit. The writer had photos of female students taken from a distance while they were going about their daily lives. Sometimes just ripped off their Facebook profiles. Underneath they wrote these diatribes about how the women were bitches and whores. How they would get what was coming to them. I guess today you'd call it a kind of incel manifesto. I hadn't come across that term back then."

"Mandy and Hannah were featured on this blog?"

"Sure. But so were dozens of other girls. That student journalist wrote a story about it. Twenty or thirty kids pulled out of school thinking they were going to be next. I don't blame them."

"Is this blog still live?" Blake asked.

"No. The author took it down a few weeks after the news article brought attention to it. He probably got worried we'd be able to link it to him. But I'm sure he was the guy responsible."

"Why?"

"He wrote about the two victims after their bodies were found. Knew details only the killer could've known. Every kid on campus was reading it. I always figured he loved the attention. But it was a dead end. And then it was gone. I took screencaps, though. Every page. I'll send them over."

"Thanks. If there's any connection with your case, I'll be in touch," Blake said.

"If there is, I hope you get the bastard who killed those two girls," Sid replied vehemently. "There's two families that never got closure."

Blake killed the call and climbed out of the car. Distant cries carried on the breeze over the sound of passing cars as members of the press desperately tried to get her attention. She wondered whether or not they knew she was running the case.

Some, maybe. Mostly not.

She ignored them as she walked into the station, passing Sandy with a nod in the lobby before joining Melissa in the investigations annex. The call had left her with a few questions and not many answers. If Captain Keaton was right and his killer had attended ECU, then they needed to get hold of a list of names for everyone who'd studied there at the time. Probably faculty as well.

But there was no chance they would get a judge to sign off on a request that broad. And it was even less likely that she would be able to convince ECU to hand it over willingly. The last thing the college's execs would want was to rake up old coals—especially the blow up in their face kind.

"Bad news" was how her partner greeted her.

"Surprise, surprise. What is it?"

"I cross-referenced Austin Crawford's personnel file with the dates of those Greenville killings."

"Don't tell me he went to ECU?"

"Princeton. He was on an ROTC field training exercise at Fort Dix the weekend Mandy Yates went missing."

"Shit," Blake said, sitting down at Melissa's side and reaching for a computer keyboard. "He was definitely there?"

"As far as I can make out. So either the murders in Greenville are completely unconnected to our case or we can rule him out as a suspect."

"Or we're looking for multiple individuals working together," Blake muttered. She quickly filled Melissa in on everything she'd learned on her call with Captain Keaton as she pulled up a web browser. She typed in the search query: *Blonde Butcher Greenville*, then pressed the return key.

The page filled with ten little blue links, most of which were from a news website called the East Carolinian, and were at least six or seven years old. She clicked on the first, her eyes quickly scanning across the now-familiar faces of Hannah Sanders and Mandy Yates, whose likenesses stared out from beneath the headline in separate photographs. Hannah was wearing soccer gear. Mandy was clutching a red plastic cup. Their evident happiness seemed frozen in amber.

"You're shitting me."

"What is it?" Melissa asked, looking away from her own computer, clearly surprised by the shock in Blake's voice.

Blake moved the computer cursor. "Look at the byline."

Melissa's eyes widened. "Aaron Weller wrote this story."

Her head spinning from the discovery, Blake clicked on Aaron's name, just in case it was an improbable coincidence. But that possibility was extinguished the second a younger Aaron's headshot flashed up on his student newspaper's biography page.

"No fucking way," she said. "What are the chances?"

Melissa bit her lip, her eyes flicking up for an instant as she pondered the question. "ECU is the biggest university in North Carolina. I'm pretty sure it is, anyway. Twenty thousand undergrads. Probably even more by now. One in three students in the state study there."

Blake remembered pulling up Aaron's biography on the *Pinecone* website a couple of days earlier.

"He studied communications there," she said slowly as she

clicked back onto the search results page. She narrowed her eyes and clicked through the first half dozen pages. Almost every link was from the East Carolinian. Almost every story was written by Aaron Weller. "Focused on journalism."

"Could just be a coincidence..." Melissa said.

Blake closed her eyes and massaged her temples. A thought occurred to her that she couldn't shake.

"What if he's behind all of this?" she posited. "Eight years ago, he kills Hannah and Mandy while he's at college. Gets some kind of sick kick out of reporting on their murders. And now he's doing the same thing again. Only on a much grander scale. The terrorist angle could be just a way of bringing more eyes to the case. A way of massaging his ego."

She typed a new search query into the engine – *Aaron Weller Nina Crawford* – and set date filters that ended before either Nina or Piper went missing. Only one relevant result populated on the screen.

Community Unites for Heroes

Blake quickly took in the story, written by Aaron and dated fall 2021 and was about a charity event intended to raise money for Afghan refugees after the botched withdrawal from Afghanistan. Several officers from the 82nd Airborne, which had deployed to Kabul, had been in attendance. Initially, she couldn't see the connection with Nina Crawford, until she saw a photo of the woman at the very bottom of the page, captioned with her name.

"So they've at least met before," she said.

"It's not a lot to go on, though," Melissa commented. "Certainly not enough to put in front of a judge."

"No," Blake said as the phone on her partner's desk started to ring. "But it's a start."

"Detective Wilson." Melissa said, holding the handset to her ear for only a couple of seconds before finishing, "Thanks, Sandy. We'll be right down."

"What is it?"

"Austin Crawford just arrived."

22

"No lawyer?" Blake said as Melissa entered the observation room that looked into Interview Room 1. There was no two-way mirror. It was all done by cameras these days. Blake had a flicker of memory of sitting in an identical room just a few months back, being interrogated by none other than her current partner.

Funny how the world works.

Melissa shook her head. "He came with a friend. No one else."

Austin Crawford was sitting inside. His arms were crossed over his chest, and he stared blankly at the opposite wall. He looked exhausted. But was it from worry about his wife or strain from hiding the truth from them?

"No point making him sweat," Blake said. "We know he's a cool customer. He might have an alibi for Mandy Yates' murder, but that doesn't mean he's free and clear. Too much about his story doesn't add up."

She grabbed a notepad and a pen from a stack of stationery and slid it under her arm. The pair of them exited into the hallway, then stepped into the interview room. Austin looked up but said nothing.

"Thank you for coming in on such short notice," Blake said, setting the pad on the table in front of her.

"No problem. If it helps you find my wife, I'll do anything."

"Captain Crawford—can I call you Austin?"

He waved his hand dismissively. "Whatever."

"Austin, let's get right to the point. When we spoke to you last time, you told us you weren't aware of the specifics of Private Hicks' personal life."

He didn't react. "That's correct. I'm her commanding officer. Like I told you before, I don't have time to keep tabs on every one of my soldiers. They are entitled to their personal lives."

Blake scribbled a note on the pad in front of her and underlined it before looking back up. "Austin, are you aware that providing a false report to a North Carolina law enforcement officer investigating a Class C felony is itself a felony crime?"

His eyes sharpened. "What the hell are you talking about?"

"Austin, you lied to us when we last spoke. You told us you didn't know who was dating Piper Hicks."

"I don't."

"You're still lying. Do you want to know the maximum penalty for lying to a detective investigating a murder?"

Austin said nothing. He moved his hands underneath the table, and from the way his shoulder muscles went taut, Blake guessed he was clenching his fists.

"Thirty-nine months, Austin," Melissa said softly. "That's a long time to be away from your kids. Not to mention you'd lose your commission. No way the Army allows you to return after that long behind bars. Work with us. It'll be a lot easier."

"You should be investigating my wife's kidnapping," Austin snapped. "Not wasting time with this."

Blake's lips tightened. "We are."

She let him sit there for a moment, steam practically pouring out of his ears as he chewed over his predicament. She watched as he bit his lower lip. He wasn't so calm anymore.

"I'm guessing you lied to the FBI as well," she finally said in a conversational tone. "That's definitely not a good move. Say goodbye to your security clearance."

"What do you want?" he hissed. He looked up and matched Blake's cool stare. His eyes were blazing. She was almost rocked back by the force of his gaze. There was so much anger there.

Enough to kill?

"I want you to start talking, Austin. Quickly. Or I will place a call to CID. See how long it takes before you're suspended."

"Okay!" Austin snapped. "I was sleeping with her, all right? I told you already, my wife and I have an open relationship. Nina is okay with this kind of thing."

"So why didn't you tell us about your relationship?" Melissa asked.

"Why the hell do you think?" he said. His face was puce red. "Piper was under my command. She was an enlisted soldier. I'd lose my job if anybody found out."

Blake made a noncommittal sound. "How did it start?"

"I was out drinking one night. First date gone wrong. Piper happened to be in the same bar. She was drunk. So was I. One thing led to another, and..." He ran his fingers through his hair. "I know I shouldn't have done it, but I did. I didn't tell you because of the consequences for my career."

"But you kept on sleeping with her," Melissa said.

He grimaced, as if wondering how they knew this stuff. "She was hot. And I was weak."

"You're talking about a dead woman," Blake snapped.

Austin shrugged. "She can't hear me."

Under her breath, Blake muttered, "Asshole."

Melissa stepped in. "How long were you seeing her?"

"I don't know. A couple of months? Three? I was going to end things."

"When?"

"Soon. It couldn't go on. I'm up for promotion soon. She was too into it. I had to finish things for the sake of my career. Both our careers."

"So you killed her," Blake suggested flatly.

"What? Of course not."

"You must see how this looks to us," she said.

"I don't care how it looks. You're incompetent. You should be focused on looking for Nina, not raking up this mess."

Insult the detectives, Blake thought. *Bold move.*

"Austin, we know about the hotel room in Carthage," she said. "You booked a room under your name for three nights. You were going to spend the weekend with Piper. Maybe something happened. Did you get angry?"

"Carthage?" Austin said in disbelief. "What the hell are you talking about?"

"Don't lie to us," Melissa said. "We checked with the manager. The booking's real."

"This is bullshit!" he shouted. "Okay, I was screwing her. I shouldn't have lied about it. I got spooked. But I was looking after my kids Saturday night so Nina could go out and do her, you know, her thing. I didn't have plans with Piper. And I sure as shit didn't book a hotel."

Blake couldn't hide the flicker of surprise that crossed her face in response. He had a fair point. She kept pushing anyway, hoping he would crack. "We know everything, Austin. You may as well come clean. We have a witness who will attest that you were planning to go away with each other. What went wrong?"

Austin slid back his chair. "We're done. Get back to me when you have some proof."

Blake reached into her pocket and pulled out her cell phone. The screen powered up, and she opened the gallery.

"You should see this," she said, sliding the phone across the table.

He picked it up and stared angrily at it. "Where the hell did you get this?"

"You know we can't tell you that."

He slammed the device back on the table so hard Blake feared that the screen might crack. She studiously avoided looking down at it, instead matching his gaze.

"It doesn't change anything. I already told you we were sleeping together."

"Were you angry that Piper was telling people about your relationship, Austin?" Blake asked, making her eyes wide and innocent. "After she disappeared, you were so afraid of the Army finding out that you lied to us and the FBI to cover it up. You risked years of jail time."

He crossed his arms but said nothing.

"Here's what I think. You wanted to end things for the sake of your career, right? And then you found out that Piper was going around telling everybody who would listen your secret. Did you snap? Decide to teach her a lesson?"

"You're trying to set me up," Austin said.

"We are following the evidence," she retorted. "If you're guilty of murdering Piper Hicks, then we won't stop until we prove it."

"Then you'll be looking a long time," he said, kicking the chair aside and walking to the door. "Next time you want to speak to me, call my lawyer."

"One last thing, Austin," Blake called out.

"What?"

"How well do you know Aaron Weller?"

Austin's face screwed up with what looked like genuine confusion. "I have no idea who you're talking about," he snapped before pulling the door open and slamming it shut behind him.

Blake sat for a second, then quickly stood up and followed him. Melissa shot her a curious look, then slipped in behind.

Austin was already twenty feet down the corridor by the time Blake emerged into it. She hurried after him but didn't reach him until he was already in the small waiting lobby. A man stood up as Austin entered. He was tall and wore a blue denim jacket and black jeans. She didn't recognize him. He had dirty blond hair and a few days of stubble. He was attractive, though not exactly Blake's type.

"Let's go," Austin said loudly.

Blake realized that this must be the friend who had brought Austin Crawford to the station for his interview.

"Austin?" she said. "I just have one last question."

He swore at her without turning around. "You said that already. Fuck off."

Blake addressed his broad, muscular black instead, lowering her voice so that only he could hear. "Did your wife find out what you did to Piper? Is that why you had to get her out of the picture, too?"

"You're fucking insane," he said, spinning on his heel and twisting toward her with his fist clenched. "Get the fuck away from me. I told you, if you have something to say, tell it to my lawyer."

"Austin!" his friend said sharply, quickly maneuvering his powerful frame in between the pair of them.

Blake saw Melissa place her hand on her service weapon, though the detective didn't yet draw it. Behind his friend, the Army captain was volcanic with rage. His face was drawn back into a snarl, and his upper body was trembling. It was slightly scary, given the size differential between her and him, though Blake made sure not to display any hint that she was intimidated on her face. It was like staring down a bear.

"Go get some air," the friend said, turning and pushing Austin toward the exit. "I'll be right out."

After a long, lingering second, Austin followed his friend's advice.

"Josh," he said, stretching out his hand to introduce himself. Blake shook it. His palm was rough and callused, and he had the grip of a man who worked in construction or agriculture. She guessed he might once have been attractive but carried himself like a man who spent too much time in the gym layering muscle onto a frame that didn't really suit it.

"Lieutenant Larsen," Blake said formally. The title still felt a little strange in her mouth. It was like she'd gotten married and was getting accustomed to a different last name. Except she'd earned this one overnight, instead of having a couple of years to get used to the prospect.

"What the hell was that about?" Josh said evenly. His tone, however, was icy, and his eyes bulged in the fashion of a habitual user of anabolic steroids. "Terrorists kidnap his wife, and this is how you treat him?"

"Sir, go be with your friend. I have an investigation to get on with."

"That man's a war hero, dammit," Josh said, jerking his thumb toward the parking lot. "He's owed a little bit of respect."

Blake looked the man up and down. He was about the same age as Austin. Probably high school friends or something like that.

"I'll take that under advisement," she said.

"You should stay the fuck away from him," he said chillingly. "If you know what's good for you."

Josh muttered something that sounded a whole lot like *bitch* as he turned and stormed out of the door. She kept watching through the glass as both men climbed into a black SUV, with Josh behind the wheel. She half-expected him to peel away at high speed with his middle finger stuck out of the window, but the powerful engine gurgled slowly, almost giving off a pang of disappointment as he guided it carefully out of the parking lot.

Blake felt Sandy's gaze on her as she turned back around. The office manager said nothing but ever so slightly raised an eyebrow in question. Feeling her cheeks flush, Blake ignored the woman.

She glanced at her watch. It was 5 p.m. Nina Crawford had nineteen hours left. The pressure was building.

And they were no closer to finding her.

The worst of her anger faded after her phone vibrated to inform her of an incoming email. It was from Sid Keaton in the Pitt County sheriff's office and contained dozens of attachments, along with an apologetic cover note. *"Took me longer to dig out than I thought. Hope you make more heads or tails from it than I ever did. Sid."*

The attachments were all labeled with a woman's name and the letters SL. Blake felt a chill run down her spine as she realized what she was looking at. She scrolled down until she found the name *Mandy* and opened it.

The screenshot was of a blogging platform that had been ten years out of date a decade ago. It reminded Blake of the early days of the web. The web address was something like: SheLies.lotsanumbers.xyz.

Underneath the blog's title—*She Lies*—was a grainy photograph of a college-age blond girl sitting inside a coffee shop, reading a book. The creepy, or perhaps creepiest, part was that the photo was taken through the shop's windowfront, its subject caught completely unaware. Blake brought her phone closer to her eyes and read intently.

Mandy Yates. Number 2. This bitch won't be the last. She dresses up like the girl next door, but everybody knows it's just a front. She says she has a boyfriend, but that doesn't stop her when the whole football team comes knocking. Not even her parents will miss her when she's gone. Not now they know her true colors. The best of her could have gone away to college. But instead she sent the worst.

There was another photo underneath the paragraph of text. Blake recognized the location from the crime scene photographs she'd pulled off the FBI's database. But these were taken with a much lower quality camera. The season was different, too.

Now she lies here.

Blake shivered. She wondered whether the photo had been taken before or after Mandy was murdered.

"What are you looking at?" Melissa asked.

Blake handed her the phone silently. She watched as her partner's expressions cycled through interest, then intrigue, then plain horror.

"Damn," she muttered. "Whoever wrote that is deeply unwell."

"You can say that again."

"Come on, we need to get suited up," Melissa said, tossing the phone back. "There's spare riot gear in the back. We'll find something that fits you."

Blake tipped her head back for a moment. She'd almost forgotten about Dwaine Hilton's hate rally. After the day she'd had, part of her almost hoped that he and his buddies would cause trouble tonight. She needed to burn off some stress.

And a racist thug's face would make a perfect punching bag.

23

Blake felt ungainly and overbalanced in a set of riot gear that was very obviously designed for a man's frame. Her knees and shoulders were protected by plastic guards, and her upper body was encased in a suit of thick, padded black armor. A heavy metal helmet and face shield hung from her belt by its chin strap. The gear all still bore the markings of the now-defunct Northern Pines Police Department.

Another reminder of the decimation the department's ranks had suffered following the corruption scandal was that assistance had been called in from a variety of neighboring towns and counties. Blake saw deputies from Richmond and Montgomery counties mingling with newly sworn Monroe County deputies, as well as officers from a number of neighboring towns.

More than two hundred local residents and out-of-towners had gathered on the corner of Hardin and Pennsylvania Avenue, waving a variety of posters, banners, and flags, mostly homemade.

GET OUT N' DON'T COME BACK was her favorite so far. It was succinct and to the point. More Northern Pines residents were arriving every second to join the counterprotest. It was a noisy, happy atmosphere, despite an undercurrent of tension at what was to come.

"We don't want you," rang out a singsong chant over and over again. It was led by a woman with white hair and a bullhorn. She looked like anybody's grandmother, but she was whipping up the crowd like a seasoned pro.

Blake turned and glanced at the community center the counter-protesters were ringed around. It was the same building she'd attended for the town council meeting just a couple of nights earlier. The thought almost made her dizzy. Things were moving too fast.

The Douglass Community Center was one of two buildings that the online event invite had referenced—the other being the charity office that stood in the lot next door. The charity had taken the lead in town in helping clothe, feed, and house the Afghan refugees that had arrived a couple of summers earlier. Ergo it was a target.

Assholes, Blake grumbled. She wondered how many of the protesters on the anti-refugee march that day had actually served in uniform. Most every soldier she'd ever served with had lived by the motto *Never leave a man behind*. That went double for the Afghans who had saved their lives over and over again in the field for far lesser reward.

Captain Rogers placed her fingers between her lips and let out a powerful whistle. She caught Blake's eyes as the other officers and deputies gathered around her.

She shot her a quick wink and muttered, "Hell of a first week, huh, Larsen?"

"No kidding," she said in reply.

Rogers clapped her hands together. "Okay. We don't have long. The protest march from the Downtown Park has just begun. It's a twenty-minute walk, but early reports from the scene indicate that some of our brave, manly protesters aren't exactly in fighting shape…"

A series of low chuckles rang out around the circle. Blake counted almost thirty personnel around her, all dressed in riot gear. Another forty or so cops were accompanying the march along Pennsylvania Avenue. It should be more than enough to keep the protesters in check.

But she still had a nervous feeling in the pit of her stomach. The kind of guys who turned up to a march like this on a weekday evening were often looking for any excuse for a fight.

"... so it could take a bit longer," Roger said, quickly wiping the smile off her face. "That's the good news. The bad news is that we're looking at almost 90 protesters. FBI and SBI have both assisted with intel packets, and we've got about twenty troublemakers in the pack known to be associated with white nationalist and prison gangs. The rest are a rabble of disaffected local residents and bottom-of-the-barrel types from neighboring towns.

"The even worse news," she continued, "is that a dozen of them are armed. Long guns as well as pistols."

This time, a low groan echoed around Blake. She felt the anxiety in her stomach ratchet up a gear.

"This could get very messy, very quick," Rogers said, raising her voice over the hubbub. "Our job is to make sure that doesn't happen. Snatch teams, raise your hands."

About a dozen men raised their arms into the air. Blake knew that their job was to rush into the crowd and pull out troublemakers who were whipping the mob into a frenzy. Herd mentality could be a scary thing once it got going. But riot policing was increasingly becoming a science, not just an art.

"Good. You know what to do. We've got spotters on the buildings and dotted around the march. The second you're passed a target, don't hesitate. Get in and out fast. If the target's too deep into the crowd, you knock it off. Capiche?"

Affirmative grunts echoed all around Blake.

"Good," Rogers said. "Anyone who's come in from out of town to help us today, you have my thanks. We'll buy you a beer when this is all said and done. Now let's get to our positions."

Blake slapped her baton against her thigh pad. All around her, law enforcement personnel were doing the same. It created an eerie, almost tribal sound that momentarily drowned out the chants from the counterprotesters around the community center.

"Done this before?" Rogers murmured to Blake as the majority of the officers filed away.

She shook her head. "Not too many riots in the Army, Captain," she said. "Besides, that would have been the MPs' job. I did a few days training at the FBI Academy, but that's all."

"Well, that makes two of us," her superior admitted. "So let's hope nothing goes wrong..."

Blake took a deep inhale as the captain walked away. She let it out slowly. Her breath clouded around her mouth from the cold. It was now fully dark, and the streetlights were doing their best to battle the midwinter gloom.

But something about the dark all around her sent a shiver running down Blake's neck. People lost their inhibitions after night fell and did things they would never contemplate doing in the light. That was especially true when people had been drinking—and reports from the park indicated that many of the protesters were more than a little worse for wear.

She walked to her own position, behind the street-facing side of a metal barrier that separated the counterprotesters from the route of the march. Her job was to keep the two groups away from one another. Her secondary task was to act as a spotter and to indicate to the snatch teams who needed to be hustled away fast.

"Radio check," her headset crackled.

Blake checked in. One by one, all the officers and deputies onscene confirmed that they were all on the same channel.

And then all there was to do was wait.

Periodically, reports came from the officers guarding the march. The news wasn't good. The crowd was already unruly and getting more violent by the minute. The core group of known troublemakers was holding flaming oil torches, which reportedly made it difficult to keep track of all the weapons.

"We've got incoming," a voice announced on the radio. "Everybody look sharp."

Blake squinted down the street. She thought she could see a faint glow about a hundred yards back, but it was difficult to separate from the streetlights. A couple of minutes later, she could definitely see them.

And more to the point, hear them.

A loud, booming voice echoed down the street. "Af-ghans, go home!"

It was greeted by a chorus of ninety voices all hurling the same line back. She shivered. There was so much hate embodied in their tone. Blake couldn't remember feeling that much rage for anyone her entire life. Not even the monsters who killed her brother. She'd long ago decided that you couldn't keep holding on to anger. It was like poison that dripped from generation to generation, killing everything it touched.

"Okay," she called out, projecting her voice as she turned to the deputies to her left and right. They were spaced every few feet. "Stay nice and calm. They want you to get mad. Don't give them what they're looking for."

"Yes, ma'am," a voice she didn't recognize replied. "And what if they step over the line?"

She shrugged. "Give 'em hell."

An appreciative rumble rang out. Blake tightened her jaw, swallowing the flicker of apprehension in her gut. She turned back to study the approaching mob. The twenty armed men in the center moved with a semblance of order. Their backs straight, they marched instead of walked, holding their flaming torches high. The flickering flames cast unsettling shadows on the all-white faces below.

"Hilton is the one with the bullhorn," her radio crackled. It was Melissa. "He's right in the center."

"Copy that," another deputy replied.

Blake knew that the heads-up wasn't just for her, but also the many law enforcement personnel from out of town, but she appreciated it nevertheless. She narrowed her gaze and focused it on Dwaine Hilton. He stood a few inches taller than most of the men marching in the center around him. He wore all black. As far as she could see, he didn't have a long rifle but did have a pistol holstered on his hip. Every few paces, he raised the bullhorn up to his lips and shouted out a hate-filled epithet.

Were the torches your idea? Blake wondered as a twinge of pain from the burn she'd suffered earlier almost brought a tear to her eye.

On the edges around the main troublemakers were a much larger number of protesters. Instead of wearing all black, they were dressed in a wide variety of clothing. They came in all shapes and sizes: short, tall, fat, thin, even one guy on crutches. Down each side of the marching protest was a line of riot police geared up just like Blake herself, about fifteen or twenty on either side.

As they approached, the chorus of counter-chants from the locals defending the community center and charity building redoubled in strength. The counterprotest had drawn at least twice the strength of the mob rolling up in front of them. But as far as Blake knew, only the guys with torches were armed.

"Here we go, ladies and gentlemen," Captain Rogers announced over the radio. "Stay sharp."

Almost as though he could hear her, Dwaine Hilton once again raised the bullhorn to his lips. He called out, "Company, halt!"

Blake actually rolled her eyes. She'd scanned Hilton's police file. He had a rap sheet as long as the flaming torch he was carrying in his left hand, but the only thing he'd ever served was a prison sentence. Why did these losers always try and cosplay soldiers?

"What a douche," someone grunted over the radio.

She hid her smile as she pushed the transmit button on her radio. "Keep your personal opinions off the channel," she said. "Even if we all agree with them."

The protesters brought their right thighs up parallel with the ground, then thrust their feet toward the ground. If they had executed it in time, it would have produced a nice, crisp smacking sound.

They didn't.

Instead, their march stumbled to a halt one by one about twenty yards away from where Blake was standing, and they did it in an uneven gaggle. It sounded like a short hailstorm beating against the road.

"Look at them!" Dwaine yelled, his face contorted into a rictus of hate. "Pick a face and just look at them. Do you know what I see?"

He was greeted by an uneven return chorus of barely audible yells.

He ignored them. "I see cockroaches!"

The hair on the back of Blake's forearms stood on end. Rational people could and mostly did disagree with each other. She had no problem with that. Where her patience ran out was when men like Dwaine reduced their opponents to caricatures. Treated them as something other than human. Mankind had traveled down that road many times before.

It never ended well.

Someone screamed, "Burn them!"

That, Blake thought, was exactly the thing she was worried about.

"I ain't got no problem with Afghans," Dwaine yelled out. "Long as they stay in their own country. They have no right to come to ours."

"You think they want to be here?" she said under her breath, accompanied by a tight shake of her head.

"Company!" Dwaine shouted. "Advance ten paces. Look these cockroaches in the eye. Show them you aren't afraid. There are more of them. But we have right on our side."

More yells. Someone threw a half-full soda bottle through the air. It cartwheeled, spewing out foam as it impacted somewhere in the throng of counter-protestors.

"Mobile units, keep nice and tight," Rogers instructed over the radio. "Face front. I want whoever threw that bottle out of there now."

"I see him," one of the spotters reported. "Red ski jacket, north side. He's making his way into the mob now."

"Bravo copies," one of the snatch teams radioed. "We have eyes on. Moving in now."

Blake raised herself onto her tiptoes in an attempt to make out the activity on the opposite side of the crowd. She watched as a group of three riot cops closed their plastic shields around each other and surged toward the mob. Their task was made easier for them by the fact that the protesters had neither tightened up nor stood shoulder to shoulder. They were arrayed like a cheap Swiss cheese.

The protesters reacted quickly as the snatch squad entered, barging men aside. She couldn't see their target, but she could hear the abuse that was being hurled at them.

"Got him," a pained voice radioed, accompanied by shouts and curse words. "Extracting."

On the far side of the crowd, half a dozen riot cops from the mobile team that had accompanied the protest from the Downtown Park jogged up to the protest. Blake finally made out the guy in the red jacket. He was squashed right in the center of a triangle composed of the three members of the snatch squad. Two of them faced into the crowd, and the peak of the triangle forced his way out.

The mobile team pushed protesters on the edge of the crowd roughly aside, then formed ranks around the snatch squad, who were finally free and clear.

"Good job," Rogers radioed. "Get him out of here."

Blake let out a deep breath she hadn't realized she was holding. Every moment like that was a dangerous one. Mob mentality could turn on a dime. It was especially dangerous with so many guns on the scene.

"They should be defending *us*, not them," Dwaine yelled through the bullhorn. "Look at them. The police aren't your friends. They're *traitors*."

Gee, thanks, Blake thought dryly.

"Got another thrower," a spotter radioed urgently. "Center of the crowd."

Blake swiveled her gaze and quickly searched the center of the throng. It was much more difficult from ground level. Her view was blocked by way too many bodies.

"Shit, it's a Molotov cocktail!" the same spotter yelled, a note of tension in his voice.

Blake swiftly squatted down and grabbed one of the spare plastic shields that was lying on the ground around her. She hefted it with her left hand and brought it across her body. She blinked and let out a shaky breath as flashes of her near-escape from the burning building earlier that same day sped across her mind.

"Stay calm," she muttered.

"He's throwing!"

Blake's chin came up, and she watched a candle of flame soar through the night sky. It looked so pretty it was hard to believe that it could cause so much damage. She followed its path through the sky, gritting her teeth with horror as she realized the intended target.

The counter-protesters.

She spun and yelled, "Look out!" knowing even as she did so it was almost certainly already too late. Yells of dismay and fear rang out around her, then the bottle smashed against the ground somewhere in the center of the crowd of locals. It exploded into flame, and suddenly people were running in every direction to escape it.

She held her gaze, searching to see if anyone was injured. A woman ran with flames licking at her back before another protester pushed her to the ground and forced her to roll over. Thankfully, the fire was doused in seconds. No one else appeared hurt. But that couldn't last.

"Push them back!" Rogers ordered. "Twenty yards. Let's go!"

Blake tested her grip on her baton. Her palm was slick with sweat, but she felt no fear at what was to come. For some reason, her gaze automatically searched for Dwaine Hilton. His face was even more contorted with anger than before, and she watched as he drew his arm back and threw his flaming torch through the air. For a second, she thought it was another Molotov cocktail.

She stepped forward, forming a line with the deputies on either side of her. It took all her self-control not to turn to the chaos behind her. Her only job was to look out for the cop to her left and the cop to her right. You couldn't afford weak links. Not on a scene like this.

"Let's move," she called out, surprised by the strength in her voice.

As one, the line of cops she was in stepped forward toward the protest mob. Another Molotov cocktail came spinning through the air. On either side of the crowd, the mobile teams were moving forward, squeezing the mass of people into a thin line, where their weight of numbers was negated.

One of the deputies to her left rattled his baton against his shield. She copied the action, repeating it over and over, surprised by how much the drumbeat steadied her nerves and breathing. It was like the boom of some kind of ancient war drum.

"Push!" she yelled as her line came into contact with the scattered forward elements of the protest mob.

Blake tried to pick Dwaine Hilton out of the crowd, but it was impossible now. She reached out with her baton and dealt a nearby protester a hard but restrained jab in the stomach just as he was bringing back his fist to strike. He fell away, stunned. As she stepped over him, she saw him being dragged through her own legs by a second line of cops behind. She heard him yell out in anger as he was cuffed and then marched into a nearby holding area.

Her heart raced from the adrenaline. Her chest heaved, still suffering the after-effects of her earlier smoke inhalation. But she barely felt it. It was almost impossible to resist the urge to give in to her animal instincts and rain powerful blows down into the crowd. But she knew they couldn't beat the mob by becoming one of their own.

Another jab. This time, the protester staggered back. He picked up a flaming torch from the ground and wielded it at her. Sparks flew through the air. Blake resisted the urge to step back.

Keep your shield locked, she growled at herself.

She drew back her right arm and jabbed her baton forward with all her strength. It bounced off his midriff and caused him to bellow with pain. He fell back as the line of cops continued grinding forward.

"Keep going," Rogers radioed, her voice unfailingly calm amid the chaos. "They're breaking."

Blake's left arm was exhausted. Her right forearm felt like it was on fire as the act of jabbing with her baton dislodged the dressings around her burns. A protester fell to the ground in front of her.

"Push!" a deputy to her right yelled out, his voice strangled from exertion. "Come on. Push!"

She did, though her legs and arms and feet were exhausted. Every couple of moments, a different protester stopped falling back, yelled something unrepeatable, then charged at the line of shields. This time a short but stocky man chose Blake's.

Just before impact, she dipped her left shoulder and forced her lower body into a squat. He slammed into her, the force of the impact rocking her half a foot back. But she kept her shoulder forward, and as he bounced off her shield, the deputies on either dragged him back and got him into cuffs.

It was the last desperate act of the mob. As Blake stopped to recover her breath, they broke ahead of her. The protesters turned tail and ran as one, sprinting away from the line of cops behind them.

Behind them, they left almost a dozen fallen, groaning protesters who were either suffering from injuries suffered at the hands of the cops or had been trampled in the crush of their fellow marchers.

"Hold!" Rogers's voice echoed over the radio. "Let them run."

Blake ground her molars together. Anger burned inside her. She swept her head left and right in search of Dwaine Hilton. He wasn't the cause of all this anger and hate. But he had brought it here, to the center of Northern Pines.

To my home.

Her eyes widened as she realized that Dwaine had fallen. He was dragging himself to his feet, favoring his left leg. She called two deputies over to her and pointed at the ringleader of the day's chaos.

She spoke with unbridled venom in her voice. "I want him in custody. *Now.*"

24

"My name is Detective Lieutenant Blake Larsen, Monroe County Sheriff's Department. I'm accompanied by Detective Melissa Wilson for the interview of suspect Dwaine Hilton. 8:21 p.m. Monday 17 April. For the record, the suspect has signed a document attesting that he understands his Miranda rights."

Blake finished speaking and fell silent. She steepled her fingers on top of a manila folder on the tabletop and didn't say anything for a full minute, instead letting her suspect sweat. He was clearly off balance: perspiring slightly at his temples, shifting position every few seconds, his right hand formed into a tense fist.

"Get going already," Dwaine finally snarled. "Ask what you want to ask."

"Why do you think you're here, Dwaine?" Blake said.

"Because you're corrupt. All cops are."

"Did your mom drop you on your head as a kid, Dwaine?"

"Huh?"

"Just wondering how someone forgets they were arrested for participating in a riot."

"It was a protest."

"No doubt that'll be your defense." Blake nodded earnestly. "The thing is, Dwaine, we have you on film throwing rocks at law officers. And some of your buddies fired fireworks at us. We're working up a charging packet right now. So if there's anything you want to tell us..."

"Spit it out," he grumbled. "I know you're itching to say your piece."

"Thought you'd never ask," Blake said, flipping the folder open and spinning it around. A glossy, printed mug shot peered out at him.

"You recognize Ralph, right? Good friend of yours. He was at tonight's protest, I think."

"I know him," Dwaine replied noncommittally. He returned to staring at the wall.

"Not the sharpest knife in the drawer, is he?" Blake said, directing the comment at Melissa.

Another anxious flicker of attention.

"That he is not," Melissa remarked dryly.

Blake turned her attention back to Dwaine. "Just so we're all on the same page, you should know that Ralph has a warrant outstanding for his arrest. He hits his wife, did you know that?"

"I ain't his keeper," he fired back defensively. "What goes on between a man and a woman behind closed doors ain't none of my business."

"That's part of the problem," Blake said. "But that's a whole different kettle of fish. We don't have time to get into it now. The thing is, Ralph's real anxious to talk. He's looking at a couple years behind bars. Wants to cut a deal."

This caught Dwaine's attention. He narrowed his eyes and took a few seconds to frame his response. "Let him. Like I told you, I'm innocent. I got the right to, you know, freedom of assembly. Nothing wrong with political protest. It's in the Constitution. You should read it. Anyway, what's Ralph gonna say: that I organized today's march? I admit it: I did. And I'm not ashamed of it."

"See, that's the thing," Blake replied, reaching forward to drag the folder back across the table. "Ralph told us you arranged the protest several days ago."

Dwaine frowned, then shook his head. "I only put the event up on Facebook yesterday."

Blake flipped to the second page in her folder. It was a printout of the text messages from Ralph's phone. She read the first out loud: "Make sure you're free Monday night. It's important."

She looked up at her suspect to gauge his response. His poker face needed work. His eyes darted between Blake and Melissa like a trapped animal searching for escape. She let the silence drag out, hoping that he would take the bait and say something incriminating, but he stayed silent.

After about thirty seconds, she continued, invisibly pinching her thigh underneath the table to manage her mounting frustration. Her face remained implacable.

"*It's important*," she repeated. "Why did you say that?"

Dwaine licked his lips. "I don't remember."

Blake hiked an eyebrow. "You don't remember? You sent that message four days ago. That's not a long time."

"My memory gets hazy. I probably wanted to go out for a beer."

"So why not say that?" Melissa asked, her tone soft and reasonable. "You see how it looks from our perspective, right? Like you organized this protest before you had a reason to. Which makes us think maybe you knew something big was coming. Something like the video that went viral yesterday."

"That's right." Dwaine nodded, the cogs visibly turning in his mind. He nodded to himself, the movement so slight it was almost invisible. "I remember now. I didn't know it was coming."

Blake leaned forward. "What?"

Dwaine's handcuffs rattled against the steel table as he adjusted his position on the intentionally uncomfortable chair. He nodded a second time, as if convincing himself that he'd chosen the correct strategy.

"I didn't have to. Something like this was bound to happen," he said. "You let a bunch of Arab terrorists into your town, what do you expect? Rats are rats. You invite them into your home, don't be surprised if they chew through the wires. Ain't no different with Arabs. These kidnappings, it's in their DNA."

Blake gritted her teeth. "They're not Arabs."

"Huh?"

"You know how to read a map, Dwaine?" she said acidly.

He tried crossing his arms belligerently, but the handcuffs stopped him short. "Course."

"Apparently not. Afghanistan is in central Asia. The people who live there are Pashtun and Persian, not Arabs. They don't even speak Arabic."

"Whatever," he said dismissively. "They're still terrorists. They don't have education there. They are just taught to hate America. You think it's a coincidence a couple white women get taken hostage just after they arrived?"

Blake felt a spout of anger building inside her. She consciously wrestled it back.

"I'm not sure they are the ones who need education," she said. "You see, Dwaine, you just contradicted yourself."

"What?"

"Did you organize the protest yesterday, or did you organize it four days ago?"

He grimaced, then stared back at the wall. "Both."

"Dwaine, where were you on Friday night?" Blake asked, drilling her gaze at him. That was when Piper had last been seen.

He looked up sharply. "Why you asking?"

"Answer the question."

"Working. Then I headed home."

"You have an old lady, Dwaine? Someone who can attest to your movements?"

"I live alone."

Remembering the vitriol of the *She Lies* blog posts, Blake bounced off his previous reply. "You have a problem with women, Dwaine? Besides your ex-wife, I mean. We both know you have a problem with her."

He looked confused. "What? No. Linda hit me first! I was just defending myself. I guess I just ain't exactly a catch right now."

That was the first accurate statement he'd made all night. "Ever been to Greenville?"

"Huh?"

"It's a town, Dwaine."

"No, I ain't never been."

"Did you go to college?"

He snorted. "Fuck no. I don't like books."

Blake eyed him, wondering if he was playing her. But she didn't think so. She got no sense that Dwaine was covering. And she didn't buy that he was intelligent enough to write those blog posts. The Ponzi scheme he'd attempted had been half-assed. And that was being polite.

She changed tack. This line of questioning wasn't getting her anywhere. "What did you do when you got home? Did you cook dinner? *Read a book?*"

He fired her a sardonic look. "I watched TV."

"What show?"

"I don't remember."

"You don't remember a lot, do you?"

"I had a few beers to unwind," he protested. "I told you already, my memory gets hazy when I drink."

Blake looked him up and down. In the right light, he could be the mystery guy she'd seen in the footage from the bar the night Nina went missing. "What about Saturday night? Ever been to The Coal Yard bar in Pinehurst?"

"This is bullshit!" he exploded. "I didn't take neither of those women. I told you, it was the Arabs. The Afghans," he corrected quickly, perhaps seeing the sharp look on Blake's face. "Stop wasting time with me and go arrest them."

He stopped, panting heavily from the exertion of defending himself.

"Just answer the question, Dwaine. Where were you?"

"Asleep, probably. Shit, I don't know. I usually get home, crack a beer, pass out in front of the TV. I work retail, last thing I want to do is see people when I'm done. I don't go out at night. Least, not in the week. Don't stay up and do the crossword puzzle, either."

"If we get a warrant to search your house, what are we going to find?" Blake asked.

"Nothing. I didn't do it. You ain't pinning this crap on me. I want a—"

Sensing what he was about to say, Blake fired out a Hail Mary. "Dwaine, have you ever met a man named Aaron Weller?"

Once again, Dwaine attempted to cross his arms. And once again, the handcuffs stopped him. "Who the hell you talking about?"

"Let me tell you what I think," Blake said, staring directly at him, her expression hard and confrontational.

"I think you knew Piper Hicks was going to go missing. Nina Crawford, too. Their disappearance was the spark you needed for your brushfire to catch light. So either you're the one who took them, or you're working with the person who did."

Blake paused and ostentatiously glanced in Melissa's direction before returning her gaze to Dwaine.

"No, not with. *For.* I don't think you're bright enough to come up with all this on your own. Did you know the person you're working with planned to kill Piper, Dwaine? In fact, don't answer that. The only question that matters is this: Are you going to turn on him before he lets you take the fall?"

A strange light flashed in Dwaine's eyes. His posture tensed, and he thumped both fists against the steel table, his handcuffs chains rattling. "Lawyer. Get me a lawyer."

Flecks of spittle flew through the air and pockmarked the steel in front of Dwaine as he finished. His hands had formed fists, and his chest was heaving with anger, his lips drawn back to expose his teeth.

The two detectives exchanged frustrated glances. Blake felt as though she'd been on the verge of discovering the truth before Dwaine shut down. She cursed herself for pushing too far, too fast. It would be nearly impossible to get anything out of him now.

Blake stayed quiet. She just observed him quietly for a few

seconds. His demeanor was tense and borderline aggressive. He looked genuinely angry at the accusation that he had something to do with either woman's disappearance. And yet there was no escaping the fact that he seemed to have known that something was coming.

Dwaine leaned forward. His voice grew course and gravelly. "I said I want a lawyer. Now fuck off."

Blake rose to her feet, her jaw set. "Okay. You'll get your lawyer. But if I learn that you had something to do with Piper Hicks' murder, then I'm going to make it my mission to put you behind bars again. And this time, you won't get out. You understand that?"

Blake and Melissa rose and walked out of the interview room. They stayed silent until the door closed behind them and they'd put a few feet of distance between them and it so they couldn't be overheard.

"He's hiding something," Melissa said.

"No kidding," Blake replied. "You think he has something to do with our case?"

She scratched her chin. "I'm not sure. Maybe. He didn't react to your question about Aaron Weller, but maybe it was an act. When his lawyer arrives, we can ask him about Austin Crawford."

Grimacing, Blake said, "I went too fast."

A shout echoed down the hallway. "Lieutenant?"

Blake turned to see Captain Rogers striding toward them. She had an intense look on her face. "Captain?"

Rogers stopped in front of them. "Do you want the good news first, or the bad?"

"Just get it out of the way," Blake replied.

Almost apologetically, Rogers said, "You're going to have to cut your suspect loose."

"What?"

"Digital forensics just finished searching the riot footage. Hilton was smart. He didn't personally break the law."

"He directed the whole thing!" Blake protested, her blood pressure rising.

"Maybe. But we can't charge him for that. And I just got a call from some hotshot lawyer in Charlotte. She says Hilton's her client, and we're not to interview him without her present. Since we have nothing on him, we're going to have to let him go."

"Captain, he knows more than he's letting on," Blake pleaded.

"Maybe." Rogers shrugged. "But you have no proof. That makes anything he just said inadmissible. Besides, if there's one thing this department can't stomach right now, it's a civil rights lawsuit. If you think he's your guy, find a way of making the charges stick."

"What about the good news, Captain?" Melissa asked, perhaps sensing that Blake was spoiling for a fight.

"Austin Crawford's phone company just supplied the location data for his missing cell phone. It cuts out late Friday, but digital forensics found something interesting."

Blake frowned. Friday was the night Piper was last seen. It was two days before her body was discovered. "What?"

"Forensics cross-referenced Piper Hicks' location data with Crawford's. Both phones pinged the tower from within a two square mile grid square the east of the Pinehurst Plaza shopping mall within twenty minutes of each other, just after 7 p.m. The search area was too large before we got a second data point. Then each phone goes dead within an hour. They haven't connected to the cell network since."

25

Within seconds of Blake screeching to a halt outside the shopping mall on the edge of town, another two patrol cars pulled up, lights flashing against the late-night gloom. Motorists visibly slowed on the road to catch a glimpse of what was happening.

She ignored them and studied the landscape around them. It was wooded and covered in thick foliage and was intersected only by a few walking paths and dirt tracks for vehicles.

A number of officers were already milling around in the head-lights of one of the cruisers, apparently unsure what to do. Blake made a beeline for a man who appeared to be organizing them into a search party. Melissa followed close behind.

"Sergeant?"

"Franks. Harry Franks."

"Okay, Sergeant. I need this entire area searched with a fine-tooth comb. Bag and tag anything that looks out of place."

"What am I looking for?"

Blake shrugged. "It's like pornography, Sergeant..."

Franks chuckled. "I'll know it when I see it."

He didn't let the amusement consume him for long. Placing two fingers in his mouth, he let out a short, sharp whistle and gathered the growing crowd of police officers around him, which now included two K-9 units. He issued succinct instructions to the assorted group, quickly consulting a map of the area on his phone before assigning each pair of officers a starting point for their search.

"I know it's dark," he bellowed. "But we all know why we're here. A woman's life is on the line. She's depending on us. So don't let her down."

The hunt began without delay. Blake, Melissa, and about a dozen police officers spread out through the pine forest, gaze glued to the ground ahead of them, sweeping the beams of their flashlights left and right. The ground underfoot was soft, sandy, and threaded by tree roots that were then covered by pine needles. It was a recipe for a twisted ankle, especially in the dark.

With Melissa at her side, and another officer twenty yards or so to her left, Blake moved in a zigzag pattern through the trees to ensure that she didn't miss a single inch of ground within her corridor. Ideally, they needed more bodies assigned to the search, but the department was already stretched thin as it was.

Several times Blake spotted something that seemed out of place in the glow of her flashlight. On each occasion, she crouched low to examine the object that had attracted her attention, but mostly she discovered only litter: crushed cans of beer, probably from illicit teenage drinking, and cigarette butts. It all looked as though it had been exposed to the weather for weeks, if not months.

She kept half an ear out for the radio handset clipped to her belt, waiting for another member of the search party to report that something had been found. But as one hour stretched by, then another, she began to lose hope.

Shortly before 11 p.m., Melissa let out a yelp of surprise.

"Lieutenant!" she called out, her voice high with excitement. "You need to see this!"

Blake stabbed an empty evidence bag onto a sharp nearby branch to mark her place, then hurried over to the source of the sound. The beam of her flashlight bounced off pine trunks in every direction.

As she reached Melissa's side, she began, "What am I looking—?"

She fell silent. The cause of her partner's excitement was clear. Only a row of half dozen pine trees between where they now stood and the disguised outline of a dark blue midsize SUV about ten yards away. Whatever left it here had piled branches and leaves against it in a vain attempt to keep it hidden.

But the license plate was still visible.

"Get forensics here, now," Blake said. "We've found Piper's truck."

"Lieutenant."

Blake snapped to her left, toward the source of the unexpected sound. The crime scene investigator, Robyn, had appeared a few feet away, on the other side of the line of police tape that marked off the crime scene. She hadn't heard the woman approach.

Robyn's blue hair was tied up in a ponytail and surrounded by a net, like a food service worker. She was wearing matching blue plastic booties and gloves, like she was planning on trying out for a performance art group in Vegas.

Behind her was a trail of yellow plastic flags that had been left by the forensics team to mark out the safe path to the truck. Her partner Elijah was crouched by the truck itself, the lens of his powerful digital camera pointed at an object out of Blake's field of view. A succession of bright flashes seared her retinas as he photographed whatever it was from various angles.

Stifling the flutter of her heart at Robyn's silent approach, Blake nodded.

"I'm Blake," she said. "I guess we'll be working together from now on."

"We're right down the hallway," Robyn replied through pursed lips. "Feel free to visit anytime."

Rebuke taken, Blake thought.

Any successful investigation was like a well-choreographed band. Detectives and investigators were like the lead singers, but they were nothing without their supporting cast of forensics technicians, lab assistants, and other support staff. And too often, they forgot that. She vowed that she wouldn't let that happen. Not while she was in charge. Used right, people like Robyn were force multipliers, as valuable in their own right as another half-dozen detectives.

"What have you found?" she asked.

"Elijah has photographed most of the scene," Robyn said, setting a black plastic pelican case down on the ground beside her. "I've taken hair, skin, blood, and fingerprint samples from inside the truck. As soon as I get back to the lab, I'll start processing everything."

Blake raised her eyebrow. "Blood?"

"Just a droplet. It could've easily been missed," Robyn replied in a tone that suggested somebody else might have, but not her. "Just a smear on the steering wheel. Could be from anything. A nosebleed, maybe."

"How long until you know who it belongs to?"

"If it matches the DNA profile of either our murder vic, Nina Crawford, or anyone else in our databases, you will have an answer within twenty-four hours."

Blake grimaced. That was too long. Nina would be dead by then. "Anything else?"

"I have a trailer en route. We'll rip the truck apart when we get it back to the station. For now, nothing out of the ordinary. No evidence of a struggle, nothing to suggest a weapon was discharged inside the vehicle, and except for a small amount of blood, nothing that leads me to believe a blade was used."

Blake reached into her jacket and pulled out her notepad and pen. She scribbled her cell number on a scrap, tore it off, and handed it to Robyn. "Keep me updated. No detail's too small, no time's too late. If you think you're on to something, I want to know about it immediately. Understood?"

Robyn inclined her head slowly. "Understood."

"Good."

Blake turned away, already slipping the notepad back into a pocket with one hand and pulling out her phone with another.

Despite her mounting exhaustion, her mind was ablaze with various theories as to what had happened here, each more fantastical than the last.

But something that Robyn had said kept replaying in her mind. *"No evidence of a struggle..."*

It was possible that Piper had been attacked outside of the vehicle and her truck dumped in the woods afterwards. But her autopsy hadn't turned up any evidence of a prior attack. Everything pointed to the likelihood that Piper had known her killer. That she had met up with that individual willingly, not knowing the choice would be fatal.

Did that indicate her killer was Austin, who she was having an affair with and who might have motive to want her out of the picture?

Or somebody else entirely...

A sensation of impotence grew in Blake's chest. She whirled around, knowing that she needed to find something to do—even if only to keep her mind occupied. She doubted she would get any sleep. Not tonight.

Her gaze fell upon a dirt track. She stared at it blankly for a few seconds before a thought occurred to her. Seeing Sergeant Franks leaning against a tree trunk nearby, she called his name.

"What can I do for you, Lieutenant?"

Blake pointed at the track. "Where does that lead?"

The sergeant's brow furrowed, and his eyelids appeared to close for an instant as he considered the question. Upon opening them, he said, "A gas station, I think."

"You think they have security cameras?"

Franks nodded slowly. "Yeah, I guess they just might."

26

Blake strode into the gas station's 24-hour store, through aisles bristling with products packed full of high-fructose corn syrup, and toward a cashier who visibly paled as she closed in on him.

His reaction probably had something to do with the pungent scent of marijuana that emanated from him. Blake remembered from her recent course that possession was still a misdemeanor offense in North Carolina, though it was usually punishable by little more than a fine of a couple hundred dollars. Something about the intensity of the fog that surrounded the kid told Blake that he was carrying enough to make him eligible for a full 45 days behind bars—the maximum punishment allowable by state law.

That wasn't why she was here. But if it made the kid more cooperative, she wouldn't argue.

"I need to see your security footage."

His eyes were red-rimmed, and he reacted slowly. "Huh?"

"Cameras," Blake repeated, enunciating the words slowly and carefully. "Security cameras."

She pointed up at a gleaming black dome a few feet above his head that stared balefully out at the store. He tipped his head back in a deliberate and sluggish pace until his forehead was almost parallel with the floor.

He studied it for a couple of seconds, then said in a tone flushed with relief, "Oh, right. Yeah, we got a camera right there."

"I can see that," Blake replied, frustration rising inside her. "I need to take a look at the footage."

Behind her, the bell over the door tinkled. She didn't look over her shoulder. The sound brought the cashier's chin back down level with the floor.

"Who are you?" he said, stealing a cautious glance out at the several cop cars now parked at all angles across the gas station's forecourt.

"Detective Lieutenant Blake Larsen," she said. "With the Sheriff's Department."

He swallowed. "Sorry, I don't work here often. The usual dude didn't show up. I can show you the computer. I don't know how to work it, though."

"I'll figure it out," Blake said, drumming her fingernails against the countertop.

The kid turned, then spun back to her with a grimace on his face. "Can you wait a couple hours? I'm not supposed to leave my spot unless something's on fire."

Blake gritted her teeth. "No, I cannot wait a couple hours," she said firmly. "You're closed."

"I am?" the kid replied, confusion flushing his cheeks.

"Correct," Blake said, leaning over the counter. "Now show me the damn footage."

"Hey," a male voice called out from behind her. "What's the holdup? I'm in a hurry."

Blake heard the blood rushing in her ears. She thought of Nina Crawford locked up in some filthy hole, heard the clock ticking on her fate, and she saw red. She spun around, her hand reaching for the badge in her pocket. She pulled it out and let the solid metal emblem fall from the leather flip fold.

"Do we have a problem?" she said inquiringly, fixing the

complainer—a heavyset man wearing a moth-eaten Simpsons T-shirt, khaki cargo shorts, and flip-flops—with an intimidating stare.

He backed a couple paces away, brandishing a bag of chips and a plastic-wrapped sandwich. "No. But I gotta pay for my food. I have places to be."

"The store's closed," Blake replied flatly. "You can come back and pay later."

She turned back to the cashier. "Take me to the computer."

He nodded, seeming a little overawed by her.

"So my meal's free?" the customer called out hopefully.

"In this economy?" Blake replied without looking back at him. "You better be kidding. Your license plate's on camera. If you don't come back tomorrow morning to pay in full, I'll track you down myself."

Without another word, she strode around the counter and pushed open the door marked *Office*. She couldn't afford to waste another second. She definitely didn't have enough free time to burn coming after some dude for a dine and dash.

But you don't know that.

The smell of weed grew even more intense as the office door swung closed behind her. Blake guessed that this was where the workers came to smoke, since they couldn't light up outside, near the pumps. It was still definitely against a couple dozen sections of the fire code, but that was a problem for another day—and one for Chief Donahue to handle, anyway.

"So where is it?" she said, looking around at the cramped space inquiringly. The walls were stacked with crates of energy drinks, and the desk in the center of the room was piled high with envelopes and forms.

The cashier took an experimental sniff of the room's atmosphere, and his expression paled even further. "I don't usually come back here," he lied.

"Sure you don't," Blake muttered. She shouldered him aside and started searching the desk herself. She found a laptop computer weighed down by what seemed like at least a decade's worth of invoices. She held her breath as she lifted the lid, wondering if the ancient machine would even start at all. Judging by the condition of everything else in the store, it didn't seem likely.

Happily, though, the computer's fans began to whir. A moment later, the screen powered up directly onto the desktop.

"What now?" Blake asked.

The cashier simply shrugged. "I told you already, I've never used it."

"You can go," she said in response.

He didn't need to be told twice.

Blake returned her attention to the computer. The desktop was littered with icons of downloaded files, payroll documents, invoices, and other detritus. She spent a couple of minutes studying it without any luck, then maneuvered the mouse to the start button. In the list of recently used applications that populated on the left, she saw an image of a security camera.

"That was easy," she muttered as she clicked it.

The underpowered laptop computer took a full ninety seconds to load the software package. When it popped up on the screen, however, it was surprisingly user-friendly. There were over a dozen numbered cameras on the property, all of which appeared to feed directly to an on-premises server. According to a setting on the main screen, the footage went back seven days before it was automatically deleted to free up space. The first thing Blake did was disable this feature, just in case.

A slider at the bottom of the screen enabled her to scroll back through time. She used the trackpad to pull it left and watched as each of the small boxes that contained a camera feed moved in sync. Cars drove backwards, customers sped blindly back out of the store. Blake realized that there was a camera inside the back office, just over her head. A couple of times she watched as different members of staff came back to light up clouds of smoke that collapsed in on themselves.

Finally, she neared the time window in which Piper's phone had pinged the nearby cell tower. She brought the slider five minutes

ahead and then set the video to play at double speed. After so long
watching the world in reverse, it took her brain a few seconds to
readjust.

Blake's eyes jumped from camera feed to camera feed. The light
from the screen reflected back off her retinas. There was too much
information for any mind to truly process, so for the first scan, she
focused only on the store's internal feeds. It was dark outside anyway,
lowering the resolution on the external cameras—few of which
appeared to be working.

"Come on," she muttered, returning to drumming her fingers on
the desk. It was still so blanketed with paper that the action made
only a muffled crinkling sound.

A steady stream of drivers entered to buy snacks. About a third
wore some kind of headgear: either a beanie hat to protect against the
cold or else a baseball cap. She peered closer at the screen a couple of
times as the footage sped by but saw no one matching Piper's
description.

As she watched, she mentally reviewed everything they knew.
They had Piper's financials. If a charge had popped up at this gas
station, law enforcement would already have checked the place out.
The pumps were card-operated, so it was unlikely she'd stopped for
gas. It was possible—likely even—that Piper had never been here at
all. The fact that her truck had been dumped a few hundred feet
away might easily be a coincidence.

Blake was so wrapped up in the details that she almost missed the
flash of blond hair entering the store. The security system wasn't
equipped with microphones, so there was no sound. Her brain filled
in the tinkle of the entrance bell anyway.

She jerked her hand toward the trackpad and hurriedly returned
the playback speed to real-time. She kept her eyes glued to the screen
as the blond woman paced around the store, taking her time
perusing the aisles before picking up a large can of what appeared to
be an energy drink.

"Come on," Blake muttered, "look at the damn camera."

Unfortunately, the target of her frustrated ire couldn't hear her.

She strolled toward the counter, apparently without a care in the world. At ten paces away, her face was too pixelated to make out any detail. At five, Blake was just barely able to make out the outline of her nose and mouth.

She reached into her purse and pulled out an object that looked like a credit card. She slowed two paces in front of the checkout counter. Her face began to come into focus.

Blake could barely contain her anticipation. She slammed the pause button down hard, freezing the video on a frame of the woman's face, then zoomed in on the image, so that only she and the cashier were in shot.

A wave of disappointment washed over her. It wasn't Piper. This was yet another dead end. And Nina was running out of time.

Blake slumped back against the office chair, momentarily numbed by this fresh failure. She stared glassily at the screen, barely taking it in.

Purely by chance, her eyes happened to focus on the two figures frozen on the monitor. And then they went wide with shock. There *was* something familiar about the cashier after all.

27

"Captain," Blake practically yelled into the mouthpiece of the cell phone as she sprinted for her vehicle. "Tell me we still have Dwaine Hilton in custody. Or at the very least, that we know where he is right the fuck now."

"That's a negative, Lieutenant," Rogers replied. "We tossed him out on his ass hours ago. What's the fire?"

"He works a few hundred feet away from where Piper's car was dumped," Blake said, her chest heaving from exertion as she neared the makeshift parking lot of police vehicles. Her head swiveled on a pivot as she searched for her partner. On sighting Melissa, she waved wildly for the woman's attention. "His alibi isn't worth shit."

Silence answered her. Blake felt almost lightheaded at the possibility that they had released a dangerous murderer back into society, free to kill again. A wave of frustration at the system's rules and safeguards buffeted her. Logically, she understood the purpose for them. But sometimes you knew, just knew that someone was bad.

But even as she was rocked by frustration and regret, a nagging doubt pricked her subconscious.

Dwaine Hilton was most assuredly an unpleasant guy. He was a fraudster, a racist, and a thug.

Was he a killer, too?

"I need his home address, Captain," Blake said firmly, dispelling all doubt from her mind. She could resolve any unanswered questions later. When they had Dwaine in custody. Until then it was just noise.

Melissa ran toward Blake, who jerked her finger pointedly at the car as she pulled open the driver's side door. She started the engine, then flicked the button that activated the flashing blue lights built into the grille of the unmarked car. The engine revved way too hard as she stepped on the gas, spinning tires sending stones and grit flying and bouncing off the underside of the cruiser with the sound of falling hail.

Blake filled Melissa in on what she'd learned at the Speedway gas station as her partner punched Dwaine's address into the vehicle's built-in GPS unit. A couple of seconds later, the directions flashed up on the screen. They were seventeen minutes out.

"What about backup?" Melissa asked cautiously.

Blake considered the question for a moment. She wanted nothing more than to bust Dwaine's door down, jab her elbow into his nose, and beat the answers she needed out of him one way or another. A woman's life was on the line, and every time she glanced at her watch, she grew more aware that Nina's time on this planet was fading away.

But that wasn't—couldn't—be the way she did things.

"Get dispatch to send a patrol car," she finally answered. "Have them park at the end of the street until we arrive. The last thing we want to do is spook him."

"Got it," Melissa said, reaching for the radio.

They made the seventeen-minute journey in twelve. Blake weaved through traffic like a woman possessed, either braking or accelerating at each junction and stop sign on pure trust as Melissa called the play from the passenger seat as though they were a well-oiled rally team.

When the GPS display announced they were three minutes out, she killed both her siren and her lights to approach more carefully. Dwaine lived on an unremarkable street of one-story houses several miles outside of Northern Pines. Each of the residences was spaced about fifty yards apart, and the land in between was studded with pine trees and other foliage that must have made for almost complete privacy.

As Blake crawled down the street, she passed yards marked off with chain-link fence and signs warning visitors to beware of dogs. She felt an uneasy sensation crawl up her spine. This wasn't the kind of neighborhood that welcomed outsiders.

Especially not cops.

When she rounded a bend and an NPPD cruiser came into view, Blake slowed to a stop and killed the vehicle's engine completely. She opened the door and climbed out, rounding the rear of her vehicle and popping the trunk. Both detectives retrieved their department-branded protective vests and shrugged them over their shoulders.

Blake idly wondered when—or if—they would get around to replacing the town's logo with that of the sheriff's department. She clipped her radio to her belt and glanced briefly at the canvas long gun case on the base of the trunk before deciding to proceed with only her side arm.

"Lieutenant, Detective Wilson," a low male voice greeted her as they approached the waiting cruiser. Two officers—now deputies, she corrected herself—stood by their vehicle, peering toward a house she guessed belonged to Dwaine. "We only got here a minute ago. Stayed out of sight, per instructions from dispatch."

"What's your name?" Blake asked the cop who had addressed her. Melissa nodded her own greeting. His partner was a Black woman with her hand on her unbuttoned holster, short where he was tall. Neither looked nervous.

"Reeves," he replied. "Charlie Reeves."

"Kayla Oakley," his partner replied with a quick nod. "Nice to meet you."

"Likewise," Blake replied.

"Kayla, Charlie," Melissa said to the two patrol cops. "I'm glad it's you guys."

"Expecting any trouble?" Kayla asked.

"The suspect shouldn't know we're coming," Blake replied after a moment's thought. "But you should consider him dangerous until further notice."

"Armed?"

"He has a concealed handgun permit," Melissa stated. "And we know he owns at least one pistol."

"Okay. How do you want to play this?" Charlie asked, worry-lines deepening at the prospect of an armed confrontation. His gun hand moved subconsciously toward his holster.

"Right now, we don't have sufficient evidence to arrest our suspect," Blake said, gritting her teeth at the insanity of it. "He probably knows that. And he's retained some fancy lawyer who will definitely know that him lying to us about meeting our murder victim doesn't constitute probable cause. But we're running out of time. I want you covering the rear just in case he runs. Detective Wilson and I will take the front. If everything goes well, he'll admit to everything and come with us peacefully."

"Right," Reeves snorted. Blake watched as both patrol cops drew their weapons. Apparently, they didn't think much of their chances of this ending up without a fight.

"Let's go," she said. "Remember, if he's our guy, then we need to take him alive. Nina Crawford's life might depend on it."

All three of the faces watching her paled at the mention of the stakes, but she saw determination written on all of them.

Dwaine's house was about a hundred yards farther down the street, bracketed by the customary pine trees that gave most of the towns in the area their names. The vegetation meant that the majority of their approach was shielded from view. Only the final twenty yards or so could be seen from the front of the house. The two cops peeled away from Melissa and Blake and headed down the side of the property line through the trees.

"Radio check," Blake said, lifting her handset to her lips and speaking softly. She narrowed her gaze and studied the house intently. A couple of lights were on inside, but they weren't exactly blazing out onto the front yard. A prickle of unease ran down her spine.

"This is Reeves," a crackled reply came a moment later. "We've got the property's rear exit in sight. No evidence of movement inside. Blinds are down on all the windows on this side. A vehicle is parked in the carport around the back of the building."

"Roger that," she replied. "Approaching the front now."

She returned the radio to her belt and loosened the clip securing her holster, then drew her weapon. She flicked the safety off and heard a corresponding sound behind her as Melissa did the same.

"Cover the windows," Blake murmured as they reached about twenty yards from the front door. "See anything?"

"Looks quiet," her partner replied, taking up a position a few feet behind Blake and several steps to her right. She took a step forward, then held her movement as Blake failed to copy her. "What is it?"

"I'm not sure," Blake replied softly. She cautiously swept her gaze left and right across the front of the one-story building, wondering if she was overthinking things, seeing imaginary dangers in the shadows. But something didn't feel right.

"Nice and slow," she said at last after nothing jumped out at her.

She took a few steps toward the front door, then held up her left hand in a fist. Melissa stopped immediately.

"The door's open," Blake whispered. She heard a rustle of clothing behind her and saw Melissa nodding in acknowledgment out of the corner of her right eye. Her partner stiffened.

Blake scanned the house again. There was only a crack separating the door from the frame, but it was definitely unlocked. A thin candle of light spilled out. It didn't necessarily mean anything, but people didn't usually leave their front doors open.

Something's not right.

"Mr. Hilton?" she called out in a loud voice. "It's Lieutenant Larsen from the Monroe County Sheriff's Department. We met earlier. Are you home?"

There was no response. Just the fluttering of a bird's wings as it launched itself from the canopy of a nearby pine tree. A light breeze rustled needles and branches all around her.

"Look sharp," she radioed to the two cops around the rear of the property. "Something feels off. Front door is ajar."

As Blake and Melissa crept forward, fine hairs stood on end on the back of her neck. Once she reached a few feet from the slightly raised front porch, she called out Dwaine's name a second time.

"Blinds just moved," Reeves' voice crackled through the radio. "He's inside."

"Mr. Hilton, we just want to talk," Blake yelled, feeling a prickle of sweat on her temple. Her hands were clammy on her service weapon, and she quickly wiped them on her pants to dry them.

Blake and Melissa traded glances out of the corner of their eyes. They said nothing, but an unspoken communication passed between them.

What next?

Before either had a chance to decide, the unmistakable bark of a gunshot rang out, quickly followed by shattering glass. Blake heard one of the two cops on the opposite side of the building cry out in alarm before another several rounds were fired off. She couldn't tell if they were returning fire, or whether they were coming from the first shooter.

"Shit," she swore, bringing her pistol up and charging toward the front door. "Let's move."

Melissa followed without hesitation. Blake brought her right leg up and drove her heel through the front door at just below waist height, slamming it backward. She was through the frame before the door rattled against the wall.

More gunfire. The sound registered in Blake's mind as coming from a rifle, rather than a pistol. That wasn't good.

She heard Reeves call for backup over the radio and inform dispatch that officers were under fire.

"This is Detective Wilson," Melissa added from behind her once the cop finished his broadcast. "Officers inside the property. Hold your fire."

Time seemed to slow around Blake as the adrenaline kicked in. She raised her weapon and swept it left and right as another half-dozen gunshots rang out from somewhere inside.

The inside of the house looked like it had emerged from the 1980s stillborn. The floor was covered by a worn brown carpet, and the place stank of stale cigarette smoke and old cooking oil. The front door opened into a hallway that ran right to the back of the building. There was a single door on the left-hand side and two on the right. All three were open. The closest was the first door to Blake's right.

"Dwaine," she yelled through a break in the gunfire, "it doesn't have to go like this. Put your weapon down and lie flat on the floor. We can talk this over."

"This is Reeves," she heard a low, panting voice hiss over the radio in the silence that followed. "Oakley got hit."

Blake reached for her handset with her free hand.

"Get her to safety," she ordered, her own chest straining as she sucked oxygen into a furnace that never seemed satisfied. "Now!"

Her hands were clammy again. A third voice crackled through the radio. Dispatch. Backup was six minutes out.

Shit.

"Okay," she whispered. "Change of plan. Let's get the hell out of here and wait for help."

It was too late.

Another rattle of gunshots rang out. This time, instead of splintering wood and glass on the other side of the building, they stitched a line of holes through the drywall just a few feet to Blake's right. They had punched through the other side of the wall. The shooter was firing blind, but he had two advantages on his side: a larger magazine and heavy caliber bullets.

Blake motioned at Melissa to get down, but her partner was way ahead of her. As she crouched low herself, she reached for the radio a second time. "Reeves, can you give me any covering fire?"

"Shit," a strained voice replied. "Oakley is bleeding pretty bad. She took a round to the hip. I pulled her twenty yards back, we're in a streambed in the woods. I'll do what I can."

"No," Blake radioed. "Your first priority is keeping your partner alive. Understood?"

"We got pressure on the wound. I'll give you a full mag and then book it straight back to her."

"Copy that," she replied. The blood rushing in her ears made it difficult to hear. Another three rounds smashed through the drywall, right over where she and Melissa were both crouched. A shower of plaster rained down on them. They were two feet too high, but their good luck wouldn't last. The shooter had them pinned.

Three more rounds. He was methodically stitching gunshots left and right. These were lower and closer to the front door. He was cutting off their way out.

That settles it, Blake thought, a rush of anger deadening her fear. If this bastard wanted to kill them, he was going to have to go through her first. And she was in no mood to make it easy for him.

"Incoming in ten seconds," Deputy Reeves radioed. "Keep your heads down."

But that wasn't what Blake had planned. She counted out the seconds in her head, breathing in deep to refresh her tense, straining muscles. This was going to be their only shot.

Ten, nine, eight...

Once again, time seemed to slow. Her heart no longer felt like it was about to explode. She was ready.

Three, two, one.

More smashing glass. This time, the gunshots sounded farther away, the sound muffled by the construction material separating them. The second Reeves opened fire, Blake crawled forward toward the door to her right. She counted out eleven full rounds, the last of which cracked out just as she reached the door frame. She heard Melissa's heavy breathing just behind her.

"I'm bugging out," Reeves radioed. "Good luck."

"Ready?" Blake whispered, glancing over her shoulder. Melissa's expression was pale but determined. She nodded.

For a moment, Blake heard only blessed silence. There was a lull in the gunfire. Then a scrape from the other side of the drywall.

With a powerful surge from the thighs, Blake thrust herself upright, squeezed her grip tight against the pistol, and spun around the doorframe and into the room beyond.

It was empty. The door was open to the backyard, still swinging on its hinges. Blood was everywhere. Some kind of deranged message was scrawled in glistening red on the wall, written in a language that definitely wasn't English.

And Dwaine Hilton's severed head sat sightless on the floor.

28

Blake slouched numbly against one of the many cruisers that had responded to the call of officers under fire. The night was lit by their flashing blue lights. Hilton's property was cordoned off by a row of police tape and was now an active FBI crime scene. The Bureau's forensics people were twenty minutes into their work. Somewhere overhead, she could hear the dull thump of a helicopter's rotors as it searched for the shooter.

But they were too late. Whoever was responsible was long gone.

An FBI agent had just finished taking Blake's statement. Melissa's was ongoing. Blake knew she should pull herself out of her fugue state, but she couldn't find the energy. It felt like every time she thought she'd caught a break in the case, things only grew more complex.

She was on the verge of simply giving up.

Due to the background clamor of an active crime scene, it took Blake several long seconds to realize that her phone was vibrating in her pocket. She reached slowly for it, not bothering to check the name on the display before she answered.

"Blake? Are you okay?"

Her shoulders slumped forward as she recognized the voice on the other end of the line. "Ryan?"

"Yeah. I saw what happened on television. I'm checking out of the hotel now. I'll be back as soon as I can. Late afternoon tomorrow, I think. How are you holding up?"

The emotion was so alien to Blake it took her a little while to process what she was hearing. *Concern.* He was worried about her.

"I'm fine, Ryan. Really," she said automatically, not stopping to interrogate whether she was being truthful to herself. "You need to look after you. What about your foot? And Axe?"

"Screw my foot," he said strongly. "I've hopped along just fine all this time without it. Besides, the techs need time to make a few adjustments. I'm just hanging around like a bad smell. Axe is doing great. The vet gave him a clean bill of health."

Blake opened her mouth to brush him off a second time, to tell him he couldn't help her, but when she reached for the words, she didn't find them. The truth was, she needed some human comfort. Just a firm, warm hug would do. Every time she blinked, she saw Piper's sightless eyes staring back at her, and now Dwaine's gruesome murder scene would doubtless haunt her dreams.

"Okay," she whispered simply.

"Okay," he repeated, as if surprised he'd beaten her down that easily. She realized he knew her better than she thought. "I know you're busy. I'm not planning on getting in the way. But I'll be there, if you need any—"

"Tell me what I'm missing, Ryan," she said, cutting across him. "I'm working a case looking for terrorists, but half the evidence points toward a serial killer. My new vic might have met my first one, but now he's too dead to tell me why, and I'm pretty sure he didn't kill Piper Hicks. I feel like I'm trapped in an endless plug hole, swirling round and round in a circle but getting nowhere."

"How did he die?" Ryan asked. "Same MO as the other murder?"

Blake knew she was bending the rules by sharing this with Ryan. But also that she had no need to swear him to secrecy. He was the walking embodiment of a green flag. She trusted him completely.

"Similar," she said slowly, replaying the sight of the crime scene in her mind. "But messier. More violent. It felt angry. Like a punishment. Maybe I'm overthinking things."

"Trust your instincts," he said. "I do. You said it was like a punishment. What for?"

"If I knew that, I wouldn't be asking you," she said instantly.

"No," Ryan pressed. "I mean, why would somebody *want* him dead?"

The answer floated into Blake's mind. Because Dwaine knew something. And the killer was worried he might spill whatever that was to the cops.

That led to one final question. Who knew that she'd interviewed Dwaine earlier that day?

Blake's eyes widened as she recognized a familiar face on the opposite side of the police tape line. Another answer presented itself. "Ryan, I have to go."

She hung up without another word, a tidal wave of frustration at repeatedly banging her head against obstacles in the path of solving this case sweeping over her good sense. She made a beeline for the man she'd seen.

A journalist.

A suspect.

And a man who'd been lingering outside the station when Dwaine was brought in.

"What the hell are you doing here, Aaron?" Blake hissed as she approached the tape.

He took a step back, visibly stunned by the vehemence in her tone. Reflected blue light flickered off his features. He looked strained. Concerned. "Huh?"

She jabbed her finger at him, stopping short just a fraction of an inch before making contact with his rib cage. "Answer the damn question."

Aaron stammered in response, "This—this is a crime scene, right? I'm doing my job. I heard over the scanner that shots were fired and a police officer was hit."

Blake inhaled sharply. The fresh air helped mellow her temper, though just barely. She knew her anger was irrational, that she needed to keep a cool head rather than give in to her emotions. But it wasn't always possible to hover above the waves without being hit by the spray. This was one of those times.

She had nothing on Aaron. Certainly nothing concrete. Just a cocktail of suspicion and distrust. But he kept popping up in all the wrong places at all the wrong times. Even as a student, he'd been the first journalist to pick up on the Yates and Sanders murders. He'd come across—then made famous on campus—the *She Lies* blog.

He was the first reporter to be contacted by the terrorists. He'd attempted to insert himself into her own orbit, dangling the possibility of an exclusive interview in front of her—why? To keep tabs on her investigation?

And now he was here.

"Where were you Friday night, Aaron?" she asked bluntly, narrowing her gaze to drink in every detail of his response.

He blanched, clearly understanding exactly what she was really asking. "Are you serious?"

"Answer the fucking question."

"What time?"

"Seven in the evening."

He closed his eyes to think. "At the office. I worked late. Then I stopped to pick up Chinese. You can check the security footage at work and my bank statements to confirm both those things if you need to. But I'm not your guy, Lieutenant. I'm not responsible for any of this. I have an alibi for Nina Crawford's disappearance as well. Not that you asked."

Blake fixed him with a piercing glare as she paused to think. A facial muscle pulsated nervously on his jaw. He was worried about something; she was certain of that.

But what?

First of all, she could rule out his direct involvement in Dwaine Hilton's horrific execution. There was no way he'd had enough time to escape, soaked head to toe in blood, then clean himself up sufficiently to return to the scene of the crime. Besides, if he was responsible, why come back at all?

And assuming he wasn't blowing smoke up her ass, and his alibis checked out, where did that leave her?

She reasserted control over her behavior as the white heat of her earlier anger began to fade. She couldn't exactly come out and ask him about the Greenville killings. He might be a suspect, but he was definitely still a journalist. Accusing him of that would be handing him an exclusive scoop on a plate.

Blake raked him with a stare. "What aren't you telling me, Aaron?"

His fingers clenched anxiously into fists and back again at his sides. He glanced toward Hilton's house, now lit up with floodlights as FBI forensic technicians swarmed all over it. His chest rose and fell with frantic rapidity. Blake guessed if she took his pulse right now, it would be off the charts.

"Nothing," he insisted. "I swear."

"Why do you look so anxious?"

"I don't!" he protested before steadying himself and adding in a more measured tone, "I'm not."

"Not the way things look from where I'm standing, Aaron. Are you worried about something?"

"No," he said, though his features told a different story.

"This is the only chance I'll give you to come clean," she said coldly. "I suggest you don't waste it."

His eyes cast around wildly. But when his gaze returned to Blake's face, her hopes sank. He'd made his decision. "If you have an issue with the free exercise of the press, Lieutenant, I suggest you take it up with my editor. Until then, I have somewhere to be."

29

A piercing whistle split the packed Hercules Fitness Center. It felt as though every federal agent and cop in the state was present. But the sound wasn't necessary. The entire room was almost silent. A heavy air of resignation clouded the large hall.

"It's 5:30 a.m.," ASAC Granger called out. "Assuming the terrorist's demand is correct, Nina Crawford has seven and a half hours left to live. It's our job to do something about that."

Blake knocked back the second half of a cup of bitter, crappy black coffee. It seared the delicate flesh at the back of her throat as it went down. She was so tired it was a little like patching the hole in the hull of the Titanic with duct tape. She'd managed a couple hours of sleep following the previous night's events. Only enough to put a crick in her neck.

"Northern Pines," Granger said. "Where are we?"

Clutching the empty coffee cup to her chest, Blake swallowed. Her mouth felt foul. She couldn't remember the last time she'd brushed her teeth.

"We believe that Dwaine Hilton and Piper Hicks might have come into contact the night our first victim went missing," she said. "However, we do not believe they had any prior relationship. Neither do we have any evidence that he was responsible for her kidnapping or murder, except for the fact that the victim's truck was found near his place of work."

Granger gestured her to continue.

"Upon leaving the station yesterday evening, Hilton made a single phone call lasting just under ninety seconds," she said, speaking from memory. "The number he dialed appears to be a burner. Our working theory is that he was an associate of the killer or killers we are looking for. It's possible they considered him compromised after we interviewed him."

"You think he was working with the terrorists?" somebody called out.

"If that's what they are," she replied.

"What about Nina Crawford's husband?" Granger asked.

Blake glanced at Melissa, who was standing at her side, looking equally strained by the frantic pace of the investigation.

"We re-interviewed him"—she paused to glance at her watch—"four hours ago, after Hilton was found dead. He claims that he lost his phone the day before Piper went missing. That lines up with what he told us in his initial interview. We've got a cruiser sitting on his house, but beyond that, he's looking like a dead end."

"And he definitely wasn't responsible for the Hilton killing?"

Melissa interjected before Blake had a chance. "We had officers sitting on his house the entire time. He's got a strong alibi."

"So much for your serial killer," somebody stage-whispered from inside the crowd.

Blake whipped around, eyes flashing in the direction the voice had come from. She scanned the sea of innocent faces. "You got something to add?"

Nobody had the balls to front up.

"Cool it," Granger snapped. "We are all batting for the same team. The bad guys want us to turn on each other. So don't fall into their trap."

He singled out another agent in the crowd, who pulled up an

image of the Hilton crime scene—specifically the message that had been daubed on the wall in blood—on the projector at the far end of the room.

"It says, *There is no God but Allah, and Mohammed is his messenger,*" she said. "The language is Arabic. It's one of the most common phrases in Arabic usage, but it's also important to note that it is the message found on the black flag used by ISIS."

Blake frowned. An echo of her conversation with Dwaine the previous day floated freely in her mind.

"But they don't speak Arabic in Afghanistan," she interjected loudly. "Not beyond insular religious communities, anyway. You'd expect to see a message like that in Dari or Pashto if it was written by an Afghan."

"Or the terrorist we're looking for is a foreign fighter," the agent contended quickly. "The best estimate we have from the CIA is that the Taliban had several thousand Middle Eastern fighters in their ranks by 2021."

Blake frowned. It was possible, but unlikely. Over the previous forty-eight hours, the Bureau and every other three-letter agency had double, triple, and quadruple-checked the list of every refugee known to have entered the United States. Agents had knocked on hundreds of doors across the country. Not a single one of those leads had panned out.

She raised her voice again. "We don't have a single piece of hard, incontrovertible evidence that the terrorist angle that's had us chasing our tails for the last two days is anything other than a fantasy. No chatter. Nobody claiming credit. What if it's just a smokescreen? A misdirection designed to have us looking in the wrong direction until it's too late?"

The same voice piped up again. "Where's *your* evidence?"

"We have two cold case murders with an almost identical MO that took place within a hundred miles of here. Piper and Nina both fit the same physical profile: young and blond. Our perpetrator courts attention, first through manipulating the student newspaper, now the national media. There are too many similarities to simply dismiss out of hand."

"What are you suggesting, Lieutenant?" Granger asked.

The truth was that she had no good answer to give. She needed more time.

"Our best bet is that the perpetrator of the ECU murders was a student. The *She Lies* blog feels too inside baseball for him not to have been. We need to pressure the university for a list of their student body, then cross-check it against anyone living within at least a twenty-mile radius of Northern Pines."

Granger shook his head curtly. "Eight hours from now, Nina Crawford will be dead. You might not like it, but we have neither the time nor the resources to waste running down your wild goose chase. You need to drop it. That's my decision. And it's final."

For a few seconds, Blake heard only a strange ringing in her head. She saw Granger turn to the cyber forensics team talking but didn't take in a single word that was said. A wave of helplessness threatened to overwhelm her.

Get it together.

As Blake shook herself out of it, she felt her phone vibrate in her pocket. She reached for it with slightly numbed hands, still feeling paralyzed by the enormity of a future she felt powerless to prevent. She glanced at the phone's screen before answering it and placing it against her ear.

"Medical examiner," she whispered in reply to Melissa's inquiring glance as she made a beeline for the nearest door.

"Doc, tell me you have something," she said as soon as she exited the fitness hall and emerged into an empty hallway. Melissa followed half a step behind her, apparently deciding like she had that there were better ways of using her time.

"I can tell you that this victim didn't die like the others," Scott replied. "I found evidence of blunt force trauma on his skull. Somebody knocked him cold."

Blake squeezed her eyes shut. A tiny wave of nausea tested the strength of her stomach as she remembered the blood-soaked crime scene.

"The victim's neck was severed with a saw, like the others. I'd go as far to say it was the same implement used on Piper Hicks—or at the very least, the same brand. There is one critical difference, however."

"Go on..."

"The cuts occurred while the subject was still alive."

"That explains the blood spray," Blake said. She'd guessed as much. "Do you have anything else?"

"Not much," Scott admitted. "Other than a small deposit of crystalline silica on the subject's skin."

"Crystalline silica?"

"Otherwise known as silica dust," Scott confirmed. "It's a major constituent of construction materials like stone, brick, and tile. It's produced when those materials are cut or drilled. Beyond that, I couldn't say."

Blake frowned as a small piece of the puzzle slotted into place in her mind. It was only a hunch. Maybe she was wildly off base. But doing something had to be better than waiting around for a woman to die.

"Thanks, Doc. Can you do me a favor?"

"Sure."

"Update the task force for me."

"Dispatch told me you were there already," he replied, sounding slightly surprised.

"I was," Blake replied, already striding down the corridor in the direction of the parking lot outside. "But I've got somewhere else to be."

30

"You sure he'll even be up this early?" Blake asked as they pulled up in front of the gate that led into Gabriel Hartmann's property—the CEO of Hartmann Construction.

"That's what his assistant said," Melissa confirmed as it swung slowly open. "I guess he's an early riser."

As they drove up the road toward Hartmann's home, they passed a black SUV coming in the opposite direction.

"You think that's him?" Blake asked curiously as it passed. She saw the briefest flash of the driver—male, and nothing more.

"It would be a weird power play," Melissa said back. "Maybe his wife."

Blake drummed her fingers on her thigh. Even she would admit that her reason for being here was tenuous. If silica dust was produced by activities like drilling and sawing, it was clearly likely to be found on construction tools like those used to separate Dwaine Hilton's head from his neck. No evidence specifically pointed to Hartmann Construction.

Except... there was something here.

Abdul-Malik Azizi's house had been constructed by Gabriel's company. And somebody had gone to the effort of burning it down—

almost as though they were sending a message. And then there was the white pickup truck she'd seen speeding away from the scene of the crime. At the time she thought she'd seen a logo on its side.

A Hartmann Construction logo?

Blake's working theory was that Dwaine Hilton had known who was responsible for Piper's murder and Nina's kidnapping—had in fact been involved in one or both herself. That suspicion only intensified following learning of Hilton's potential encounter with Piper and redoubled after his own vicious murder. Then there was the dust found during his autopsy, and the likelihood that he'd been murdered after the mastermind of the whole plan got spooked that he might snitch.

Sure, Blake knew she didn't have much to go on. But she'd solved harder cases with less. Gabriel Hartmann ran the largest construction company in fifty miles. If anyone could shine some light on the construction connection, it was him.

But this was what investigative work was about: slow, painstaking effort, in which filling in any individual piece of the puzzle yielded no reward. You just had to hope that in the end it would come into focus.

As they approached the front of an enormous mansion, the large, heavy front door swung open. It was painted in a glossy black and bracketed on either side by large windows. A man stepped out, wearing a neatly pressed gray suit despite the early hour.

"Can I help you, Officers?" he asked calmly after both presented their badges. Blake felt his gaze sweep across her body, pausing for a moment at the weapon holstered at her hip. She didn't detect anything more than interest in his eyes.

Clipping her badge back onto her belt, Blake extended her hand. "Lieutenant Larsen," she said. "I was hoping to ask you some questions."

"Gabriel Hartmann," he replied as he shook. "I take it you're here about the arson incident? You'll find I'm an open book. Fire away."

The response caught Blake a little short. She adapted quickly and rolled with it. "Among other things, sir."

"Please, Gabriel."

"Okay, Gabriel. Do you have any idea who would have cause to burn down one of your properties?"

Gabriel held up a finger. "Not mine," he said quickly. "That's important. It was Abdul's home that was set on fire. Once I handed over the keys, it became his home, not mine."

"Still, any ideas?"

The construction CEO shook his head sadly. "I wish Abdul had come to me about those letters. I don't know what I would've done. Advised him to call the police, probably. It sickens me that people would write such awful things after everything his family has been through. But no, Lieutenant, I have no suggestions for you. We have a no assholes policy here at Hartmann Construction."

Sensing he was looking for a response, Blake raised her eyebrow.

"I don't hire assholes," he said proudly. "Everyone who works for me is someone I would want my grandmother to meet, may she rest in peace. They are all on board with our mission. About a third of my contractors are veterans themselves. They know what these Afghans have gone through."

"Tell me about your foundation," Blake said, not certain where this was going. Maybe it had nothing to do with her case, after all.

"Lieutenant, are you a believer?"

"What?"

"Do you believe in God? The Savior, Jesus Christ, all that stuff?"

"Depends on the week," Blake replied. Faith was a touchy subject for her. Sometimes she wanted to believe. And then she looked at the ashes of her life, remembered that everyone she'd ever loved was gone, and pushed the thought out of her mind.

"That's what this is for me," Hartmann said intensely. "Not in a religious way, I don't mean that. I've fucked a lot of things up in my life. My first two marriages. My relationship with my son. I've made a hell of a lot of money over the last couple decades. More than I can use. But nothing's given me satisfaction like building two dozen homes just to give away.

"All the company's profits will be funneled back into the Foundation. For as long as it takes. This is my way of giving back. Leaving some kind of mark on the world. Do you understand?"

Blake thought she did. Perhaps it was a midlife crisis, but if it was, then it was a damn sight better than buying a sports car.

"You care about them. Your... beneficiaries."

"Deeply," Hartmann replied, a shadow crossing his face as he perhaps realized that he'd shared too much. "I personally interviewed every single one of the individuals and families who will receive or have already been given the keys to their first home in America. I wanted to know whether they were good people. Invariably, they were. Every single one."

Blake relaxed the intensity of her stare. She was certain that Gabriel Hartmann was telling the truth. She didn't detect any reservation in his demeanor.

"What about your employees? You said they are all on board with your company's new direction. How do you know that for sure?"

"This company's like a family to me," Hartmann said. "I know that my success isn't just my own. I've known most of the people who work for me for years. They are all good people."

Raising an eyebrow, Blake said, "I hope you don't mind me saying, Gabriel, but I've heard that story before. In the end, every organization has grudges and bad apples."

"What are you suggesting, Lieutenant?" he replied flatly.

"I'm guessing your employees must have taken a hit after you started giving away houses," Blake said, studying him intently as she waited for a response. "It's not exactly great for the business model."

"You guessed wrong," he fired back. "The Hartmann Foundation is funded by my share of the company's profits, along with generous donations from local residents and businesses. No one lost a penny as a result of my decision. Besides, this is the hottest construction market in years. If anybody was that disgruntled, they could get a job elsewhere in a matter of hours."

Blake shifted tack.

"You said the company's partly staffed by veterans. You must have people working for you who deployed to Afghanistan. Is there any possibility that one of them harbors a grudge after the things they saw out there?"

"No," he said bluntly.

"You seem pretty confident about that. I doubt they would come right out and say it in front of the boss. So how can you be sure?"

"We made the decision together," Gabriel explained. "I called an all-hands meeting. I made the proposal to the entire company. Asked for a show of hands. I don't remember a single person being against it."

"Are you sure about that?" Melissa asked.

For just a fraction of an instant, Blake thought she saw a flicker of doubt cross Gabriel's face. By the time she blinked, it was gone.

"Damn sure," he insisted. "Let me tell you, Lieutenant, I'm getting real tired of hearing you question the integrity of my people. Unless you have something more substantial to bring me, I'm going to ask you to leave."

Blake abandoned the line of questioning. It wasn't getting anywhere.

"Mr. Hartmann," she said. "Are you aware that a man was murdered last night?"

He blinked. The surprise on his face indicated that he was not.

"The reason we're here is that we found evidence at the scene that was potentially linked to your business," she said, stretching the truth a little.

"What evidence?"

"I'm not at liberty to disclose that. It might affect an ongoing investigation," she white-lied. "I get it. You trust your people. And you're probably right to. But, Gabriel, a woman's life is on the line here."

She glanced showily at her watch, then looked back into his eyes. "We have about seven hours to save Nina Crawford's life. That's it. Once the clock runs out, she's dead. She has a husband. Two kids. Do you want her life on your conscience?"

"You think this murder is connected with Nina's disappearance?"

"I believe so." Blake nodded. She saw Gabriel wavering and sensed this was the time to strike.

"All I need from you, sir, is a list of your employees and their whereabouts yesterday afternoon. Please. It might help save Nina's life."

31

Blake drummed her fingers anxiously against the surface of one of the desks in the open-plan suite of detectives' offices. A live stream of a national news channel was playing silently on one of the computer monitors. The only subject that any of the anchors were talking about was the impending murder of Nina Crawford.

The message on the chyron at the bottom of the screen, *HOPE FADES*, was doing nothing to improve her mood. But it wasn't like she was in a position to deny the truth of it. Even she was beginning to give up hope.

Almost two hours had passed since their visit to Gabriel Hartmann. After returning to the station, they'd spent the intervening time going over the case file in microscopic detail, hoping to find something they'd missed on the first go-around. After over an hour of poring over the already-thick ring-binder, Blake had turned her attention to the Yates and Sanders cases.

"Let's go over what we know again," she said, pushing her keyboard aside. She closed her eyelids and massaged them, fruitlessly fighting against a budding migraine.

"Austin Crawford was at home when Dwaine Hilton was

murdered. The officer in the cruiser outside his house saw him taking out the trash at 9:15 p.m. That doesn't leave enough time to get to Hilton's residence and back. So he's clean."

"And Aaron Weller can't be our suspect either," Melissa said, looking up. "Security camera footage places him outside the station at about the same time."

"He was wearing the same clothes when he turned up at the crime scene, too," Blake said, thinking out loud. "If he was Hilton's killer, he would have been soaked in blood. That was a messy way to kill a man."

"Our only other suspect was Hilton himself," Melissa said. "But since I'm pretty sure he wasn't the one to hack off his own head and then daub a terrorist message on his living room wall, we'll have to rule him out."

Blake snorted darkly.

"He was involved, somehow," she said. "Unless the FBI are right. Maybe we've been wrong this whole time. Maybe there really is an ISIS cell running around Northern Pines."

"I don't buy it," Melissa said. "The task force hasn't picked up any chatter on transnational forums or on the dark web. None of the usual suspects have claimed credit. And every single terrorist suspect the Bureau generated a couple of days back had an alibi for either Piper's disappearance or Nina's. Mostly both."

"Then we're missing something. Follow up with Hartmann Construction again," she said, frustration evident in her tone. She pushed her keyboard aside. "We need that list."

"On it," Melissa replied. "Wait, I just got an email from Gabriel's operations manager. It's here."

"What took so damn long?" Blake grumbled. "Okay, forward it to me. Two sets of eyes have to be better than one."

Blake waited expectantly for the Excel file to drop into her email inbox. The moment it arrived, she double-clicked it. The problem with the list of Hartmann Construction employees, contractors, and their whereabouts became apparent within moments.

"They punch out at 6 p.m.," Melissa said, apparently coming to the same conclusion. "Dammit."

The list itself was extremely detailed. Over two hundred different names reflected back off Blake's eyeballs as she scrolled down the page. They came complete with the worksite to which that individual was assigned, the time they'd signed in, and the time they'd signed out. Gabriel Hartmann's operations manager had at least done a thorough job.

Unable to resist glancing at the news feed on the desk opposite, Blake grimaced as she saw that it was almost 9 a.m. It was now possible to count the remaining hours of Nina's life on one hand.

"At least we found our haystack," she said, attempting to sound optimistic.

"But we don't even know if our suspect is in it."

"No, we don't," Blake agreed. "But we have to try. You take the top, I'll go up from the bottom. Check the criminal records for every single name on that list."

"On it."

Blake blinked as another thought occurred to her. "Google them, too."

"What am I looking for?"

"Whether they ever lived in Greenville, Aden, or Bethel. Or studied at ECU."

Melissa nodded.

Both women turned their attention back to their respective computers. The work itself was dull, repetitive, and yet required extreme, unbroken focus. In short, it was like most police work.

On her first pass, Blake immediately discounted every female name. Unfortunately, since it was a construction company, that only knocked five individuals out of her half of the list, leaving a little over a hundred remaining.

Jake Moretti. No criminal record. Didn't study at ECU. Next.

Blake closed her eyes for a second. A muscle just underneath her left eyelid was twitching from the strain of staring at the computer screen. She was startled when Melissa spoke.

"Who's JH?" her partner said.

"Huh?"

"Halfway through the list. Cell, um, A57. You see it? Weird, right?"

Blake highlighted the name she was looking into so that she didn't lose her place, then scrolled back up the Excel file. She saw the cell that Melissa was referencing instantly. The entire row looked out of place.

"Unassigned?" she muttered.

"Right?" Melissa said. "He's the only person on this entire list who doesn't have a specific worksite assigned to him."

"And no punch in/out times, either," Blake said. "Weird."

A neuron fired somewhere in her brain, but the signal was fuzzy and indistinct. JH. Why did that ring a bell?

"Could be he's out sick," Melissa suggested. "Or maybe it's just a data entry error? Shall I ask the operations manager?"

"Can't hurt." Blake shrugged. She winced as the action sent a spike of pain surging through her skull. She turned her attention to her desk, hoping a pack of Advil would miraculously appear in front of her.

Instead, her cell phone vibrated. Her head slumped forward. She was running on fumes, her body hacking and coughing as it struggled to make it through the day. She reached for it anyway, narrowing her gaze as she looked at the screen.

Isn't that Aaron Weller's number?

Blake's finger hovered over the screen. She didn't have time to fob off the journalist's current request for information. Not right now. She tapped the red button, though there was a part of her that respected his persistence—especially after the raking-over she'd given him the previous night.

Seconds later, the phone vibrated a second time. Any lingering respect dissipated in an instant as Blake snatched up the device and answered the call.

"Aaron, fuck off," she snapped, drawing a surprised glance from Melissa, who had her own phone pressed to her ear. "I don't have time to deal with you right now."

There was a moment's silence, then, "What? No, this is Gabriel Hartmann."

Blake barely had time to register the shakiness in his tone, so unlike the firm confidence she'd detected earlier, before a wave of embarrassment collided with her. She closed her eyes, feeling like she should clap her head in her hands.

"I'm sorry, Mr. Hartmann—"

"Lieutenant, I—somebody has my wife."

"Say that again," she said, not fully registering the import of his statement. "Somebody what?"

"I don't know. Shit. I was on the phone with Lara when she screamed. There was somebody in the house. I tried to call back, but it was too late. And I can't connect to the cameras, either. I'm blind!"

"Did you call 911?" Blake asked, her headache instantly disappearing as fresh adrenaline amped up her system.

"What? No. I called you first."

"Where are you, Mr. Hartmann?"

"At work. I'm getting into my car now. I have to—"

"Stay where you are," Blake said firmly, rising from her desk and reaching for her gun. "We're on our way, sir."

"She's my wife! I have to be there!"

"You'll get in the way," Blake said bluntly. "If you want to keep your wife alive, stay where you are. Can you think of any other details that might help us?"

"No, that's everything I know."

"I have to go, sir."

Blake killed the call and looked up at Melissa as she slid her service weapon into its holster. She was so amped up by the news that she almost didn't notice the strange expression on her partner's face.

"What is it?"

"JH," Melissa said. "It stands for Josh Hartmann."

The neuron that had fired in Blake's brain a few moments earlier exploded with intensity. She sat down with a bump, snatching for the keyboard. She pulled up a search window and typed in *"Josh Hart-mann, Aaron Weller."*

The page hung for a moment before a list of blue links populated on screen. The second led to Aaron Weller's Facebook profile. But that wasn't the one that attracted Blake's attention.

She clicked on a link to an archived story on the East Carolinian student newspaper's website. She remembered reading it a couple of days earlier, shortly after Nina Crawford had disappeared.

Blake scan-read the entire story in a matter of seconds, frowning when she didn't find what she was looking for. She was about to click away from the story, figuring she'd mis-remembered, when her eyes passed over the image on the page. It was a nighttime shot of a memorial made up of candles and flowers in the background, with the backs of a man and a woman in the foreground.

But it was the caption that caught her attention.

"ECU students Amber Whitmore and Josh Hartmann pay their respects."

A sensation of dread gripped Blake's stomach as she tore her attention from the screen. As she met Melissa's gaze, she mumbled, "It's him."

32

Blake rocketed round the corner. They were now less than a mile from Hartmann's property. Probably less. She stepped on the accelerator, feeling her chest compress from the force as the cruiser leaped ahead.

Perhaps it didn't matter. Already almost every sheriff's deputy, police officer, SBI, FBI, ATF, and homeland security agent, along with God only knew what other components of the alphabet soup, was heading flat-out to the Hartmann residence. It was unlikely that they would be first to arrive.

But Blake had wanted to try. *Needed* to try. To somehow expunge from her soul the stain of failure for not figuring it out all this time.

As the nose of the vehicle rounded the final corner before the Hartmann residence, she was surprised not to see any other law enforcement vehicles. No other vehicles at all, in fact, though an orchestra of sirens was audible in the distance.

"Unit 19 is on scene," Melissa reported over the radio as Blake screeched the car to a halt not far from the main gate. It opened with agonizing slowness. "Entering the property now."

The instant the gate was open wide enough for the unmarked cruiser to squeeze through, Blake gunned the engine again. A metallic screech sounded as the iron gate tore the paintwork off both doors, but she ignored it as she accelerated up the hill that led to the mansion itself. Fifteen seconds later, with her heart pounding and breath ragged, she braked hard and stopped in front of the main entrance.

Both detectives jumped out of the vehicle. Blake went straight for the trunk, popping it open and retrieving the rifle inside, along with several magazines of ammunition, which she stuffed into every free pocket. The weight of the long gun felt reassuringly familiar. The Army had taught her to fire one that wasn't much different from the one she now held.

And after spending a month refreshing her skills at the range, she knew she was damn good at it.

"Let's go," Blake hissed, flicking off the safety and bringing the weapon up. She swept it left and right across the front of Hartmann's mansion, only sparing half a second for each of the many windows. It was a Herculean task. A shooter could be hiding behind any one of them.

The two women ran in a low crouch toward the front door. Blake kept the rifle high and ready to cover Melissa as her partner tried the handle. It was unlocked and swung open easily.

A crunch underneath Blake's soles caught her attention. She looked down to see that she was stepping on large shards of broken glass. Narrowing her eyes, she glanced around to see where they had come from. The window just to the left of the front door was shattered, creating a hole large enough to fit a man's torso through. She wondered if it was how the intruder had gained access to the house. Something didn't feel right about it, but she pushed the thought out of her mind. She needed to focus.

"Sheriff's Department!" Melissa yelled. "We're entering the property. Mrs. Hartmann, Lara, are you in there?"

Blake listened for a response with every fiber of her being, gritting her teeth with frustration as the howl of police sirens began to increase in intensity in the distance. It sounded like thousands of cops would soon swarm on the property. This was about to be a very dangerous place to be for their killer.

And us, she realized.

There would be a lot of trigger-happy cops on-scene any moment now, fired up and raring to shoot themselves a terrorist. She offered up a prayer that dispatch had successfully informed all the various police departments and federal agencies now converging at this location that friendlies were inside. It was one hell of a game of Chinese whispers.

Melissa looked back at Blake and shook her head. She mouthed, *Nothing*.

Blake nodded. She jabbed a thumb at her own chest to indicate that she would be the first through the door. She sucked in a deep lungful of oxygen to steady herself, nestled the butt of the rifle in the crook of her shoulder, then pressed herself flat against the left-hand side of the door frame. Melissa was opposite her.

"Three…" she whispered.

"Two."

As she said, "One," Blake pivoted around the doorframe, immediately bringing the barrel of her rifle up and sweeping it across the mansion's vast entrance lobby. Despite the somewhat old-fashioned style of the exterior of the property, the interior was light and modern. The space was filled with a large coffee table, weighed down by heavy, no doubt expensive books of photography.

The coffee table was bracketed on either side by a pair of dark gray couches. Behind the furniture, at the corners of the back of the large room, were two doorways leading out into the remainder of the house. Both doors were ajar, but neither was fully open.

Blake grimaced. This place was massive, and if the outside was anything to go by, it was probably a maze inside. She regretted not asking Hartmann for a basic layout of the interior.

She gestured silently at the left-hand doorway, picking it for no other reason than she had to make a choice. The two women moved quickly through the room, Melissa covering her six as Blake led.

Hearing a sound behind her, Blake froze. She glanced back to see

Melissa gesturing at the cream-painted wall to her left. A smudge of blood at about shoulder height. It was about the size of a man's hand.

Is it Lara's?

There was only one way to find out. Blake covered the door as Melissa reached out and pulled the handle back. It swung open, and they stepped through, into another large sitting room. This one was homier, with shelves around the walls that were neatly, almost sparsely filled with framed photographs and other mementos. Unlike the couches in the entrance lobby, the ones here—even larger—at least had depressions in them that looked like they had been carved by human features.

The carpet in here was pale. There was another stain of blood on it, in fact a trail of footprints. Again, they looked more like smudges than splashes, as if whoever left them had stepped in a pool of blood and then tracked it through the house.

As they crouch-stepped through the living room, Blake glanced at the photos out of the corner of her eyes. She caught glimpses of Gabriel Hartmann and a much younger-looking blond woman, probably taken on vacation somewhere. It was sunny in the background, and both looked tanned and relaxed.

Lara?

And then they were gone. As the sirens grew louder in the background, Blake and Melissa stepped into a large open kitchen. Another crunch underfoot.

Blake looked down and saw she was stepping on smashed porcelain. She froze and held up a clenched fist. Melissa followed her lead. The two women scanned the vast, marble-topped space. It was open and modern, and there was nowhere to hide.

But something had happened here, nonetheless.

Two internal doors led out from the kitchen, along with a large set of glass sliding doors that fed onto a large, neatly maintained yard. As far as Blake could tell, no one was out back. She and Melissa each covered a different doorway as they drank in the details of the scene.

A barstool was pulled a couple of feet away from a kitchen island. A couple bottles of condiments—mustard and ketchup—sat on the marble countertop, along with several plastic take-out boxes. A set of cutlery was also laid out, slightly askew.

Blake guessed that the smashed porcelain was a dinner plate. Someone, presumably Lara, had been eating here when the intruder entered. Before the line went dead, she'd told her husband over the phone that she'd seen someone inside the house. The plate must have smashed either as she tried to make a getaway or as she was being chased. One of the shards was covered in still-glistening blood, where it must have cut her.

Only one of the interior doors was open. It was on the opposite side of the kitchen. Blake gestured at it with two fingers. As they passed the other doorway, the two women stopped to clear it. Blake's finger caressed the trigger as Melissa pulled back on the door handle and opened it up.

"Clear," she hissed a second later. It was a large, well-stocked pantry with heaving shelves around the walls that contained every manner of food from seemingly every corner of the known universe.

But there was nowhere inside for a person to hide.

As one, they spun back toward the other, open doorway. Despite their best efforts, the smashed plate crunched underfoot as they moved. They stepped through, and a staircase opened up in front of them.

Melissa gestured at the wall leading up and murmured, "More blood."

The longer the search went on, the more Blake's heart was hammering in her chest. She was soaked in adrenaline, her nerves jangling with every innocent creak made by the house and every tiny scrape and sound as they moved through it.

Another doorway past the staircase led farther into the first floor of the house. But the blood led upstairs. Lara must have sprinted for the stairs.

She pointed up. Melissa nodded.

Blake gritted her teeth. Her breath was coming in sharp, uneven gasps. She knew that staircases were kill zones in a house clearance.

If someone was at the top, they had the high ground. Better shooting angles. They could see you before you saw them.

But there was no choice.

She took the first step, sweeping the rifle left and right in search of targets. Nothing. As they reached the top, Blake could only hear an all-encompassing, stifling quiet. It compressed her lungs and deadened her senses. She felt barely able to breathe.

It was another letdown. Nobody was waiting for them.

They followed the trail of blood to the master bedroom. Here, the smudges were smaller and less frequent. It didn't make any sense. If Lara Hartmann was dead in there, perhaps decapitated like all the other victims, then it would have been bathed in blood. The killer couldn't possibly have done it cleanly. Not on this compressed timetable. Less than fifteen or twenty minutes had passed since Gabriel Hartmann had first spoken to his wife.

Blake and Melissa formed up just ahead of the door into the master bedroom. They didn't wait. Blake surged around the frame, bringing the rifle up, preparing to fire.

But nobody was inside. The door to what looked like a large walk-in closet swung wide open. Behind it was a much larger, thick steel vault door. A panic room, Blake quickly grasped. It was a few inches ajar and was making a quiet beeping sound, perhaps protesting that it was unlocked.

Lara had made it to the threshold of safety. But she had been too late to get inside. Now she was gone. Blake tipped her head back, a wave of frustration coursing out of her. As she looked up, she saw that a security camera was installed directly overhead, looking down.

Amid the darkness pressing in all around her, she felt a flicker of hope. Perhaps they would finally get a glimpse of the individual they had been chasing all this time, even before they knew who they were looking for. Find out for certain whether Josh Hartmann was behind the kidnappings and murders that had torn a town apart.

But one question was foremost in Blake's mind.

Why?

33

"Let him through," Blake called out as she ran through the quickly growing thicket of cop cars now sprouting outside Gabriel Hartmann's home. She ducked underneath a line of police tape that had somehow already been stretched between two trees on either side of the road.

When the cop at the gate didn't respond, Blake bared her teeth and yelled, "I said let him through, dammit!"

"What is it?" Hartmann said as he approached, his footsteps now leaden. His face was pale, and he looked like he was going into shock. "Nobody will tell me what's going on."

"Gabriel, Lara may be alive," Blake said. Instantly she saw a flare of hope in his eyes. "But I need your help to keep her that way."

"Is she hurt?"

"She's missing. She didn't make it into the panic room in time."

"You need to find her! My God. Did the terrorists do this?"

"Gabriel, focus," she said, not yet willing to deliver the blow that their prime suspect was his son. "You have a security system installed in your house, correct?"

He nodded. "Cameras in most rooms. Not the bathrooms, obvi-

ously, or the guest bedrooms. But everywhere else. The insurance
company demanded it."

"How do I see the footage?"

Hartmann blinked but quickly pulled himself back. "It's online.
There's a portal. I couldn't access it before."

"Show me."

He reached into his suit jacket pocket and pulled out his cell
phone. He held it in front of his face and then navigated through a
series of screens on his phone. He was about to turn the phone
around to show the two detectives when his face screwed up in confusion. "What the hell?"

"What is it?"

"It's gone."

"What do you mean?"

"I can't find any footage from the last twenty-four hours."

"How is that possible?"

Hartmann made a guttural, keening sound and sank onto his
haunches. The phone fell limply to his side. "Lara knows the code,"
he whispered.

"Is there any way of retrieving the footage?"

"I don't know. I..."

"I'll call digital forensics," Melissa said, pulling out her own cell
phone and stepping away.

Blake nodded. She closed her eyes and massaged her temple with
her free hand. She felt her earlier migraine returning with full force.
She was sick of butting into closed doors, of lines of investigation
closing all around her.

What the hell did Lara Hartmann have to do with any of this?
Why had Josh Hartmann taken her?

She let out a short, sharp breath, then pushed away her frustration. It wasn't productive. The last few hours of Nina Crawford's life
were ticking away as they stood there. Now perhaps Lara would join
her. Blake couldn't stop searching. Not until it was over.

"Tell me about your wife, Gabriel," she said.

He was crying now, thick, heavy tears sliding down his face as his body sobbed silently.

"Gabriel, stay with me," she said, squatting down in front of him and reaching out to grab his shoulder. She squeezed hard, hard enough that his expression registered a wince of pain. But she had to cut through.

"What about Lara?"

"Is she the woman I saw in your photos? She's blond and..." Blake trailed off, feeling a pang of awkwardness as she broached the topic. It was ridiculous, given the gravity of the situation, but she was relieved anyway when Hartmann took up the baton.

"Younger, I know," he said. He blinked rapidly several times in succession. "I didn't—it was never my intention. I know how it sounds, a wealthy guy with two previous marriages. It's a cliché. But Lara is never embarrassed by it. By us. I wish I could say the same about myself."

"Walk with me," Blake said, ushering him toward the mansion. It was a crime scene, but right now, there were more important considerations than preserving the scene. Their killer was clearly escalating. Nina's deadline was drawing to a close, Dwaine Hilton lay dead in a pool of blood, and now this man's wife was missing—his own son the likely culprit.

Blake frowned as an image of Nina crossed her mind, the same one she saw every time she closed her eyes. She'd only caught a passing glimpse of Lara Hartmann in a framed picture, but the woman bore a resemblance to Nina, didn't she? Young, pretty, blond.

Piper was all of those things, too...

Was it a coincidence? Maybe. But their suspect had killed Dwaine immediately. The only victims he'd kept alive fit those three categories. All three women kidnapped.

"You have to tell me," Hartmann said, stopping and gripping Blake's arm. "Does this have something to do with Nina's kidnapping? I can handle it. Please just tell me."

Blake didn't pull her arm away from his grip, though she frowned as she thought over his statement. He hadn't used Nina's full name.

Nor had he done so when they'd interviewed him earlier that morning. If anything, he'd said it with a measure of familiarity.

"Do you know Nina Crawford?"

"Of course," he said as though it was the most obvious thing in the world. "Not well, but she's how I met my wife."

"What?" Blake asked sharply.

Hartmann's hand dropped away from her side as though he'd touched a hot pan. An ashen look crossed his face, and he began to stammer. "I should've told you. I didn't know it was relevant."

"Stay with me, Gabriel," Blake said calmly. She couldn't have him giving way to shock now. "Take me right back to the start. Tell me everything."

"I'm a philanthropist, I suppose. You know, the Hartmann Foundation. But for years, it was more of a tax consideration. When you're a man of my means in a town this small, it's just part of the deal."

Blake didn't want him to go *right* back to the start, but she dared not interrupt now.

"So I've bumped elbows with pretty much everyone who's involved in charity around here. Nina volunteers with an informal network of Gold Star wives and families. Just helping out. Doing whatever needs doing. We met at cocktail parties more than once over the years. She always asked for a big donation. I obliged. With a smaller one."

Gold Star wives were widows of military service personnel lost at war, Blake knew. She had no idea where he was going with this, though.

"Lara lost her first husband five years ago. They were high school sweethearts. She wanted to honor his memory by getting his translator a place to live. Somehow she met Nina, and Nina introduced her to me."

"So you built the guy a house?" Blake interjected, her eyebrow raised.

"Lara's persuasive," he snorted, momentarily appearing to forget that she was missing. His expression dropped, and he met her gaze once again. "You'll see."

"I'm sure I will."

"She bugged me for months about that damn house. This was before the fall of Kabul, about a year earlier. Finally, I cracked and went to dinner with her. A year later, we were married, and somehow my foundation wasn't just a tax write-off anymore."

Blake's brow furrowed. It was a great story and filled in a number of gaps in her knowledge, but she didn't see how it was connected.

"What about Austin Crawford?" she asked. "Nina's husband."

"He's been a friend of my son Josh's for years, though I never had time to really meet him. I regret that now. That cocktail party was the first night we ever actually spoke. The photographer took a shot of us five. Somehow, Lara tracked it down and had it printed and framed."

Blake's eyes widened, though she attempted to conceal her interest. "Can you show me?"

Hartmann looked doubtfully at the police officer guarding the front entrance to his house. "If you can get me inside."

Blake did just that, ignoring the protest of the cop guarding the crime scene. This was more important. Her subconscious was throwing out theories. Perhaps Austin was connected with this after all. Could he have been sleeping with Lara, along with Piper, and of course his wife?

She stopped dead in the entrance lobby, ignoring Hartmann's curious look, and reached for her radio handset and cranked up the volume. "Dispatch, this is Larsen."

A couple of seconds passed before a crackly voice replied, "Go ahead, Lieutenant."

"Do we still have a car sitting on Austin Crawford's house?"

"Sure do."

"I need a door knock. Right away."

"Hold please."

Blake waited what felt like an interminable length of time as the call went out over the radio. The cop in the cruiser sitting outside Crawford's house reported first that his car was still sitting in his driveway. She insisted that they get firsthand evidence that he was actually inside.

"Dispatch, this is Madison," the cop's voice said over the radio. "The, ah, subject is no longer in his residence. Say again, the subject is no longer in his residence."

"Madison, give me a play-by-play of exactly what happened," Blake said urgently. "When did you last see the subject?"

"An hour ago," the cop replied hesitantly. "Two at most. His mom came to pick up the kids. Then a friend stopped by for, I don't know, five minutes? I watched Crawford close his front door after the guy left."

Blake's eyes widened. "What friend?"

"I noted down the license plate," he replied. "Running it now. But like I said, the guy didn't stay long, and he drove off alone. Both the Crawfords' vehicles are still in their driveway. He can't have gotten far."

"Get me that name, Madison," Blake said. Somehow Austin Crawford had given his minders the slip. And she had a strong suspicion that he'd had help."

"The vehicle is registered to a, uh... Aaron Weller."

"Fuck," Blake swore as her mind cast about wildly for an explanation as to how all this fit together. Were Aaron, Austin, and Josh all working together? How could such a conspiracy possibly come about? "Dispatch, I need all units looking for the pair of them. They are our highest priority."

Feeling Hartmann's gaze on her, Blake pulled herself together.

"You think Austin has something to do with my wife's disappearance?" he asked, his lips tightening.

"Show me the photo, please," Blake said simply.

Hartmann led her silently into the living room. He paused in the entranceway, as if to remember where to locate the photo, then continued to a sideboard on the far wall. A vase filled with fresh flowers sat on top, bookended by several photo frames. He stopped in front of it, and his gaze flicked from side to side before he reached out and picked up one of the images on the left.

"Here," he said, glancing at it quickly before handing it to her.

Blake had to resist the urge to snatch it from his grasp. She peered at the group in the photograph, all dressed to impress. The men wore sleek tuxes, the women party attire. Her gaze first flicked to the woman who could only be Lara. She was wearing a figure-hugging shimmery gold dress. It wasn't Blake's style, but she looked good in it.

The other woman Blake knew well, if only by sight. Nina Crawford. She looked calm and relaxed, her eyes staring right into the camera lens. She was arm in arm with her husband. Nothing about either of their postures indicated that anything was off. They looked happy.

Blake's gaze swept past Hartmann. He was standing to the right-hand side of the photo, his left arm tucked flat against his side, as if he subconsciously dared not risk it brushing up against Lara. She wondered if he'd known that he was attracted to her then.

To Hartmann's right was another man. Someone Blake had now come across several times, even if she'd been too dense to realize his importance. A memory of the first time she'd caught sight of Hartmann's son—behind the wheel of his work truck when he'd swung by the Crawford residence to pick up Austin—flitted across her mind's eye. Then the next time, when he'd visited the station after Austin's interview.

She'd thought he was just protecting his friend. But now she suspected his overt interest in the case sprang from a far more personal source.

"Who's that?" she asked in a casual tone, tapping the familiar figure.

"Huh?" he grunted. "Oh, that's my son, Josh."

Blake blinked as another thought occurred to her. When she and Melissa had first entered the Hartmann residence, she'd stepped on broken glass. But it was on the outside of the porch, not inside the house—as if the window had been smashed from the inside. Perhaps it was an afterthought, designed to make Lara's kidnapping look more realistic. Just poorly executed.

She strained to keep her tone casual. "Does he live with you?"

"In the pool house. It's on the other side of the property. He moved there a couple of years ago, after I married Lara. We had a disagreement, but we're working through it."

"Does he know the code to the security system?"

"Of course. He—" Hartmann said before falling silent. His gaze snapped up to meet Blake's once more, eyes wide. "What are you saying?"

Blake stared back at him without blinking. "Gabriel, does Josh have any reason to wish harm to your wife?"

34

Hartmann shook his head. "No, no he wouldn't. He couldn't."

But Blake sensed something in the man's tone that indicated he wasn't so sure. She twisted the knife, probing, hating the hurt on his face but knowing she had no other choice. "Gabriel, Lara's life depends on this. And if your son is mixed up in something, the best way to get him help is to tell me everything. I can help you. And him."

Once again, Hartmann appeared unsteady on his feet. He swayed as if struggling to process this fresh blow, coming after all the others. He reached out and gripped the sideboard for support.

"He wouldn't," he repeated as much to himself as for Blake's benefit.

"This morning you told me that you'd ruined your relationship with your son. What did you mean?"

She saw his knuckles turn white. But he seemed to steady himself.

"We argued," he finally said.

"About what?"

"The foundation. Most recently, anyway."

"What about it?"

"Josh had troubles after college holding down a job. He tried everything under the sun. Even set up a paintball field. But nothing worked out. Eventually I offered him an opportunity in my company. Working with his hands. Figured the structure and routine might help make something of himself. Not everyone's suited to a desk job."

"Did it?"

Hartmann shrugged helplessly. "He's past thirty, and he still lives at home."

"How long's he been working for you?"

"The past six years. Seven, maybe. I guess at some point, he figured he would inherit the company. We never spoke about it. I certainly never promised him anything like that."

"You said he went to college. Where did he go?"

"ECU. In Greenville."

"And then you started giving away your money. Building houses for the refugees. Is it possible that he saw this as you wasting his inheritance?"

"I know he did. He screamed that at me, in front of Lara. We didn't speak for a month. A few weeks back, he apologized. Seemed to understand that he was in the wrong."

He trailed off. Blake took in his pale, sightless expression and hoped like hell that her suspicion was wrong. If it wasn't, then this man might have lost a wife and a son in the blink of an eye.

But though she didn't yet see the full picture, there were enough pointers to indicate she was on the right track. Josh and Austin were friends. They went way back. Josh knew Austin's wife. Perhaps at some point, he had met Piper, too. Or Austin had told him about her. Either way, it didn't matter.

She frowned as another thought occurred to her. *Does—did—Josh know Dwaine?*

Blake still didn't understand how he fit into the picture. Or what role Aaron played in all this. But figuring out the precise details of how this all fit together could wait. Nina's time was almost up.

"Gabriel, we need to track down your son. Do you have any idea where we might find him?"

Hartmann's eyes closed, and he brought his open palms up to his face. He rubbed them against his cheeks while wearing an expression of anguish underneath. He looked like he might be having a nervous breakdown.

"Gabriel, this is urgent. Lara—"

"Just wait!" he snapped.

His hand formed a fist, and he smashed it hard against the sideboard, causing the vase to topple and shatter against the ground. Glass scattered everywhere, followed by a wave of liquid as the water inside washed outward. The flowers lay limp and flat on the ground.

The moment of silence that followed probably only lasted a couple of seconds, but it felt much longer. In that time, he made his decision.

"If my son has got a hand in this, I won't defend him," Hartmann said coldly. "I've tried with that boy. I've given him everything."

Blake just nodded, not knowing the kind of pain he must be feeling. Not wanting to know.

He beckoned at her. "Come with me."

He led her through the house into a room that must have been his home office. Blake wanted to radio dispatch and put an APB out on Josh Hartmann but didn't dare break the spell, just in case Gabriel reconsidered turning in his son.

"Sir, we don't have long..."

Hartmann sat down in front of a sleek aluminum and glass computer. He leveled his gaze at her. "Promise me you'll give him the opportunity to come in peacefully. This might all be some horrible misunderstanding. I can't have his death on my conscience. Not if he has nothing to do with this."

"I will. I swear."

"I hope so," he said before his fingers raced across the keyboard. Blake walked around to the side of the desk so she could see what was happening on screen.

"I lease all the company's vehicles from the same dealership," he explained as he opened a web browser and typed in a URL. "Work trucks and my personal vehicle. Same for Josh. They all have a GPS tracker installed for insurance purposes."

"You can see where they are?"

"I can," he confirmed as he logged into an online portal. He scrolled down the list, then selected an entry labelled *Josh Hartmann*. Double-clicking on it opened up another screen with icons for two different vehicles: a white work truck and a black Mercedes SUV.

Blake's mouth fell open at the sight of the first. All this time, she'd assumed deep down that Dwaine Hilton was responsible—directly or otherwise—for burning Abdul-Malik Azizi's home. But what if she'd gotten everything wrong? What if *Josh* was the one responsible?

"Gabriel, has your son ever expressed any racist sentiments?" she asked. "Something more than his displeasure at your plans for your wealth."

He looked up. "How did you know?"

"I didn't," Blake replied softly, replaying in her mind the memory of hurtling around that corner on her way to Azizi's address and passing what in hindsight was clearly a speeding white work truck just like the one Josh Hartmann drove.

He shot her a strange look but returned his gaze to the computer. "His truck is... at the office. He probably parked it there. He usually drives his Mercedes in."

"Where's that?"

Hartmann clicked on the icon of the black SUV. The screen hung for a second before a map flashed up. He frowned and muttered, "Huh?"

"What?"

"Looks like he's at the Waterford site. But that makes no sense."

"Why not?"

"I bought the land two years ago. We broke ground, put up the shell of the building. Then some environmentalists discovered a rare frog or something. The project's been held up in a bureaucratic nightmare of permitting approvals ever since."

"Show me," Blake said, leaning forward and feeling her pulse race.

The map was set to a satellite overview. The images had been taken on a sunny day. She watched as Hartmann zoomed in on an isolated location surrounded by trees. A line on the ground indicated a shadow thrown by a section of fencing that surrounded the entire site. It was several acres in total. And half a mile away from the next nearest building.

In short, it was the perfect place to stash a kidnap victim.

Blake knew this was it. It had to be. She reached for the radio handset clipped to her belt, then pulled her fingers away.

"Can you access his historical location data?"

"Sure," he said slowly. He jerked the mouse slightly to the right, then the left, as if he wasn't exactly certain how. Blake figured he probably didn't spend much of his life tracking his employees' precise locations. "Wait, here."

He clicked an option on a drop-down at the top of the screen and pulled up a list of different journeys taken by Josh's Mercedes.

Both he and Blake fell silent as he scrolled through it. His visits to the construction site began several weeks ago, then ceased for about ten days. The next occasion was the day before Piper Hicks went missing. Then before her body was found. They lined up with Nina's disappearance, too.

And now Lara's kidnapping.

Pulling out a notepad, Blake scribbled down the address of the construction site. Eyeballing the location, she guessed it was about a twenty-minute drive away.

"He did this, didn't he?" Hartmann said, slumping back against his chair, his voice strangled.

Blake didn't reply. What could she say? The entire state—probably half the country—had been following Nina Crawford's disappearance and the subsequent apparent terrorist deadline. Gabriel Hartmann would have known when Piper and Nina had disappeared, just as she did.

As she turned to leave, she felt his hand grip her arm. He fixed her with an intense, powerful stare. She found she couldn't tear away.

"Bring my wife home safe," he whispered. "Please."

Blake tore herself away without saying a word. She couldn't promise something she didn't know she could deliver.

She glanced at her watch again, her mind ablaze with theories. Had Lara's kidnapping been part of Josh's plan right from the start? Had he always intended to snatch her at this time and perhaps use the attention on his execution of Nina to cover up another, different crime: removing the threat to his inheritance?

After all, Lara had been the driver of Gabriel Hartmann's decision to donate all his time and money to his foundation.

With her out of the way, she guessed the intention was for the money to find its way to Josh, perhaps after Gabriel himself became yet another victim of his son's madness.

"Shit," she muttered under her breath.

She knew she had to call in the FBI. Monroe County didn't have the resources to deal with a takedown like this. They would need to get reconnaissance units on scene in the next few minutes to get a sense of what kind of tactical situation they were dealing with. The county had its own SWAT team, but it would take them more time than either Nina or Lara had left just to suit up, let alone arrive on scene.

And she had no doubt that the Bureau's Hostage Rescue Team, which had been on standby the past few days, was both better trained and equipped. They were the best of the best.

But still, calling them in was putting the two women's lives on the line. With this little time to plan an operation to rescue them, whatever happened had the potential to turn into a crapshoot.

"It's not like you have any other choice," she said as she reached into her pocket to pull out her cell phone.

Half a dozen missed calls flashed up on the screen, all from within the last half hour. They were all from the same number. It rang again just as she brought it up in front of her. This time, though, Blake's eyes widened as she stabbed the answer button.

"Detective?" a muffled voice whispered. "Can you hear me? God, please..."

"Aaron?"

"Thank God," Aaron Weller whispered. He sounded nothing like the confident reporter she'd met previously. He was terrified. "My signal isn't—"

The line crackled. Blake lost the next few words to the ether. She made a fist, her nails biting into the fleshy part of her palm.

"Aaron? I didn't hear that. What's going on?"

The line solidified once more. "It's Josh, Josh Hartmann. He's lost his mind. He's the one who kidnapped Nina. Now he's got Austin. And he's going to kill Lara, too..."

Aaron trailed away.

"Where are you?" Blake asked urgently.

He didn't answer the question, gasping instead as he moaned, "I figured it out after seeing you last night. Most of it, anyway. He's been playing me for days. I thought he was asking about the case for Austin's benefit. But he was just using me to keep tabs on your investigation."

"Who has, Aaron?" Blake asked.

"Josh! We went to college together. We were friends. He always had this thing about women, I guess, but—fuck, I think he fractured my skull." Aaron groaned in pain. It sounded like the adrenaline of successfully placing the phone call was wearing off. "He did it, didn't he? He killed those girls back at college..."

"Stay with me, Aaron," Blake said. "What happened?"

"I went to Austin this morning with my suspicions. We came up with a plan to test Josh. Austin didn't want to go to the cops. Not at first. I got him to meet me. Said I had something important to tell him. That the police had a suspect."

Blake's jaw tightened as she remembered encountering Josh's black SUV on the way out of his father's mansion earlier that morning. He would have realized they were cops. Maybe the subsequent meeting with Aaron had convinced him the game was up. Perhaps they had inadvertently accelerated his timetable.

"He was pissed when I didn't give him a name," Aaron continued, panting heavily. "Drove off in a hurry. We followed him to a construction site. But before he entered, he seemed to change his mind and peeled off in a different direction. We tried to follow, but we lost him. So we turned back to check out the site."

"Are you outside Waterford?" Blake said quickly.

"Yeah, how did you know?"

"No time. Tell me exactly what you saw."

"Not much. Josh hit me in the head with a shovel. I've been drifting in and out for, I don't know how long."

"Where's Austin?"

"I don't know. We just made it over the fence when Josh came back. He had Lara Hartmann with him!"

"We know, Aaron," Blake said soothingly. She saw Melissa reproaching and beckoned her over urgently. "What else can you tell us? Every detail is useful."

He groaned. "I don't know. My head..."

"It's okay, Aaron. We're on our way."

"No, you can't!"

"Why not?"

"The last thing Austin told me was that they're in a shipping container. It's rigged to blow. Josh shot him!"

Blake's voice went up an octave in shock. "Explosives?"

"Yeah," he replied almost silently. "You can't send in SWAT. If you do, they'll all die."

35

"What do we do?" Melissa asked.

The truth was, Blake had no idea. But the question jolted her into action nonetheless. Standing here in an already obsolete crime scene would do nothing to help save three innocent lives.

"Get the FBI on the line," she said, limbering up into a jog and running for the car. Melissa hesitated for a second, then followed. Blake could feel her questioning gaze on the back of her neck. "They need to spool up HRT now."

She took a peek at her wristwatch as she ran, dodging a startled uniformed officer as she did so. Nina Crawford's life was now measured in minutes, not hours. The location where she was being held was at least a fifteen-minute drive away.

The odds were not good.

If Aaron was right and the location where the two women were being held really was rigged to blow, she didn't see how they could possibly both get to the location and defuse the explosives in the time remaining.

Blake found the keys still in the car, though the engine wasn't still running. She pushed the start button and heard it grumble into life.

"What do I tell them?" Melissa asked, her phone pressed to her ear.

"Ask if the HRT squad is air mobile," Blake replied as her partner's door thunked closed. Her teeth ground together as she surveyed the cluster of messily parked cars both in front and behind her. There was no way out. At least, not by sticking to the road.

She put the car into gear and powered up her lights and sirens. After a quick glance into a mirror, she gunned the engine and drove straight onto the lawn, pulling a one-eighty on the grass and speeding back down through the grounds toward the gate. All around, uniformed officers and detectives stared curiously at them.

Blake ignored it all.

"They've got a bird ready to roll at Monroe County Airport," Melissa reported a couple of seconds later. "Where am I telling them to go?"

The entire vehicle rocked as Blake guided it back onto the asphalt. The seat reared up underneath both of them and slammed them in the ass.

Blake needed a few seconds to think. If the Hostage Rescue Team rolled right up to the location in the chopper, Josh Hartmann might blow the shipping container to kingdom come.

"What about the bomb squad?" Blake asked to buy time.

Melissa relayed the question.

"That'll take longer," she replied a moment later. "Nearest one's at Bragg."

"Shit," Blake swore. "Tell them to get suited up and rolling, stat. I know where Nina and Lara are being held. Josh Hartmann's the one who kidnapped them both. But he's got them rigged up with explosives. Aaron's drifting in and out of consciousness, and Austin may or may not be alive."

Melissa blanched but didn't hesitate as she communicated this to the FBI's control center. Blake did the math in her head as she did so. From Bragg to Waterford was a fifteen-minute drive. By the time the bomb squad were suited up, they would barely have a couple of minutes on-scene to forestall disaster—if Josh planned to hew to his original timetable.

She exhaled edgily, meeting Blake's gaze in the rearview mirror. "It's Granger. He says it's your call. He wants to know what to do."

Blake only hesitated for a second. "Get the bomb squad moving. Get HRT in the air but hold the chopper outside of audible range. Don't do anything to spook the perp."

Melissa nodded quickly, phone still pressed to her ear. "What's our plan?"

Before Blake could respond, her own phone rang. She pulled it out of her pocket with her left hand, glancing at the screen briefly before returning her attention to the road. Foliage flashed past on either side, and she was weaving between traffic like a woman possessed. Strangely, her heart was no longer racing. It was as if her body had accepted that this was the new normal.

It was Aaron.

Blake gestured at Melissa to kill the sirens. When her partner did so, she put her own phone on speaker and answered the call.

"Aaron? Are you okay?"

For a moment, she heard only heavy breathing.

"Hello, Lieutenant," Josh Hartmann said slowly.

"Who is this?" Blake asked, playing for time.

"You know."

"Aaron?"

"Don't play games with me, woman," Josh spat down the line. "You know who this is. Don't fuck around. You know what I'm prepared to do."

Blake winced and bit her lip. In just a brief few seconds, Josh's tone had oscillated between eerily calm and viciously angry. She answered calmly, in a steady tone of voice, hoping that it might help modulate his emotions. The last thing she needed was an unstable serial killer with access to a ready supply of both victims and explosives.

Out of the corner of her eye, she saw Melissa move her own phone closer so that the FBI could listen in on the call.

"This is Josh Hartmann, right?" she said softly. "Austin's friend. We met the other day."

"Yeah, and you're the bitch trying to ruin a good man's life," Josh snarled.

"Why do you say that?" Blake asked. The important thing was to keep him talking. She glanced quickly at the speedometer. She was doing over a hundred miles an hour. At this speed, they would arrive at the abandoned construction site inside seven minutes.

Though she still had no idea what she would do when she got there.

"I told you not to play games," he replied, once again turning cold. The shift in his mannerisms sent a shiver up Blake's spine. "It doesn't matter anyway. I should have let you. He's weak. *Worthless*."

"Are you strong, Josh?"

"You know I am," he replied, sounding like a teenager trying to prove their worth. "You've seen what I can do."

The investigator in Blake itched to get Josh to confess to his crimes here and now. The Bureau was doubtless recording every second of this call. But with lives on the line, there were more important things to worry about than a future conviction.

"I'm impressed," she said, taking a leap. In an ideal world, she wouldn't want to get an unstable serial killer talking about his previous kills, not when he was in the position to murder again. But perhaps she could develop a rapport with him. Or at the very least, buy time.

"Impressed," he snorted. "You can't even comprehend what I've done."

"Tell me how this ends, Josh," she replied solicitously, her stomach convulsing with revulsion at having to pander to this man-child's twisted ego. "You must have a plan."

"I did," he said, rage building again. "Until Austin fucked it up. He was supposed to understand. I did this to help him!"

He ended sounding almost hurt by Austin's betrayal. Blake dodged another car up ahead, wishing she was able to envelop her own vehicle in the protective bubble of sirens, rather than just lights. She frowned, trying to think.

What does he mean, help Austin?

She thought quickly. Her current working theory of the case was that Josh had come up with an insane plan to remove—permanently —the obstacles in the way of his inheritance and shift the blame elsewhere.

But maybe she'd been too hasty. Why kidnap and murder his supposed friend's lover—then the same man's wife?

He's just crazy.

Blake pushed the thought aside. Josh was definitely crazy. But something else was at play here as well.

Keep him talking.

She braked as she approached a sharp bend in the road, then accelerated the moment she passed the apex. Her chest constricted from the force of the acceleration. "What didn't he understand, Josh?"

"That bitch was humiliating him," he hissed back. "She was sleeping around. Half the fucking town knew she was whoring herself out."

"You're talking about Nina?"

"Of course! What kind of man lets his wife screw other men? It's a beta thing to do."

The choice of the word 'beta' pushed aside any lingering doubt in Blake's mind that Josh was also responsible for the Yates and Sanders murders. It was a term used in the incel—or involuntarily celibate— community. It was an ideology that combined self-disgust with hatred of women. But incels were more than just a strange curiosity. The loneliness and social isolation of many adherents made them suitable targets for radicalization, just as with Islamic terrorism.

Blake guessed she was now no more than three minutes away. She just had to keep him occupied until then.

"Austin told me that he was in an open relationship. Nina had his permission to sleep with other men."

Not that she needs it, she thought silently. She wasn't pro-adultery.

But she was definitely against the idea that any husband should or could control his wife.

"She manipulated him," Josh replied quickly. "She must have. She messed with his brain."

"What about Piper, Josh? What did she do?"

"That slut?" Josh replied dismissively, as though he barely thought of her. "She disgraced herself. I did the world a favor."

"Did Austin tell you he was sleeping with her?"

"Of course," he replied, almost bragging. "He tells me everything."

Blake thought she understood now. Josh had a sickness of the mind: a barbed self-loathing paired with a hatred of women. She would bet money that if she went back and re-interviewed witnesses in the Yates and Sanders murders, she'd learn that they'd either turned Josh down or been friends with women who did. Years later, he'd seen Austin, a man who he must have believed had everything: a successful career, a family, desirable enough to attract not only a wife, but other women, too.

Then Lara had come into the picture. Perhaps Josh believed that she had corrupted his father, like Nina had apparently done with Austin. Or perhaps he was just angry that his own father could attract a young, desirable woman when he could not.

And finally, he had been faced with the loss of his inheritance.

The precise motivation was irrelevant. Maybe he'd killed again since college. Or maybe he'd lain dormant all this time. Some toxic combination of all the above had pushed him back over the edge. All that mattered was that it had twisted him beyond repair.

Even conversing with a mind this broken filled her with revulsion. But Josh held more innocent lives at risk.

Blake swallowed, knowing she had to tread carefully but also that she was running out of road. She had to make a move, or he would kill again. She quickly weighed up what she knew. Josh wasn't special. He was jealous and insecure, and those personal failings had turned toxic. In that way, he was like many men she had met.

But she could use those emotions against him. Men like him were crying out to be listened to; they just didn't realize they had nothing worth hearing. But if it would save lives, she would listen.

"They deserved it, Josh."

He sounded suspicious. "What? Who did?"

"Mandy and Hannah. They didn't understand you. Not like I will."

"I don't know what you're talking about."

"Of course you do. There's no shame in what you did. No shame in any of it. It's time somebody finally stood up. You were the only one with the balls to do it."

"What are you talking about? Do what?" he said.

She parroted the vitriolic screed he'd written on his blog, years before, hoping that she was right. This was a gamble she could only make once.

"The world is a sick place, Josh," she said. "Men and women have forgotten their rightful places. Men have become weak, lost in video games and porn. Women dress like sluts, giving themselves up for a few cheap likes on Instagram and TikTok. Right?"

As the pause drew out before he replied, she winced, wondering if she'd pushed too quickly. But after several seconds of heavy breathing, he muttered, "Right."

Blake clenched her fist with relief and triumph. "I put it together, Josh. Not many women could, but I did. The world doesn't know how smart you are, but I see you. You're going to go down in the history books. Let me be there by your side."

"What do you mean, you put it together?"

"I know where you are, Josh. I'm coming there now."

"Stay the fuck away," he snarled. "I'll kill all of them."

"Just give me a chance, Josh," Blake said, continuing to chip away at his defenses. "I'll come in alone. Unarmed. You'll see that I'm telling the truth. I know you can read people better than almost anybody else. I can't hide the truth from you."

"I'll know if you're lying," he said.

That's not a no, she thought.

"I know. That's why I trust you, Josh. Because you're smart enough to see through the bullshit."

"Come through the front gate," he said, his tone short. Blake wasn't sure whether or not she'd lost him. "Alone. If you try and screw me, I'll put a bullet through your brain."

The line went dead.

Blake took her foot off the gas. She knew she could only be about thirty seconds out. She was pretty sure that after a bend in the road up ahead, the worksite would come into view. The car began to roll slowly to a halt.

"What the hell are you doing?" Melissa gasped. "You can't go inside. He's unhinged. He'll kill you!"

"Maybe," Blake said, feeling a twinge of uncertainty in her stomach. "But we don't have a choice. He's got four innocent people in there with him. He'll kill all of them if we don't do something."

"Don't get out of that car, Lieutenant," ASAC Granger growled through Melissa's phone. "That's an order."

Blake reached for her belt and unbuckled it.

"Lucky for me, you're not in charge," she said with a false cheerfulness in her tone. "Where's the bomb squad?"

"Sixteen minutes out. Stay the fuck inside your car until they arrive. They'll handle it."

"There's not enough time," Blake replied, glancing at the display behind the steering wheel. "You need eyes inside that compound for them to know what they are dealing with. That's the only way they've got a shot at defusing whatever Hartmann has rigged up on that shipping container."

When only silence answered her, Blake said, "You know I'm right."

"I can't ask you to do this, Larsen," Granger said.

"Good," she replied, reaching for the door handle. "Because you didn't."

36

Blake let out a shaky breath as the walls around the construction site came into view. Despite knowing that dozens of people were probably listening to her words via the cell phone tucked as discreetly as she could manage in the short time available into her bra, she muttered, "Well, this was a stupid idea."

For just a second, she closed her eyes and pictured Piper's final moments. The woman must have known she had no hope of survival. Blake just prayed that her end had come quickly.

"I'll make him pay for what he did to you," she whispered under her breath, this pledge for her ears only.

I promise.

The sound of her footsteps scraped against the road as she walked, making it impossible to hide the fact that she was approaching the compound's front gate. As she got closer to the fence, she saw that there were dozens of chinks of light shining through gaps between the different sections. Josh could and probably was hiding behind one of them, watching her right now.

The thought made her skin crawl.

But Blake did not stop. She didn't even slow. She kept her posture easy and relaxed, knowing that if the twisted killer on the other side of that gate saw her acting any other way, then he would know that she was playing him. And the risk of her gambit was that a character that fragile might explode after such a realization.

Still, her mouth was dry. She grew more apprehensive with every passing step. As she closed within twenty feet, it was all she could do to stop herself from turning and sprinting in the other direction.

"Stop right there!"

The voice came from somewhere to her right. She did as Josh commanded and turned in the direction the sound had come from. She caught a flash of movement before her eyes focused on the end of a rifle barrel poking out through the fence.

"I came, Josh," she called out. "Like I promised I would."

Blake saw the flash of light and smoke erupt out of the barrel of the gun a fraction of a second before the first of the two rounds sparked against a rock a few inches away from her left foot. Or maybe she didn't, and her brain simply filled in the details, knowing from bitter personal experience what she would've seen.

Either way, she jerked away from the gunfire out of instinct, stumbling several unsteady steps backward before she tumbled to the ground. Somehow, she had the presence of mind to hold on to her chest as she fell, knowing it was vital she kept her cell phone in place. If it slipped out, then this was all for nothing.

"I'm okay," she whispered as loudly as she dared without attracting Josh's attention as the ringing of the gunshots died away. "He was just testing me."

"Get up!" Josh yelled, his angry voice carrying in the near-silence that followed. "Walk closer to the fence. Slowly. Count out every step. Move!"

Blake slowly pushed herself to her feet, intentionally facing away from the madman with the gun. She took a second to brush her palms against her jeans to knock off the dirt and tiny stones that had stuck against them in her fall. A little trickle of blood dribbled out of the cut at the base of her left palm, and the burn on her forearm screamed from the impact. She breathed in deeply, then quickly touched the cell phone against her breastbone, probing as if checking for bruises and scrapes. It was still in place. She just prayed the FBI had heard her whispered message.

"Quit messing around!"

She turned back to the fence, raising her palms up in front of her in a calming entreaty. She walked toward the fence, counting out each step as instructed.

When she came within about six feet of it, Josh yelled out again, "Hold right there."

Blake could see his eyes now through the crack in the fence. They were vicious and beady, dark little orbs glinting from within a twisted face.

"Take off your jacket," he said, his voice a bit calmer but no less chilling. "Nice and slow. Don't try anything stupid."

"You don't have to do this, Josh," Blake said as she followed his instructions, casually lifting her hands through the air until they settled on the lapels of her jacket. She shrugged it off and slowly tossed it to the ground. It settled with a whisper, not a thud.

She met his gaze. "See? I'm not armed. I wouldn't do that to you."

"Lift up your top," he instructed next, his gaze still shifty and untrusting.

Blake picked up the hem of her top and lifted it, holding her breath as the cloth came up to the level of her bra. She lifted it still further, so that her undergarments were almost on full display.

Almost.

Using sleight-of-hand, she covered up the bulky rectangle shoved into the front, edges digging into her skin. Without being asked, she shuffled in a full three hundred and sixty degree turn to show Josh that she wasn't hiding anything.

"I told you I wasn't lying," she said when she was facing front again. She didn't drop her top, though she felt the heat of Josh's stare burning the skin around her navel.

For several long seconds, Josh said nothing. His gaze flickered around her. She sensed that he wanted to believe she was telling the truth but was fighting against an instinct that he was being played. She prayed he didn't realize he was right.

"Now your pants," he called out.

Blake let out an audible sigh of relief as she dropped her top back down. She clamped her mouth shut as soon as she realized what she had done, but thankfully, he didn't seem to notice.

"Is that necessary?" she replied, reaching down and pinching the fabric between her thumb and forefinger. It barely pulled away from her skin. "I couldn't hide a razor blade underneath these, let alone a gun."

He stared back at her suspiciously for a second. She used the time to unbutton the fly of her jeans, then roll them down a couple of inches to show that she wasn't hiding anything underneath. Again, she felt his attention probing farther down than she would like. She pushed her distaste aside.

Conscious the time was ticking away, she pulled her jeans back up before waiting for his say-so, buttoning them with one hand as she sank down into a crouch to show that she wasn't hiding a backup piece on either ankle.

Finally, she stood back up, her posture easy, feet shoulder width apart. She waited for his judgment.

"Okay. I believe you," Josh finally said, a strange pining in his voice. She got the sense that he was like a beaten dog, just desperate for love. It was strange to reconcile the thought with the knowledge of the horrors he had committed.

"I knew you would."

"I believe you're not armed," he fired back a second later, distrust prickling in his voice and on the scraps of his expression she could see through the fence. "And I'll let you inside. But if you try anything..."

37

"What's your plan, Josh?" she asked as she followed his instructions to chain and padlock the gate shut behind her. As the lock mechanism clicked, she felt a prowling unease in her stomach for the first time.

There was no escape. Not anymore.

As she turned to face him, she saw him unobscured for the first time. He was standing about fifteen feet from her, leveling a semiautomatic rifle at her chest. His face flickered with unease, distrust, and a pained, pathetic longing.

"Why are you asking?"

After glancing ostentatiously at her watch, Blake looked back at him. "We don't have long."

He stared back at her suspiciously. "What do you mean *we*? Don't have long for what?"

"The FBI are going to find us," she said, neatly sidestepping his first question. "We need to get out of here before they arrive. You'll never escape the dragnet. Not now that they know your identity. Not without my help."

As Josh appeared to deliberate how to respond, Blake used the opportunity to scan her surroundings. The shell of a large condo building stood in the center of the site. Not far from where she was currently standing, there were several large piles of sand, each almost the height of a man. Other assorted construction supplies were scattered around the yard, weathered by age, wind, and rain.

Where are they?

Blake quickly looked back at Josh. The last thing she needed was for him to begin to suspect she was up to something. Had he already moved Austin and Aaron into the shipping container? Or were they tied up elsewhere?

Or worse, dead.

"How can you help me?"

Blake grimaced. She didn't want to remind him that she was law enforcement, not now that he seemed to have forgotten that key piece of information, but it was her only card to play.

"I'm a cop, remember. The FBI is setting up roadblocks and checkpoints all around here," she said. It wasn't exactly a lie. They probably were. And if they weren't already, they definitely would now that she'd suggested it.

"My badge is in my jacket outside. We can use it to get through the checkpoints. They won't search a cop's car."

As Josh processed her statement, Blake allowed her eyes to drift again. This time, she thought she saw the squared-off ends of a faded red shipping container sticking out from behind the shell of the building. Her pulse quickened. She needed to get closer to it. The longer she procrastinated, the closer the bomb squad would get. And their proximity would present Granger with a choice.

If he held off on sending them in and waited for her Hail Mary to play out—and things went sideways—his career would be over. By contrast, if he ordered the bomb squad in and they were unable to defuse the IED in time, then at least he'd tried *something*.

No matter that everybody dies.

"Why are you doing this?" he said. "Why help me? I'm deranged. That's what the news will say, right? They'll tell everyone I went crazy. That only a psychopath could do the things I've done."

"But they don't know the truth," Blake fired back quickly, feeling her breath tighten as she made a leap of faith. "They don't know that what you are doing is necessary. That sometimes strong men need to do hard things."

"You really understand."

"That's right," she said.

After one last flicker of hesitation, he turned toward the shipping container. "Come on. We don't have long."

They hurried toward then through the half-finished building. A concrete floor had been poured but not smoothed. Dust and small stones were scattered everywhere. Their footsteps crunched against them as they walked.

Blake gasped out loud as she saw an inert frame slumped against the building's far wall. The man's ankles and wrists were bound with silver tape.

"Who's that?" she asked, staring at him as long as she dared. Was he breathing? Or was he already dead? And where was Aaron?

Josh barely spared Austin's unmoving body a glance. His lips curled back as he spat, "A traitor. You've met."

"Austin?"

"Yeah. I thought he would understand. I did this to help him. Partly, anyway. But he turned out to be a bitch."

Blake kept her tone even. "Oh?"

"Nina fucked dozens of men. Flaunted what she was doing in front of him. And still he begged me to spare her life. All I had to do to get him onto his knees was threaten to detonate the explosives."

"But he was sleeping around too, right?" Blake asked. She regretted the comment as soon as she said it.

Josh turned back toward her, his posture tense, eyes flashing accusingly. "So he should accept the way that bitch was emasculating him?"

"Of course not," she assured him.

"I could've slept around like he did. Loads of girls at college wanted me," Josh boasted. Blake sensed he was embellishing the truth. "But real men don't take pride in fucking easy women. So I took the high road."

"You did what you had to," she replied.

"Mandy was a whore," he said in a faraway tone. "She would open her legs for anyone. That's why she had to die."

But not you, Blake thought. *Mandy rejected you, didn't she? I'm betting so did Hannah. And Piper and Nina were just reminders of what you couldn't have.*

"Then that bitch new wife of my dad's thought it was her place to give away what was rightfully mine to a bunch of fucking Arabs!"

"Disgusting," Blake murmured.

"But Lara offered me the opportunity to paint my masterpiece," Josh said, building on his theme. "When life gives you lemons, make lemonade, that's what they say. So I did. I worked out how to turn the whole town against those fucking refugees. And in a few minutes, when Lara's dead, my dad's money will be mine again."

Blake felt open-mouthed at the insanity of his plan, even as he spoke as if it was the most rational sequence of events imaginable.

"What about Dwaine?" Blake asked. "Why take his head while he was still alive?"

Josh bared his teeth. "He was a moron. I made a mistake when I chose him. He made too many mistakes. He was supposed to burn Piper's car. He worked a shitty job at a gas station, he should have at least been qualified for that. Instead, he left it in the woods like an idiot. He admitted it to me before I killed him. Begged for mercy."

"But you didn't grant it," Blake said slowly.

"He would have cracked," Josh snapped. "I saw it in his eyes. Even after I told him I'd hired a lawyer for him, I still saw it. He was weak. So he deserved to suffer. That's just the way of the world."

"Right," Blake muttered, a sick feeling in her stomach.

"I'll take care of you, you know that," Josh said quickly, shifting gears as they exited the shell of the apartment building. "No matter what happens with the inheritance. I'd never cheat on you."

"I know, Josh," Blake said.

She finally tore her attention away from him and took in the shipping container for the first time. Two sixty-gallon plastic cylinders were stacked on either side of the locked doors. They appeared to be wired up. Cables led from each through a hole that had been drilled through the steel then inside the container.

"What's in those barrels?" she said a little louder than before.

He grinned mercilessly. "Insurance. Anybody tries coming after us, those things are rigged to blow. Took me a while to get enough fertilizer together, but I got it done. Good thing I'm not an Arab, right? Someone would have reported me for sure."

"It's like an IED?" Blake narrated. "How did you figure out how to do it?"

"You ask a lot of questions," he said irritably. "You can learn anything on the Internet."

As they drew closer, Blake detected the scent of petroleum in the air. Her heart sank. It dispelled any hope she had harbored that Josh's IED was a bluff. Ammonium nitrate—fertilizer—mixed with fuel oil was a simple but deadly effective form of explosive. It was the substance that had been used in the Oklahoma City bombing and was a favorite of ISIS as they conquered and then defended their short-lived caliphate.

She was no explosives expert, but she figured a hundred twenty gallons of the stuff would be enough to flatten not just the shipping container but anyone and anything within a decently sized radius.

Josh hooked his rifle over his shoulder as he reached for a keychain from inside a jacket pocket. Blake tensed. She was standing only a couple of feet behind him. Was now the moment to take a chance?

Wait.

She breathed out. She had to be patient. It was possible that Josh had rigged himself up with some kind of dead man's switch. It wasn't likely, but neither was it a technically difficult feat. She couldn't take the risk until she knew for sure.

Besides, the odds were still tilted against her. Perhaps inside the container, with space at a premium to help level the playing field, she would find something to use as a weapon.

Josh glanced over his shoulder before pushing the key into the padlock that held the shipping container's two doors closed. His expression was oddly torn. Blake didn't react; she just looked at him expectantly, almost fawningly. Her only goal was to reinforce his preconceptions. A man like Josh didn't really see women as equals or consider them capable of conscious thought. Their only role was to stand behind a man and provide him support.

He turned and twisted the key.

"You ready?" he said without looking at her.

She didn't have to feign the excitement in her voice. "You bet."

He lifted the padlock out and tossed it onto the ground, then unbolted both doors. He paused for a few seconds, presumably for theatrical effect, then swung them open with a flourish.

Blake gasped out loud as light spilled into the container. The scene inside was horrific. Bloody footprints speckled the plywood floor. A steel table occupied the space nearest the entrance, on top of which were stacked bottles of bleach, other forms of cleaning supplies, and various knives and construction tools. It looked like a mortuary table.

But that wasn't what drew her attention. Her gaze settled on the true cause of her horror: the three figures shackled to opposite walls at the far end of the container. Two of them, Lara Hartmann and Aaron Weller, seemed to be either unconscious or dead. Neither stirred at the disturbance.

But Nina Crawford did.

She was wearing a dirty orange jumpsuit, on which Blake saw more bloodstains. Though she'd only been held captive for a few days, she seemed paler and skinnier than in the photos her husband had provided the investigation. Unlike Lara and Aaron, who were slumped on the floor, Nina was seated on a steel chair that appeared to be bolted to the wall. She didn't look up as the doors opened.

"You really did it," Blake whispered, momentarily lost for anything else to say.

"Did you doubt me?" Josh scoffed.

"Of course not," she covered quickly. "But seeing it in person is... different."

Her stomach turned at the role she had to play. It sank still further as Nina flinched, her eyes darting toward the sound of voices. There was a momentary flash of hope in them, then a deep morass of despair as she realized that Blake and Josh were standing side by side.

Blake wished she could somehow communicate her intentions to Josh's terrified captive. But she could not. His trust in her was still tenuous at best. She couldn't do anything to risk it. She tore her gaze away from Nina's, not trusting herself to follow through.

"You built all this?" she said, needing to get him talking. Every detail might be useful to the bomb squad. She tried to guess how far away they might be but realized that she'd lost track of time. The adrenaline pumping through her veins was skewing her grip on reality.

"Yeah," he said, seeming to focus his attention on Lara's prone form. He positively radiated hatred. Blake saw that he was almost trembling with it. "I've been planning this a long time. Ever since that bitch weaseled in to steal what's rightfully mine."

Blake wondered if she should protest she would never do such a thing. But she sensed that would make her sound more, not less suspicious to Josh's skeptical mind.

"Can we set the charges to blow from a distance?" she asked instead.

"Why do you want to know?"

There was that suspicion again. He wanted to believe she was with him. But he didn't yet. Not truly.

"We need to cause a distraction to help make our escape," she said. "But I'm sure you already thought of that."

"Course I did," Josh insisted. He shot her a boastful look as he reached into his jacket pocket and pulled out a cell phone. "I thought of everything."

He only gave her a glimpse of the phone before shoving it back into his pocket. But Blake saw enough to know that it wasn't a cheap burner. It looked like an iPhone. That complicated things. Programming an app to detonate the explosives would be a trivial task—not even requiring any coding skills.

Any number of conditions could trigger an explosion: anything from Josh's cell phone leaving a predetermined GPS grid box to not typing in a code after a set length of time. She guessed it was even possible that he could be wearing a heart rate monitor—even a cheap fitness watch—with the bombs programmed to detonate the moment his heart stopped.

"Get inside," Josh said, jogging her train of thought.

She did as instructed, grimacing as he swung the container doors closed. He'd installed a deadbolt on the inside and slid it across. Her skin crawled at the prospect of being locked inside this torture chamber for any length of time.

It also complicated her backup plan. Significantly.

"Can you open the doors?" she said, faking a gasp and pressing a hand to her chest as she narrated for the sake of those listening in. "I'm not good in tight spaces. Especially not when I'm locked inside."

"You'll get over it," he said dismissively. "You'll need to toughen up if you want to stay with me."

You're a real charmer, she thought.

With that option at least temporarily blocked, Blake started reconsidering her position. She glanced around the space properly for the first time, taking in details she'd missed earlier. She hadn't noticed at first, but the interior of the container felt smaller than it looked from the outside. She soon saw the reason why: Josh had constructed a drywall partition about two thirds of the way down. A small doorway, more of a hatch, really, led to the other side.

Blake guessed that was where he'd filmed the hostage videos.

Josh began walking toward Nina, reaching once more for the keychain in his pocket. He grabbed the shock of her now-dirty blond hair and yanked it backward so her head collided with the container's steel wall. She let out a dazed groan, head lolling as he crouched to unlock the chains that bound her ankles and wrists to a makeshift lock belt around her midriff.

As he did so, he muttered something that sounded suspiciously like "Fucking bitch."

Blake forced herself not to react. She kept probing her surroundings, and as her gaze passed across the table once more, taking in the half-dozen or more knives and saws arrayed there, an idea struck her. It was a risk, but she was out of other options.

And time.

"Can I do it?" she said softly as the first, then the second set of chains fell away from Nina's ankles and wrists.

"Do what?" Josh asked without turning.

"I'm not stupid, Josh," she said. "I want you to trust me. Truly. And I know you won't. Not unless I dip my hands in blood."

As he dragged Nina upright, he twisted back to her. A look of confusion crossed his face, then surprise. "You want to kill her?"

"If you'll allow me."

Blake studiously avoided looking at the weapons on the table. Josh had to think giving her one was his idea. Even then, he might see right through her ploy.

He hesitated for a second, then jerked his chin at the hatch. "Open it."

She shuffled past the table, itching to pick up one of the knives but not daring to make her move. The threat of an explosion condemning them all hung heavy over her. She felt the weight of his gaze on her every step of the way.

She crouched in front of the hatch and twisted the handle. There was no lock. It opened and swung away from her.

"Go through," he instructed.

She did.

Nina came through a second later, tumbling through with forced, careless momentum. She lay moaning on the floor. Blake resisted the urge to pick her up and comfort her. Josh followed quickly, his hand resting on his shouldered rifle as he scurried upright.

Blake gauged her surroundings. The space back here was much more cramped. Josh had built a wood and drywall room inside the shipping container. On the far side of the space was a camera on a tripod wired up to a laptop, as well as a bundle of clothing: another orange jumpsuit, a variety of seemingly hand-painted ISIS flags, and a black balaclava. A chair stood in the center of the space, which she recognized from Nina's first video.

It was constricted. Messy. There were three bodies and a variety of obstacles in a space that couldn't comfortably fit all of them. It all meant that it would be harder for Josh to wield his weapon effectively.

"You know she has to die," he said as he yanked Nina upright then pushed her into the chair. Her bruised and filthy orange jump-suit-clad frame now separated Blake and Josh.

"I know. Let me do it."

He bound her with a fresh set of chains that were bolted to an anchor point on the floor. Nina looked up with pleading eyes that seemed to say, *"Why are you doing this?"*

"You will be on the run forever. The FBI won't forget."

"So will you."

Blake inhaled deeply. Whenever Josh turned away, as he did now to power up the camera, she loosened her muscles, rolling her neck and filling her lungs with oxygen. She needed every advantage she could get.

"I know their playbook," Blake continued. "They won't catch us. Not if we work together."

"They won't catch me," Josh snorted. "Fine. You do it."

He sounded like he didn't believe that Blake had the stones. She looked at him expectantly. "How?"

He looked her up and down, sizing her up. Finally, he nodded, as if a decision had been made. He reached for the sheathed knife in his jacket, the outline of which she had seen earlier.

"Slit her throat," he said coldly.

The knife came spinning through the air toward her—unsheathed. Next, Josh took a step backward and assumed a position behind the camera. As Blake cautiously snatched for the weapon, praying she caught the hilt and not the blade, he brought his rifle up and aimed it at Nina's chest.

"I've got you covered," he said, ostentatiously flicking the safety on the side of the rifle. The click echoed through the cramped space.

Blake's heart began to race. Her palms were sticky with sweat. She felt an acrid tang of copper at the back of her throat as adrenaline built up in her system. She wanted—needed—to run, to fight, to kick and bite and tear some way out of this situation. If it was just him and her in this box, she would scratch his eyes out if that's what it took.

But she was in a bind.

Josh stood six feet away from her—too far away to reach before he could pull the trigger. He could kill both Nina and her, and there wasn't a damn thing she could do about it. He'd placed her in checkmate, and she'd walked right into his trap.

He glanced at the camera, then crouched and tapped a few keys on the laptop. A light began to glow near the lens.

"You're live in twenty seconds." He grinned. "Let's make you famous."

Blake gulped. She stood limply behind Nina, wondering what the hell she could do now. The blade felt impossibly heavy in her grip. It felt like she was holding Nina's life in her palm.

You fucked up.

She opened her mouth to speak, but her tongue was suddenly impossibly dry. She croaked out, "Are the bombs ready to blow? Once I do this, we'll need to move fast."

"Do you think I'm stupid?"

"No, of course not," she said in a mollifying tone.

He reached into his jacket and pulled out his phone. He tapped in a passcode, then spun the device around and flashed the screen at Blake.

It took a moment to process what she was seeing. At first it was just a jumble of numbers. And then she realized that it was a timer.

Counting down.

She had four minutes left to live.

Now 03:59.

Strangely Blake no longer felt fear, or doubt, or uncertainty. The knowledge of her impending death dispelled all of that. Now there was only one way out. It didn't matter if Josh was wearing a dead man's switch. Because they were all dead anyway.

"You'd better hurry up," he said, his tone cold, his eyes boring into her soul. She wondered if he'd ever believed a word she'd said. Or maybe he had, but he was too far gone in his hate for it to matter. "Or we're all going to fry…"

"Four minutes doesn't give us enough time," Blake protested loudly. "We still need to get out of here…"

Josh shrugged. "Time's ticking. Slit her throat. Or I'll put a bullet through your chest and do it myself."

A chime rang out from the laptop. He peeled his lips back from his teeth and leered at her in what she guessed was supposed to be a grin. "Showtime…"

Blake glanced down at the blade of the knife. She gently ran her thumb across it, wincing as this drew a trickle of blood. It was razor-sharp. She looked around desperately, searching for some other play. She thought she heard the thump of rotor blades in the distance, muffled by the walls of the container. But she was probably just imagining things.

It was just her and him.

She took a step closer to Nina. Josh was five feet away now. He brought the barrel of the rifle up an inch. Just an inch, but it was a warning. She stood behind the woman, ran her hands through her hair, and grasped it tight.

Crouching down so that her ears were close to Nina's lips, she said loudly, "Do you have any last words?"

Nina shook her head. She still looked groggy. But she still had some fight in her. Spittle flew from her lips as she swore, "Fuck you!"

Blake whispered two words into her ears before she stood and pressed the knife against Nina's throat.

"What did you say?" Josh demanded suspiciously.

She didn't reply.

Blake drew the blade across Nina's throat, feeling warm blood trickle down the woman's throat, enough to spot the front of her orange jumpsuit. Nina jerked with pain, but Blake forced the woman's head down. She let go of her hair and pressed her free hand over her mouth, locking her other arm over Nina's chest as she bucked and writhed in pain.

And then she went limp. Her chains went taut as her body slumped forward.

Blake circled Nina's chair. She looked down at the woman, at the blood now soaking her front. She leaned forward and wiped Josh's blade on Nina's knee.

Only then did she turn to face Josh. He was only four feet away now. She still felt the warmth of Nina's blood on her hands.

But she didn't look back. She smiled at him and said, "I told you..."

He looked startled, disbelieving. "Told me what?"

"That I had what it takes."

38

Blake's ribcage rattled from the blows of her heart as Josh eyed Nina's body. Blood was still dripping from her neck onto the front of her jumpsuit, and then onto the floor. But there clearly wasn't enough.

Her only hope was that Josh didn't know how much blood there should be. Severing a man's head was very different from slitting a woman's throat.

Wasn't it?

"We need to go," she said, beckoning him toward her with her free hand to distract his gaze. "How long do we have left?"

He took a hesitant half-pace toward her. Three feet, now. He was in slashing range. But still not close enough to be sure of delivering a killing blow.

She hefted the knife. The blade no longer felt heavy in her hand. Quite the opposite. It was light, energetic, free. She was hungry to put an end to this, to put an end to Josh.

The barrel of the rifle dropped a couple of inches as he came toward her, his attention no longer on Blake, but on Nina's body. Blake felt time slow around her. She knew she would only get one shot at this.

She had to make it count.

Josh took the final step. The rifle came down lower as his attention focused on her obscured face. A cavalcade of emotions passed across his. Hatred. Disbelief. Exhaustion. He reached forward and placed two fingers on Nina's chin. He started to lift.

Blake struck, bringing the knife down fast, the tip of the blade aimed for the top of his right forearm—the one carrying the rifle. She drove it down with all her strength, feeling only momentary resistance as the edge passed through the skin, cutting through sinew and flesh before it buried itself between the bones in his arm.

He roared with pain, the scream guttural and raw, flinging his arm away from him as he did so. The movement took Blake by surprise. With her fingers already slick from Nina's blood, the hilt of the knife slipped from her grasp. It came free of Josh's flesh and went skittering across the floor.

"You fucking whore!"

Josh gripped his right arm with his left, staring up at her with shock and anger coursing through him. Blood dripped freely down the limb, pooling momentarily at the elbow before coursing through the air and falling to the floor.

Blake sensed movement to her right as Nina stirred. Out of the corner of her eye, she saw the slash of red across the pale skin of her neck. She was pulling herself away from the fight, but the chains trapped her in place.

Knowing she'd already hesitated too long, Blake turned her head in search of a weapon. The knife was farther away, lying against the wall, so she went for the rifle instead, diving to the floor and feeling the cool metal meet her fingertips.

She knew the safety was off, so she rolled and brought the weapon up, searching for a target.

But Josh was already upon her. He was lightning quick, natural reflexes no doubt aided by the adrenaline pumping through his body. He formed a fist with his left hand and brought it down like a hammer as the damaged right one went for the gun.

Blake wrenched her head to the left, and he hit the floor instead.

She was saved by the fact that he was forced to use his non-dominant hand. He was less agile, his movements jerky and forced. She tried to scramble away, but he was sitting on top of her legs. He pulled his arm back and readied for another blow.

An impossibly loud crack roared through the inside of the shipping container as Blake's finger, trapped inside the trigger guard, was wrenched against the trigger itself as Josh tried to rip the weapon from her hands. A round spat free of the muzzle and buried itself in the drywall.

"Shit," she muttered with what little oxygen was left in her lungs.

Time slowed further. The muscles in her neck were wrenched, the sinews in her arms and shoulders straining as Josh tried to pull the gun from her. The only thing that saved her was that his blood was making the metal slick and slippery.

Blake did the only thing she could. She let go.

The rifle jerked upward. With her free hand, she reached for the deep wound in his right forearm and dug her thumbs inside, pressing and pushing and tearing with everything she had.

The strangest thing was it took him a second to react. It was as if the adrenaline was dulling his pain. Blake felt the strength fading from her body, exhaustion and defeat threatening to swallow her whole.

Josh lurched backward, sending the rifle flying in the same direction. His eyes went white, almost rolling in their sockets. He threw himself away from her, as if his body had simply refused to suffer any more agony.

For a moment, it was all Blake could do to lie back and suck oxygen into her lungs. She was lightheaded from exertion and lack of air.

All she knew was that she couldn't rest. She couldn't remember why.

And then it hit her.

The countdown.

The timer.

The bomb.

Blake scrambled backward. Josh's rearing frame separated her from the rifle, so she went for the knife instead. A stabbing pain in her side marked the spot where he must have kneed her in the torso as he attacked her. Maybe a cracked rib. It hurt to breathe.

She crawled, using swimming strokes to pull her along the ground as she propelled herself with strong kicks. Her vision narrowed, she saw only one thing.

Her hand settled on the knife.

As she turned back to Josh, she was hit with a wave of sound, as if her senses had been on pause all this time. Someone was banging on the exterior of the shipping container. She heard muffled voices, and definitely now the chatter of helicopter rotors. But it was impossible to focus on any of it, not in detail. Not over the sound of Josh's angered, pained roaring. Didn't they know what was about to happen? They needed to run!

But they didn't, couldn't know.

Fresh hits of adrenaline rocked her system, pumped out of already-drained reservoirs. She saw Josh reach for the gun. He was bringing it up to fire.

Don't you dare die like this.

Hearing her own chiding words echoing in her skull, Blake did the only thing she could think to do. She launched herself through the air, knife gripped solidly in her right hand, the blade arcing down. Josh's eyes went wide. He tried to bring the rifle's barrel up, but he was too slow, his injured hand making his movements too clumsy.

She fell on him, bringing the tip of the blade down with all her might. It punctured his jacket just below the right shoulder, and the blade buried itself to the hilt in his flesh. He didn't scream, but instead inhaled sharply, wheezing as he breathed.

Blake didn't stop. She couldn't stop. His fingers were still wrapped around the rifle, still struggling to maneuver it into a firing position.

So she pulled on the knife. It grated on bone as it emerged from his body, a horrific scraping noise that was barely dulled by Josh's cries of agony. She pulled her elbow back and sank the knife into him a second time, this time aiming lower, for the stomach.

He bucked, trying to push her off him, but already his strength was fading. Blood flowed freely from his many wounds. Blake was covered in it. It soaked her clothes, stained her skin, and coated her so thickly it felt like it would stick there until the day she died.

She scrabbled away from him, horror at what she had done overcoming her. The sight was horrific. He was still breathing, air bubbling from the wound on his shoulder. The blade must've gone down through his rib cage and punctured his lung.

He could barely move. But even in death, his vindictive evil won out. She saw his uninjured left hand tremble, then begin to move as he reached inside his jacket. It took Blake a moment to realize what he was doing.

The phone.

Fresh energy gripped her. She'd forgotten all about the countdown. How long had the fight swallowed up? Twenty seconds? A minute?

Two?

"Shit," she swore, shock fading from her system. She propelled herself upright, clambered onto Josh's quivering, dying body, made a fist, and brought it down against his nose. She heard it crack, then a deep, resonant thud as the back of his skull bounced off the floor. She ignored it, reaching instead for the phone.

She ripped it out of his jacket pocket and brought it up in front of her face, hope filling her that the device would be unlocked.

It didn't last.

The screen was lit up, demanding a passcode. She tried waving it in front of his face, but either he didn't have facial unlock set up, or the device didn't recognize him underneath all the blood.

Neither was there a timer. She didn't know how long she had left.

Burying a wave of revulsion, Blake pushed her thumb inside Josh's shoulder wound. His flesh was torn yet forgiving. He screamed in agony, his throat raw and hoarse.

She ignored him. Instead, she lowered her face over his and hissed, "Tell me your fucking passcode."

39

Blake flinched with surprise. Josh was gone. There was no light left in his eyes. The shock of the last wave of pain must have tipped him over the edge.

She tossed the phone aside in disgust. She didn't have time for regret. She needed to get the hell out of here.

Ignoring for the moment the banging on the outside of the container and the muffled voices which she could barely hear over the ringing in her ears after her exertion, Blake looked up at Nina. The two women's eyes met. Nina was exhausted, the shallow cut on her neck still oozing red. It would leave a nasty scar.

But she was alive.

Her chest heaving, starved for oxygen, Blake pushed herself upright and staggered over to the bound woman. "Please tell me," she panted, "that the bombs aren't real."

Nina shook her head sadly. "They're real. At least, he told me they were. He was real careful with them, that's for sure."

Blake searched Josh's body for his keychain, anxiety building when she didn't find it on his person. She breathed a sigh of relief a second later and snatched it off the floor. "Then I don't know about you, but I think we'd better move."

"Sounds good to me."

There were half a dozen keys on the chain. Blake cycled through them, her fingers slippery with blood, wishing she'd paid more attention when Josh locked Nina up in the first place. She quickly discounted three of them, reasoning the padlocks were too large.

In the only stroke of luck she'd had all day, the first key she tried popped Nina's ankles free. She dragged the chain free of the bolt on the floor, then heaved Josh's former captive upright.

"Let's deal with your wrists later," she said, pulling Nina toward the hatch, then pushing the woman through it. She scrambled through a moment after, leaving a streak of blood on the floor behind her.

"I'll get the bolt," Nina said, sprinting for the locked doors, the chains of her wrist jangling with every step.

Every nerve in Blake's body was telling her to run. But as her eyes passed over Lara's still unconscious body, she knew that she could not. She heard a squeal to her right, more muffled voices, movement. Nina had the door open. People were rushing in.

"Get the fuck out of here!" she yelled, exploding with frustration that these people didn't understand the seriousness of the situation. She reached for the only two keys that were left.

The first was a dud.

Blake let out a hiss of frustration. She sank the second key into the padlock. It turned. She barely heard the click as the mechanism unlocked. She tossed the keychain aside and grabbed the prone woman's shoulder, dragging with the last energy she had left.

"I've got her!" a voice said. She felt a second set of hands close around Lara's body, lightening the load as she began dragging the woman out of the container.

Melissa's voice.

A wave of relief washed over Blake, despite the fear building inside her that the explosives would detonate any second now. With Melissa's help, they pulled Lara out of the shipping container. Austin was already pulling Nina away in the distance, limping as he headed for the shell of the apartment building about twenty feet away—but alive. A cop she didn't recognize hefted Aaron into a fireman's carry.

"We don't have long," she said with about the last air left in her lungs. "We need to get as far away as we can."

Melissa said nothing. She just grunted in response. The two women redoubled their efforts, pulling and dragging, aware that Lara's legs were scraping along the ground, the skin being ripped from her knees and shins, but knowing they didn't have any other choice.

And then the world turned white.

EPILOGUE

Blake groaned as her consciousness became consumed by an intense, throbbing headache. For a long time, she remembered nothing at all. Now only pain.

"Hey," a low, soft voice crooned. "You're back with us. Drink this."

She knew that voice, she was sure of it. But right now, both his face and name escaped her. She didn't dare open her eyes. Not yet. Everything hurt too much. Even the mention of drinking only prompted her to realize that she was suffering from a burning, seemingly unquenchable thirst.

Something hard and thin was pressed gently against her lips. The rim of a cup. Her carer tilted it, and a small trickle of cool droplets loosed into her mouth. The relief was like the feel of aloe on the skin after a long day on the beach, only a thousand times as pleasurable.

Blake sucked greatly from the cup, only for the water to make its way down the wrong pipe. Her body tensed as a painful cough wracked through her.

"Okay, that's enough for now," the voice said. He pulled the cup away from her lips. "There's more than a few guys around here who might not treat me too kindly if I accidentally drowned their action hero."

"Where am I?" Blake croaked. Her voice was raw and sounded far away.

"Womack Army Medical Center," the voice said. He sounded achingly familiar. But still Blake could not remember his name. "It was the closest trauma center. The HRT chopper airlifted you straight here."

With the intensity of the headache finally beginning to fade, Blake finally risked opening her eyes just a fraction. She peered out through a thicket of eyelashes. The room's lights were turned down low, which she was incredibly grateful for.

Blake's memory began to return to her in dribs and drabs. She remembered figuring out that Josh Hartmann was responsible not just for the murder of Piper Hickson and Nina Crawford's kidnapping, but also at least two prior killings. She'd tracked him to the abandoned construction site outside of Waterford, where she'd attempted to convince him she was on his side. A wave of revulsion coursed through her at the thought of the things she'd been forced to say.

She opened her eyes a little farther. At first, she couldn't see the source of the voice, but then she tilted her head to the left, where she sensed a presence. Ryan's face came into view. He looked tired, a little worried, and it had been at least a week since he'd trimmed his beard.

"How long was I out?" she said softly. Even speaking was easier now.

"A couple years," Ryan said. "I kept visiting. Didn't really believe you'd wake up. It's a miracle."

"What!" Blake exclaimed, her heart rate suddenly racing. She tried to push herself upright, but the movement was too agonizing. It felt like every muscle and tendon in her entire body had been ripped in the explosion.

"I'm kidding," he said, the twinkle in his eye she only now recognized for what it was quickly replaced by a look of abject horror. He placed a hand on her torso and pushed her gently down against the bed. "Just a few hours."

Blake heard an alarm sound in the distance. She glanced around and realized it was coming from a vital signs monitor near the head of her bed.

"Turn that thing off, will you?" she muttered, closing her eyes again as the pain from the surprise movement faded away. "And do me a favor?"

"Sure." He sounded deeply contrite. She heard a rustle to her side, then—thankfully—only blessed silence as the insistent mechanical beeping stopped. "What is it?"

"Keep your jokes to yourself for a while."

"Ten-four."

"What happened?" Blake asked, her heart rate still elevated. The last thing she remembered was desperately attempting to hustle Lara Hartmann out of the booby-trapped shipping container before the explosives detonated. "Did they all get out?"

"Like I said before, you're a hero," Ryan said. "Nina Crawford's in the next room over. It's just a precaution," he quickly added to forestall her next question. "Just a few bumps and scratches. Her husband took a beating, but he's not in any danger. They're going to keep Lara Hartmann in overnight for observation, but I don't get the sense the doctors are too worried about her either."

"Thank God," Blake muttered, finally relaxing back against the bed sheets.

"I think He should be thanking you," Ryan replied dryly.

The door opened, and a doctor entered. He checked Blake's vitals, shone a flashlight into her eyes, performed a battery of tests, then departed, seeming pleased with what he saw. Only a couple of seconds later, two sharp knocks sounded at the door.

"Who's that?" Blake asked. She pushed herself upright, then smiled gratefully as Ryan plumped the pillows behind her.

"Oh," Ryan remarked. "I thought I told you already. Seems like you've developed a bit of a fan club."

He stepped away to open the door. Assistant Special Agent in Charge Carl Granger was the first to enter, followed a step later by Captain Rogers.

"Lieutenant," Granger growled in a low voice. "It's good to see you doing better. You had a lot of folks real worried about you."

"I'm like a cockroach," Blake replied, wincing as a cough felt like it tore something fresh inside her. "You couldn't kill me if you tried."

"I don't doubt it." Rogers smiled. "I hope your first week hasn't made you reconsider your decision to join the department?"

"I expected more paperwork and less running from explosions," Blake said wryly. "But you'd have to pry me away with a spatula."

"Good."

Granger cleared his throat. "I do have an apology to make. I should have given more weight to your theory that this wasn't a terrorist case. I had blinkers on. Only saw the evidence I expected to."

"Forget about it," Blake said. "All's well that ends well, right?"

"Lieutenant, you're lying in a hospital bed. That's a black mark on my record," he said, reaching into his jacket pocket. He shot her an apologetic look. "Still, the job comes first. You feeling up to answering a few questions?"

"Did you search Josh Hartmann's place?" Blake asked instead.

Granger nodded. "He was one sick puppy. Looks like he met Hilton through a far-right paintball group. They got together every few months to playact their insurgency fantasies. We also found trophies from the murders of those two ECU students. A bracelet Mandy Yates was wearing when she disappeared, and a locket with Hannah Sanders' initials inside."

Blake felt tension she didn't even know she was holding seep out of her. "Someone needs to contact Captain Sid Keaton from the Pitt County Sheriff's office," she said. "Those families deserve closure."

"It's underway," Granger confirmed with a sharp nod.

"Thank you," she whispered.

The ASAC paused for several long seconds for her to compose herself before he continued. "You want us to come back another time?"

"No, shoot," she replied.

"Nina Crawford told us you spoke with the deceased suspect," he said. "Do you remember what you discussed?"

"I convinced him that I was on his side," she said, tilting her head back as she remembered. "It was a Hail Mary, but I guess it worked. Barely..."

"You can say that again," Granger said.

"The pieces all started to fall into place after I learned that Josh Hartmann and Austin were friends. I suspected from the moment I learned about the Greenville killings that whoever was behind the events of the past four days had killed before. There were too many similarities with the way the bodies were staged."

"Except the decapitations."

"Exactly. But the underlying MO was the same."

Granger furrowed his brow. "I don't follow."

"The killer in the Greenville murders fanned the flames of the community's fear by funneling information to the student newspaper. To Aaron Weller, specifically. He created a blog—*She Lies*—that effectively put a target on the backs of dozens of different women. I believe he experienced some kind of dopamine hit from being the center of attention—even anonymously."

"Like the hostage video this time," Granger said.

"Precisely." Blake nodded. She reached gingerly for the cup of water Ryan had left on her bedside table and shot him a grateful smile when he lifted it to her lips.

"Then this time, the person closest to the story was the very same reporter. That always seemed off to me. I don't know why Josh stopped killing after Greenville. That's a question for your profilers, I guess. But the catalyst for restarting was simple: He saw a woman, his hated enemy, coming for the inheritance he believed was his by right."

"Serial killers can sometimes lie dormant for years, sometimes decades." Granger nodded thoughtfully. "Until they are prompted to resume by an intense emotional stimulus. That fits the bill."

"Josh Hartmann always believed that he was superior to others," Blake said, wincing as her headache began to pick up. "Women especially. But he didn't confine himself."

Rogers picked up the thread. "Right. I read a couple of those blog posts. He harbored racist beliefs about his own genetic superiority. He thought he was smarter than everybody else. But then real life intervened. He ended up working for his dad's construction company, not running it. It must have created an intense cognitive dissonance."

Blake gritted her teeth and steeled herself to continue. "So he developed a plan that would kill three birds with one stone. First: He needed to get rid of the foundation that was wasting his inheritance. Second: His dad's wife had to go. Third: He wanted to scratch that long-forgotten itch. He wanted to kill again."

"And four, he had to get away with the heist of the decade," Granger said, scribbling a note in his pad. "Which meant he needed somebody to take the blame."

"So he invented a terrorist plot," Blake said. "Not only that, he needed to whip up anti-refugee sentiment in town, so he conspired with a local white nationalist to make his father's charity foundation's work too toxic to continue."

"We think Dwaine Hilton was a vital component of Josh's plan," Rogers said. "Robyn discovered a partial print of Hilton's on the underside of Piper Hicks' car door handle and confirmed the droplet of blood was his. Our working hypothesis is that his job was to hide the car after Josh manipulated her into meeting near the mall, using Austin Crawford's stolen phone."

"He did a pretty shitty job," Blake muttered, thankful once again for the continuing rarity of criminal competence. She closed her eyes and pictured Piper's reaction as Josh had shown up in Austin's place. Had he told her he was there to give her a lift? Assured her that everything would be all right?

"We believe Hilton also assisted in kidnapping Nina Crawford," Granger continued. "We discovered clothes matching the ones worn by the man she met in The Coal Yard in a garbage bag in his truck. We'll have her look at a picture of him once the doctors release her."

Blake glanced up at the ceiling as she processed this revelation. It made sense. Nina probably wouldn't have agreed to go on a date with her husband's close friend. But Dwaine had been tall and handsome, as long as you didn't scratch more than skin deep.

Granger scratched something on his pad. "Was Hilton's murder always part of the plan?"

"I'm not sure," Blake admitted. "I suspect Josh would always have wanted to tie up that particular loose end. But the way it happened, the violence, the lack of planning—it was sloppy. I think he got spooked when Aaron told him we had Hilton in custody. I'm guessing Josh moved up his timetable."

"And why choose the women he did? Lara Hartmann I get. Why Piper and Nina? Austin Crawford was his friend, right?"

"As far as anyone could be," Blake said. "I think it's as simple as he needed somebody, or his plot wouldn't work. Josh was jealous of Austin. He's a decorated soldier, a war hero with no trouble attracting women. Someone for whom things come easy, when Josh himself had to struggle. He was a tall poppy. So he needed cutting down."

Granger snapped his pad shut. "I think you're probably right, though I guess we'll never know for sure. I think I have everything I need right now. I'll let you rest. Although with that line outside, I doubt you'll get the chance."

Line?

Blake's unspoken question was answered a moment later as Granger and Rogers left and CID Special Agent Nathan Cooper replaced them. He lingered at the door for a moment as if asking permission to enter. A strange flicker crossed his face when he saw Ryan seated at her bedside, though it disappeared so quickly she wondered if she'd imagined it.

"How do I look?" she asked, tilting her head from side to side so that he could see the collection of bruises and scrapes she'd acquired during her brush with death.

"Honestly?" Nathan replied as he reached. "A damn sight better than I do."

Blake grinned. "I'm calling it IED chic."

"It'll be all the rage on the New York runways next season," he fired back before the smile on his face was swallowed by a look of pensive concern. "You had us real worried, right, Ryan?"

Ryan cleared his throat. He took a second to respond. "Yeah. Right."

Nathan jerked his thumb in Ryan's direction. He was smiling again, but strangely, Blake thought it was a little forced. Maybe she was overthinking things. It had been a long day...

"I'm still not sure how this guy made it past the doctors," Nathan said. "He's been stuck to your bedside like a limpet since pretty much before the chopper landed."

"Guess I still have some pull around here." Ryan shrugged before pursing his lips. "Lord knows I spent enough time in this place to earn it."

Blake shut her eyes as comprehension dawned on her. Both men were puffing out their feathers like peacocks dueling for a mate's attention. It was flattering, but she was way too tired to play referee.

"We should leave you to rest," Nathan cut in quickly, causing Blake to hide a half-smile as she wondered whether the suggestion was entirely for her benefit.

"Yeah," Ryan agreed a little more slowly. "I'll be right outside."

Blake's eyes flickered open. In truth, she really was exhausted. Whatever adrenaline had fueled her after she woke was now well and truly gone. "Can you pass me my phone?"

Nathan grabbed it off the bedside table and handed it to her like a token of his affection. It was a little dented from the explosion, and the screen had a fresh crack that wasn't there before, but it still turned on.

"Thanks," she said, letting out a deep sigh that seemed to signal to the rutting stags that it was time to leave her alone.

She opened the notifications screen, eyes widening as she saw dozens, perhaps hundreds of messages and missed calls—some from former colleagues she hadn't seen in years. She sagged back against the crinkly plastic pillows as she realized with considerable dismay that she must have become the main character in that day's new cycle while she was out.

Great.

As she toyed with the idea of giving in to the urge to sleep, one particular notification jumped out at her. It was a text message from Skip Hobson, the CID agent who had investigated her parents' murder-suicide.

I remembered something interesting. Call me.

The time stamp was from just before noon. It was now almost 9 p.m.

Blake sat bolt upright in bed, a fresh wave of energy deadening the pain this should have caused. She knew instantly there was no way she would get any rest before her curiosity was slaked. She tapped the message, then the icon to call the sender, and pressed the phone to her ear. It rang out three, four, five times before she heard a click on the other end of the line.

Then just breathing.

"Hello? Skip? Can you hear me?"

To Blake's surprise, it wasn't Skip Hobson's voice she heard. In fact, the person on the other end of the line wasn't even male.

"Who is this?" a woman's voice answered in a strangely accusatory tone.

Blake frowned, wondering if she'd somehow dialed the wrong number, though she didn't see how that was possible. Perhaps she was still groggier than she thought. "I'm sorry. Is this Skip Hobson's phone?"

"Who's asking?"

Disconcerted, Blake answered, "Lieutenant Blake Larsen with the Monroe County Sheriff's Department, returning his call. Is Skip available, or should I call back later?"

A long pause followed. Finally, the woman said, "No, my father isn't available. He's dead."

NEXT IN THE SERIES...

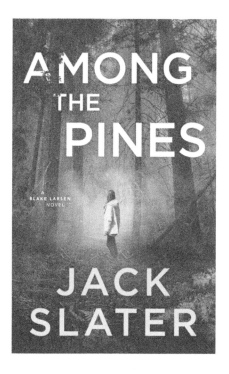

Pine Ridge is a haven for lost souls.

What happens when a haven becomes a living hell?

Lieutenant Blake Larsen is on the trail of her own family tragedy when another rips apart Pine Ridge Retreat, a troubled teen camp on the edge of Northern Pines. A girl named Chloe Perez is dead, and a missing teenager with a troubled past—Jax Mitchell—is the prime suspect. Though Blake is desperate to uncover the truth about her parents' horrific murder-suicide, duty calls.

When deputies first arrive at Pine Ridge, security refuses to let them through the gate. Why? What are they hiding—and why will no one talk? Does it have anything to do with the strange devotion the camp's staff have for their leader?

When Blake learns that Chloe's father is the speaker of the State House, she finds herself in the eye of yet another public storm. With her suspect list growing, and bodies piling up, Blake's investigation itself comes under pressure. Someone wants to shut her down. But Blake made a dead girl a promise.

Visit the Amazon Kindle store to read *Among The Pines*, book three in the *Blake Larsen* thriller series.

FOR ALL THE LATEST NEWS

I hope you enjoyed *She Lies Here*! If you did, and don't fancy sifting through thousands of books on Amazon and leaving your next great read to chance, then sign up to my mailing list and be the first to hear when I release a new book.

Visit www.jack-slater.com/updates to subscribe, and receive a FREE ebook!

Among the Pines, book 3 in the *Blake Larsen* crime series, is available now - head to the Amazon Kindle store to get your copy.

Thanks so much for reading,

Jack.

Made in United States
Orlando, FL
15 August 2024

50399179R00178